D0638219

THE CLOCKMAKER

Thomas Chandler Haliburton

THE
CLOCKMAKER

or

THE SAYINGS AND DOINGS OF
SAMUEL SLICK OF SLICKVILLE
(First Series)

Introduction : Robert L. McDougall

General Editor : Malcolm Ross

New Canadian Library No. 6

McCLELLAND AND STEWART

NOTE ON THE TEXT

The source for this reprint is the edition published under the Riverside Classics by Houghton, Mifflin and Company of Boston in 1871. The text was chosen by virtue of its clarity in paragraphing, punctuation, and other points in style.

The Canadian Publishers
McClelland and Stewart Limited
25 Hollinger Road, Toronto

0-7710-9106-0

Printed in Canada by Webcom Limited

ADVERTISEMENT

The following Sketches, as far as the twenty-first Chapter, originally appeared in *The Nova Scotian* newspaper. The great popularity they acquired, induced the Editor of that paper to apply to the Author for the remaining part of the series, and permission to publish the whole entire. This request having been acceded to, the Editor has now the pleasure of laying them before the public in their present shape.

Halifax, December, 1836.

CONTENTS

IN the course of looking for a text on which to base this reprint, I bought second-hand a few months ago an early American edition of *The Clockmaker*. Pasted to the inside of the cover was a newspaper clipping which read as follows:

ORIGINAL "SAM SLICK" DEAD

A despatch from Bangor, Maine, to the Montreal "Star" states: Jackson Young, known throughout New England as the original of "Sam Slick, the Yankee Clockmaker," written by Judge Thomas Chandler Haliburton, is dead here, aged 87 years....

Mr Young was one of four brothers who came to Maine from Vermont and travelled the State selling Yankee notions in peddlers' carts. Later they took up the clock business, and thousands of the old-fashioned brass clocks still doing duty in the farm-houses of Maine and the provinces were bought from the Young brothers.

Samuel J. Young was the last surviving of the four, the others of whom became millionaires in Western and Canadian lumbering and lands, all getting their start from peddling clocks.

Was Samuel Jackson Young in fact the "original" of T. C. Haliburton's Sam Slick? Probably not. The news item is dated 1908—which means that the Mr. Young who has died "aged 87 years" could have been no more than a teenager, with (as Sam would say) many rings to grow on his horns yet, at the time when Mr. Slick made his first bow to the public in the pages of *The Novascotian* in 1835. Moreover the best authorities, including Haliburton himself on one occasion, are agreed that there was no "original" for Sam in this narrow sense.

What the clipping does establish, on the other hand, is the remarkable vitality of Haliburton's portrait of the clockmaker —and at the same time, of course, its faithfulness to a real-life background of clock-peddling and Yankee enterprise. Sam Slick of Slickville, Connecticut, became a legend in his own time. When Haliburton visited England in 1838, Lord Abinger is reported to have raised himself on one elbow from a sick-bed long enough to ask the author if it was not true (as he firmly believed) "that there is a veritable Sam Slick in the flesh now selling clocks to the Bluenoses." To which Haliburton replied no, it was not true. But the point is that Sam was the kind of person one read about and was promptly sure that one knew, or that someone knew, in the flesh. Such vitality is proof against time. If Samuel Young, therefore, is very much dead today, Samuel Slick is not. It seems likely, in fact, that he will outlive even the very durable brass clocks which those of his calling are said to have sold by the thousands to maritimers more than a century ago.

More specifically, Sam Slick has survived because the man who created him was a capable humorist—and the tricks of making people laugh change little with the years. Reports of Haliburton refer often to his lively wit, and tradition has it that he had a special fondness for off-colour jokes. The off-colour jokes had to remain for the most part private; but the rest of his comic spirit (with just a touch of bawdiness for sauce) Haliburton successfully incorporated in the one memorable character that was to come from his pen. Above all, he made this character a reflection of his own remarkable energy of mind and imagination. His methods were the standard ones of comedy : exaggeration and disruptive turns of speech and action.

Yet universal laughter can have a special ring to it, and it is worth recalling that the American humorist Artemus Ward is said to have named Haliburton "the father of American humour." The claim, like all of its kind, is open to debate. It is certainly not one that has found much favour with American critics since Ward's time, who have generally preferred that their founding-father be home-grown. But however the case is argued, there is at any rate no disputing the fact that Haliburton is often funny in a recognizably North American way. Sam's democratic brashness, his "calculatin' " shrewdness, his colossal assurance and resourcefulness in argument, his readiness with homespun comments, with anecdotes and tall tales—all these traits were already connected with popular conceptions of the Yankee character in Haliburton's time, and most of them were well suited to humorous treatment. It is true they are traits which occur (though usually with a different twist) in English humour. But their aggregate in Sam is a distinctive mark. Davy Crockett, type of the "ring-tailed roarer" of the West, is his blood-brother; and so also is Jack Downing, Seba Smith's dispenser of axe-handles and cracker-barrel philosophy who had a wide following in these years throughout the eastern states. The legendary Paul Bunyan is a not-too-distant relative.

Certainly, if I were asked to name the qualities of *The Clockmaker* which attracted me most, I would choose two which seem somehow more native to the New World than the Old— audacity and energy. If these are not noticeably Canadian qualities, it is perhaps because Haliburton wrote long before national self-consciousness gave birth, in the strange Canadian way, to national diffidence. The qualities are of course Sam's, but they are easily transferred into a feeling one has about the whole book. The kind of spawning of comic situation that goes on in *The Clockmaker* is part of this feeling; but much more it is a matter of language—the colourful and inexhaustible speech which flows from page to page, and which in sum makes up one of the most remarkable monologues ever written. Sober critics (mostly Canadian) of Haliburton's time complained of murders committed on grammar and the proper use of words. They found that Sam, like his friend January Snow, knew English "real well," and could do "near about anything but speak it." But in the wake of slaughtered forms rise lively words and phrases, and altogether as fine an array of imagery as one could hope for in a shelf-load of contemporary writing.

Is a man crestfallen, put out, downhearted? Well, says Sam, he's "streaked" or "chop-fallen." Or, better still, he's "wamblecropt." And the words stream out into images—images bred in the barnyards, the inns, the farm-kitchens, the seacoast villages of Nova Scotia. A pettifogging justice, says Sam, is "a regular suck-egg." "They ought to pay his passage, as we do such critters, tell him his place is taken in the mail coach, and if he is found here after twenty-four hours, they'd make a carpenter's plumb-bob of him, and hang him outside the church steeple, to try if it was perpendicular." Small matter who the Grahamites were, but the man who belonged to this sect catches the eye. "I once travelled all through the State of Maine with one of them 'ere chaps," Sam says. "He was as thin as a whippin' post. His skin looked like a blown bladder arter some of the air had leaked out, kinder wrinkled and rumpled like, and his eye as dim as a lamp that's livin' on a short allowance of ile. He put me in mind of a pair of kitchen tongs, all legs, shaft, and head, and no belly; a real gander-gutted lookin' critter, as holler as a bamboo walkin' cane, and twice as yaller." See also, in one of many unflattering poses, the Bluenose—"with his go-to-meetin' clothes on, coat-tails pinned up behind like a leather blind of a shay, an old spur on one heel, and pipe stuck through his hatband, mounted on one of these limber-timbered critters. that moves its hind legs like a hen scratchin' gravel. . . ." Turbulent, sometimes overwrought, but always bold and vigorous, this language is probably the heart of the book's attraction for the present-day reader.

The passages quoted, however, will suggest that Sam Slick is often funny, not in an empty-headed way, but with a purpose. Most amusement is at someone else's expense, and the fact is that Haliburton, in his own person a bold and energetic thinker, was very much bent on satiric business when he created Mr. Slick. Indeed there were to be times in Sam's later career when this satiric business fairly drained the life-blood out of him, so that he became no more than the vehicle for political argument on questions frequently as clouded with contemporary reference as the records of our Pipeline Debate will appear to be to readers a hundred years from now. Fortunately, what is published in this reprint (which is only the first of three series of *The Clockmaker*) contains little that needs to be explained in terms of political and social developments in the Nova Scotia of Haliburton's time. An allusion, for example, to a project much favoured by Haliburton for building a railroad from Halifax through to the Minas Basin is manageable enough in its own context; and if not, there is no great loss. And for the rest, we shall do well enough if we simply approach the satirical side of the book at the ground-floor level of an attack upon pride and laziness and greed and the special vagaries of women—upon human traits, in other words, as recognizable today as they were in 1835. Still, since a specific design controlled the conception of *The Clockmaker*, it is perhaps worth doing a little more than this to pin down Haliburton's intentions.

Like the best satire, Haliburton's comes from clearly defined opinions strongly held in the face of opposing values. Haliburton was a Tory of an old and rigorous school—a school so completely overwhelmed within the last century by the triumphs of labour and democratic thought as to be almost a museum-piece now. Yet the line is pure from Burke (whom Haliburton greatly admired); and perhaps the shift of political thought to the right that has taken place in recent years makes Haliburton's outlook

more widely acceptable today than was the case twenty or
thirty years ago.

It should not at any rate be difficult for the present-day reader
to make the necessary distinction between this outlook and
that of a narrow-minded reactionary. Haliburton fashioned his
convictions into a coherent and, in its own way, enterprising
political philosophy. He came by his Tory principles honestly :
from his parents, who were Loyalist stock transplanted from
New England to Nova Scotia about the time of the American
Revolution; from his studies and associations at King's College,
Windsor, which was in his day the seat of established Anglican-
ism and social privilege in higher learning; and, perhaps most
notably, from his own thoughtful appraisals of the British and
American constitutions. On the Bench and in the House of
Assembly, it is true, he showed a certain amount of concern for
political justice and human rights. Contrary to a commonly held
opinion, however, such a concern is by no means incompatible
with the viewpoint of a true-blue Tory. With as much consist-
ency as can be demanded of any man, Haliburton made Tory
principles the cornerstone of his thinking from the time of his
first entry into provincial politics in 1826 to the time of his
death in England in 1865. He stood for the British constitution
and the perpetuation of colonial ties with the mother country;
he opposed mob rule, the levelling tendencies of his age, and the
swing towards responsible government in the Canadian provinces.

It was the particular issue of responsible government that
awoke the satirist in Haliburton. History, which saw the
achievement of responsible government in the maritimes by
1848 and the course of all the provinces set steadily in the direc-
tion of the national independence which Canada now enjoys,
has put the satirist on the wrong side of the fence. Yet Haliburton's mistrust of the initial gesture towards independence
was shared by some of the best minds of the period. When he
came up to Halifax in 1826 as a member for Annapolis Royal,
he found the House of Assembly at odds with the appointed
Executive Council. By the terms of the colonial constitution,
this Council, acting in conjunction with the Governor, could
block any legislation passed on to it by the House of Assembly.
And the Council, being on the whole a body of special privilege
whose members were tied to the Crown by the strings of ap-
pointment, was beginning to make notorious use of these
powers. For a time, when the stand taken by the Assembly

seemed to be a simple one against injustice and oppression at the hands of a privileged few, Haliburton supported the call for reform. But it was a different matter when the Reformers (as they came to be called) began to argue that the ministers of provincial government should be responsible, not to the Crown of England, but to the people of Nova Scotia. To Haliburton, as to Lord John Russell, such a conception of colonial government was completely at variance with the conception of a continued connection between the colony and the mother country. The logical outcome could only be independence; and Haliburton, perhaps because of his realistic insight into the American experiment and an accompanying fear that the United States might in course of time simply engulf the British provinces, could see no future in independence for Nova Scotia. He split with the Reformers and sharpened his quill for the attack.

Thus Sam Slick was born. Since the satire of the first series of *The Clockmaker* was veiled, and since Joseph Howe, though the leader of the reform movement, was still a good friend of the author, it was not wholly inappropriate that the sketches should appear in the columns of Howe's *Novascotian*. There arose, nevertheless, the pleasant paradox of this Yankee democrat, Mr. Slick, being fathered by a Tory die-hard and presented to the public in the pages of a liberal newspaper.

As originally conceived (for he was to prove unwieldy in later books), Sam Slick was a brilliant choice of weapon. The crux of the matter, as Haliburton saw it, was that the Bluenoses spent far too much time agitating for political reform and laying the ills of their depressed economic condition at anyone's door but their own. Nova Scotia, he argued, was a country of immense natural resources, strategically located on the sea-lanes, and a good farming province to boot, provided hard work and the right methods were applied. What better stick with which to beat the Bluenoses than Sam? He was an outsider with a plausible knowledge of the country and a plausible interest in its welfare. At the same time, he had the credentials of a "grassroots" representative of a people already renowned for their industriousness and shrewd application to practical affairs, for their bold speech and love of exaggeration. Sam was a natural for the job. It mattered little in these early days of the first series that a Yankee democrat was being put to work in the interests of Tory ideals; for Haliburton was not at this stage inclined to press the more strictly political side of his views. The ideals of Benjamin Franklin, already implanted in the American

conscience as national characteristics, were the ideals of fru-
gality, industry, and practicality. And these were ideals admir-
ably suited to Haliburton's vision of a revived agrarian economy
for Nova Scotia. The arch-Tory Swift is their common
denominator.

But the best of Sam was that he could be used to beat more
heads than one. If Sam could say that *The Clockmaker* "wipes
up the Bluenoses considerable hard," he could say also, perhaps
with more truth than he knew, that it "don't let off the Yankees
so very easy neither." The balance of the Yankee criticism was
a difficult one to maintain, since ridicule of Sam, once out of
hand, could quickly damage his authority as the homespun
prosecutor of the case against the Nova Scotians. A few touches
must suffice—a little inflation in Sam under the pressure of
some of his own hot air about the prowess of the American
eagle; a little deflation, as needed, from the Squire. It was better
that the rest of the criticism be cleared out of Sam's way and
dropped in the lap of the Rev. Mr. Hopewell. And the third
target was the British—chiefly for the pride and bull-headedness
which produced what Haliburton came more and more to see as
a badly informed and unintelligent colonial policy. In this case,
of course, it was not the problem of keeping Sam in character
(which was no problem at all), but the much stronger check of
Haliburton's fundamental sympathies that set the curb on ridicule. Over the whole of this first series of sketches, therefore,
the play of satire is remarkably rich and complex. It provides an
interesting glimpse, if only a glimpse, of a way Canadians would
later develop of looking in upon themselves with reasonable
clarity by looking out upon John Bull and Uncle Sam. By the
same token, it prophesies faintly our twentieth-century commit-
ment to the uninspiring but useful middle course. In his later
work Haliburton foresaw specifically something of the nature
and function of the Commonwealth as we know it today. It is
certainly a fair guess that he would have understood very well
Canada's present role in NATO.

Satire and humour, then, combine to make *The Clockmaker*
a book well worth keeping in print. It was, in fact, by far the
most creditable piece of writing in this line to be produced in
Canada for many years to come. The winning of responsible
government, without the severance of ties with the parent state,
must be counted one of the great events in Canadian history—
perhaps even in the history of the western world. But it took
the sharp taste out of the nation's drink. Extremes had found

their cue in compromise and were soon, duly moderated, to make a holy alliance with Victorian seriousness. Thus the springs which feed such writing as Haliburton's were pretty well dried up at their source. The country's centre of settlement and development shifted westward, moreover, and it was to be a long time before new writers could experience the benefits Haliburton enjoyed from being deeply rooted in a distinctive cultural environment. Whatever the reasons, nearly a hundred years were to pass before Canadians took freely to laughter and mockery again. Leacock was a long way off.

ROBERT L. McDOUGALL

Carleton College, Ottawa,
May, 1958

THE CLOCKMAKER

To Mr. Howe.

Sir—I received your letter, and note its contents. I ain't over half pleased, I tell you; I think I have been used scandalous, that's a fact. It warn't the part of a gentleman for to go and pump me arter that fashion, and then go right off and blart it out in print. It was a nasty, dirty, mean action, and I don't thank you nor the Squire a bit for it. It will be more nor a thousand dollars out of my pocket. There's an eend to the Clock trade now, and a pretty kettle of fish I've made on it, hav'n't I? I shall never hear the last on it, and what am I to say when I go back to the States? I'll take my oath I never said one half the stuff he has set down there; and as for that long lochrum about Mr. Everett, and the Hon. Alden Gobble, and Minister, there ain't a word of truth in it from beginnin' to eend. If ever I come near hand to him ag'in, I'll larn him—but never mind, I say nothin'. Now there's one thing I don't cleverly understand. If this here book is my *"Sayins and Doins"* how comes it your'n or the Squire's either? If my thoughts and notions are my own, how can they be any other folks's? According to my idee you have no more right to take them, than you have to take my clocks without payin' for 'em. A man that would be guilty of such an action is no gentleman, that's flat, and if you don't like it you may lump it—for I don't valy him, nor you neither, nor are a Bluenose that ever stept in shoe-leather, the matter of a pin's head. I don't know as ever I felt so ugly afore since I was raised; why didn't he put his name to it, as well as mine? When an article han't the maker's name and factory on it, it shows it's a cheat, and he's ashamed to own it. If I'm to have the name, I'll have the game, or I'll know the cause why, that's a fact. Now folks say you are a considerable of a candid man, and right up and down in your dealins, and do things above board, handsum

After these sketches had gone through the press, and were ready for Publication, we sent Mr. Slick a copy; and shortly afterwards received from him the following letter, which characteristic communication we give entire.—Editor [Richard Bentley edition, 1837.]

—at least so I've hearn tell. That's what I like; I love to deal with such folks. Now 'spose you make me an offer? You'll find me not very difficult to trade with, and I don't know but I might put off more than half of the books myself, tu. I'll tell you how I'd work it. I'd say, "Here's a book they've namesaked arter me, Sam Slick, the Clockmaker, but it tante mine, and I can't altogether jist say rightly whose it is. Some say it's the General's, and some say it's the Bishop's, and some says it's Howe himself; but I ain't availed who it is. It's a wise child that knows its own father. It wipes up the Bluenoses considerable hard, and don't let off the Yankees so very easy neither, but it's generally allowed to be about the prettiest book ever writ in this country; and although it ain't altogether jist gospel what's in it, there's some pretty home truths in it, that's a fact. Whoever wrote it must be a funny feller, too, that's sart'in; for there are some queer stories in it that no soul could help larfin' at, that's a fact. It's about the wittiest book I ever see'd. It's nearly all sold off, but jist a few copies I've kept for my old customers. The price is just 5s. 6d., but I'll let you have it for 5s., because you'll not get another chance to have one." Always ax a sixpence more than the price, and then bate it, and when Bluenose hears that, he thinks he's got a bargain, and bites directly. I never see one on 'em yet that didn't fall right into the trap.

Yes, make me an offer, and you and I will trade, I think. But fair play's a jewel, and I must say I feel ryled and kinder sore. I han't been used handsum atween you two, and it don't seem to me that I ought to be made a fool on in that book, arter that fashion, for folks to laugh at, and then be sheered out of the spec. If I am, somebody had better look out for squalls, I tell you. I'm as easy as an old glove, but a glove ain't an old shoe to be trod on, and I think a certain person will find that out afore he is six months older, or else I'm mistakened, that's all. Hopin' to hear from you soon, I remain yours to command,

Samuel Slick

Pugnose's Inn, River Philip, Dec. 25, 1836.

P.S. I see in the last page it is writ, that the Squire is to take another journey round the Shore, and back to Halifax with me next Spring. Well, I did agree with him, to drive him round the coast, but don't you mind—we'll understand each other, I guess, afore we start. I concait he'll rise considerably airly in the mornin', afore he catches me asleep ag'in. I'll be wide awake for him next hitch, that's a fact. I'd a ginn a thousand dollars if he had only used Campbell's name instead of mine; for he was a'most an almighty villain, and cheated a proper raft of folks and then shipped himself off to Botany Bay, for fear folks would transport him there; you couldn't rub out Slick, and put in Campbell, could you? that's a good feller; if you would I'd make it worth your while, you may depend.

I WAS always well mounted: I am fond of a horse, and always piqued myself on having the fastest trotter in the Province. I have made no great progress in the world; I feel doubly, therefore, the pleasure of not being surpassed on the road. I never feel so well or so cheerful as on horseback, for there is something exhilarating in quick motion; and, old as I am, I feel a pleasure in making any person whom I meet on the way put his horse to the full gallop, to keep pace with my trotter. Poor Ethiop! You recollect him, how he was wont to lay back his ears on his arched neck, and push away from all competition? He is done, poor fellow! The spavin spoiled his speed, and he now roams at large upon "my farm at Truro." Mohawk never failed me till this summer.

I pride myself—you may laugh at such childish weakness in a man of my age—but still, I pride myself in taking the conceit out of coxcombs I meet on the road, and on the ease with which I can leave a fool behind, whose nonsense disturbs my solitary musings.

On my last journey to Fort Lawrence, as the beautiful view of Colchester had just opened upon me, and as I was contemplating its richness and exquisite scenery, a tall, thin man, with hollow cheeks and bright, twinkling black eyes, on a good bay horse, somewhat out of condition, overtook me; and drawing up, said, "I guess you started early this morning, sir?"

"I did, sir," I replied.

"You did not come from Halifax, I presume, sir, did you?" in a dialect too rich to be mistaken as genuine Yankee. "And which way may you be travelling?" asked my inquisitive companion.

"To Fort Lawrence."

"Ah!" said he, "so am I; it is in my circuit."

The word *circuit* sounded so professional, I looked again at him, to ascertain whether I had ever seen him before, or whether I had met with one of those nameless, but innumerable limbs of the law, who now flourish in every district of the Province. There was a keenness about his eyes, and an acuteness of expression, much in favour of the law; but the dress, and general bearing of the man, made against the supposition. His was not the coat of a man who can afford to wear an old coat, nor was it one of "Tempest and More's," that distinguish country lawyers from country boobies. His clothes were well made, and of good materials, but looked as if their owner had shrunk a little since they were made for him; they hung somewhat loose on him. A large brooch, and some superfluous seals and gold keys, which ornamented his outward man, looked "New England" like. A visit to the States, had perhaps, I thought, turned this Colchester beau into a Yankee fop. Of what consequence was it to me who he was? In either case I had nothing to do with him, and I desired neither his acquaintance nor his company. Still I could not but ask myself, Who can this man be?

"I am not aware," said I, "that there is a court sitting at this time at Cumberland."

"Nor am I," said my friend. What, then, could he have to do with the circuit? It occurred to me he must be a Methodist preacher. I looked again, but his appearance again puzzled me. His attire might do, the colour might be suitable, the broad brim not out of place; but there was a want of that staidness of look, that seriousness of countenance, that expression, in short, so characteristic of the clergy.

I could not account for my idle curiosity—a curiosity which, in him, I had the moment before viewed both with suspicion and disgust; but so it was, I felt a desire to know who he could be who was neither lawyer nor preacher, and yet talked of his circuit with the gravity of both. How ridiculous, I thought to myself, is this; I will leave him. Turning towards him, I said I feared I should be late for breakfast, and must therefore bid him good morning. Mohawk felt the pressure of my knees, and away we went at a slapping pace. I congratulated myself on conquering my own curiosity, and on avoiding that of my travelling companion. This, I said to myself, this is the value of a good horse; I patted his neck; I felt proud of him. Presently I heard the steps of the unknown's horse—the clatter increased. Ah, my friend, thought I, it won't do; you should be well mounted if you desire my company. I pushed Mohawk faster, faster, faster—to his best. He outdid himself; he had never trotted so handsomely, so easily, so well.

"I guess that is a pretty considerable smart horse," said the stranger, as he came beside me, and apparently reined in to prevent his horse passing me; "there is not, I reckon, so spry a one on my circuit."

Circuit or no circuit, one thing was settled in my mind—he was a Yankee, and a very impertinent Yankee too. I felt humbled, my pride was hurt, and Mohawk was beaten. To continue this trotting contest was humiliating; I yielded, therefore, before the victory was palpable, and pulled up.

"Yes," continued he, "a horse of pretty considerable good action, and a pretty fair trotter too, I guess." Pride must have a fall: I confess mine was prostrate in the dust. These words cut me to the heart. What! is it come to this, poor Mohawk, that you, the admiration of all but the envious, the great Mohawk, the standard by which all other horses are measured—trots next to Mohawk, only yields to Mohawk, looks like Mohawk—that you are, after all, only a counterfeit, and pronounced by a straggling Yankee to be merely "a pretty fair trotter!"

"If he was trained, I guess that he might be made to do a little more. Excuse me, but if you divide your weight between the knee and the stirrup, rather most on the knee, and rise forward on the saddle, so as to leave a little daylight between you and it, I hope I may never ride this circuit again, if you don't get a mile more an hour out of him."

What! not enough, I mentally groaned, to have my horse beaten, but I must be told that I don't know how to ride him; and that, too, by a Yankee! Aye, there's the rub—a Yankee what? Perhaps a half-bred puppy, half Yankee, half Bluenose. As there is no escape, I'll try to make out my riding master. "Your circuit?" said I, my looks expressing all the surprise they were capable of, "your circuit, pray what may that be?"

"O," said he, "the eastern circuit; I am on the eastern circuit, sir."

"I have heard," said I, feeling that I now had a lawyer to deal with, "that there is a great deal of business on this circuit. Pray, are there many cases of importance?"

"There is a pretty fair business to be done, at least there has been, but the cases are of no great value; we do not make much of them, we get them up very easy, but they don't bring much profit." What a beast, thought I, is this! and what a curse to a country, to have such an unfeeling, pettifogging rascal practising in it! a horse jockey, too—what a finished character! I'll try him on that branch of his business.

"That is a superior animal you are mounted on," said I; "I seldom meet one that can travel with mine."

"Yes," said he coolly, "a considerable fair traveller, and most particular good bottom." I hesitated; this man, who talks with such unblushing effrontery of getting up cases, and making profit out of them, cannot be offended at the question—yes, I will put it to him.

"Do you feel an inclination to part with him?"

"I never part with a horse, sir, that suits me," said he. "I am fond of a horse: I don't like to ride in the dust after everyone I meet, and I allow no man to pass me but when I choose." Is it possible, I thought, that he can know me—that he has heard of my foible, and is quizzing me? or have I this feeling in common with him?

"But," continued I, "you might supply yourself again."

"Not on this circuit, I guess," said he, "nor yet in Campbell's circuit."

"Campbell's circuit—pray, sir, what is that?"

"That," said he, "is the western; and Lampton rides the shore circuit; and as for the people on the shore, they know so little of horses that, Lampton tells me, a man from Aylesford once sold a hornless ox there, whose tail he had cut and nicked, for a horse of the Goliath breed."

"I should think," said I, "that Mr. Lampton must have no lack of cases among such enlightened clients."

"Clients, sir!" said my friend, "Mr. Lampton is not a lawyer."

"I beg pardon, I thought you said he rode the circuit."

"We call it a circuit," said the stranger, who seemed by no means flattered by the mistake; "we divide the Province, as in the Almanac, into circuits, in each of which we separately carry on our business of manufacturing and selling clocks. There are few, I guess," said the Clockmaker, "who go upon *tick* as much as we do, who have so little use for lawyers; if attorneys could wind a man up again, after he has been fairly run down, I guess they'd be a pretty harmless sort of folks."

This explanation restored my good humour, and as I could not quit my companion, and he did not feel disposed to leave me, I made up my mind to travel with him to Fort Lawrence, the limit of his circuit.

I HAD heard of Yankee clock peddlers, tin peddlers, and Bible peddlers, especially of him who sold Polyglot Bibles (*all in English*) to the amount of sixteen thousand pounds. The house of every substantial farmer had three substantial ornaments: a wooden clock, a tin reflector, and a Polyglot Bible. How is it that an American can sell his wares, at whatever price he pleases, where a Bluenose would fail to make a sale at all? I will inquire of the Clockmaker the secret of his success.

"What a pity it is, Mr. Slick"—for such was his name—"what a pity it is," said I, "that you, who are so successful in teaching these people the value of clocks, could not also teach them the value of time."

"I guess," said he, "they have got that ring to grow on their horns yet, which every four-year-old has in our country. We reckon hours and minutes to be dollars and cents. They do nothing in these parts but eat, drink, smoke, sleep, ride about, lounge at taverns, make speeches at temperance meetings, and talk about 'House of Assembly.' If a man don't hoe his corn, and he don't get a crop, he says it is owing to the bank; and if he runs into debt and is sued, why, he says the lawyers are a curse to the country. They are a most idle set of folks, I tell you."

"But how is it," said I, "that you manage to sell such an immense number of clocks, which certainly cannot be called necessary articles, among a people with whom there seems to be so great a scarcity of money?" Mr. Slick paused, as if considering the propriety of answering the question, and looking me in the face, said in a confidential tone——

"Why, I don't care if I do tell you, for the market is glutted, and I shall quit this circuit. It is done by a knowledge of *soft sawder* and *human natur'*. But here is Deacon Flint's," said he; "I have but one clock left, and I guess I will sell it to him."

At the gate of a most comfortable-looking farmhouse stood Deacon Flint, a respectable old man, who had understood the value of time better than most of his neighbours, if one might judge from the appearance of everything about him. After the usual salutation, an invitation to "alight" was accepted by Mr. Slick, who said he wished to take leave of Mrs. Flint before he left Colchester.

We had hardly entered the house, before the Clockmaker pointed to the view from the window, and, addressing himself to me, said, "If I was to tell them in Connecticut there was such a farm as this away down East here in Nova Scotia, they wouldn't believe me. Why, there ain't such a location in all New England. The Deacon has a hundred acres of dyke——"

"Seventy," said the Deacon, "only seventy."

"Well, seventy; but then there is your fine deep bottom, why I could run a ramrod into it——"

"Interval, we call it," said the Deacon, who though evidently pleased at this eulogium, seemed to wish the experiment of the ramrod to be tried in the right place.

"Well, interval, if you please—though Professor Eleazer Cumstick, in his work on Ohio, calls them bottoms—is just as good as dyke. Then there is that water privilege, worth three or four thousand dollars, twice as good as what Governor Cass paid fifteen thousand dollars for. I wonder, Deacon, you don't put up a carding mill on it; the same works would carry a turning lathe, a shingle machine, a circular saw, grind bark, and——"

"Too old," said the Deacon, "too old for all those speculations——"

"Old!" repeated the Clockmaker, "not you; why you are worth half a dozen of the young men we see, nowadays; you are young enough to have——" Here he said something in a lower tone of voice, which I did not distinctly hear; but whatever it was, the Deacon was pleased; he smiled, and said he did not think of such things now.

"But your beasts, dear me, your beasts must be put in and have a feed"; saying which, he went out to order them to be taken to the stable.

As the old gentleman closed the door after him, Mr. Slick drew near to me, and said in an undertone, "That is what I call 'soft sawder.' An Englishman would pass that man as a sheep passes a hog in a pasture, without looking at him; or," said he, looking rather archly, "if he was mounted on a pretty smart horse, I guess he'd trot away, if he could. Now I find——" Here his lecture on "soft sawder" was cut short by the entrance of Mrs. Flint.

"Jist come to say good-bye, Mrs. Flint."

"What, have you sold all your clocks?"

"Yes, and very low too, for money is scarce, and I wish to close the consarn; no, I am wrong in saying all, for I have just one left. Neighbour Steel's wife asked to have the refusal of it, but I guess I won't sell it; I had but two of them, this one and the feller of it, that I sold Governor Lincoln. General Green, the Secretary of State for Maine, said he'd give me fifty dollars for this here one—it has composition wheels and patent axles, is a beautiful article, a real first chop, no mistake, genuine super-fine—but I guess I'll take it back; and besides, Squire Hawk might think kinder hard, that I did not give him the offer."

"Dear me!" said Mrs. Flint, "I should like to see it; where is it?"

"It is in a chest of mine over the way, at Tom Tape's store. I guess he can ship it on to Eastport."

"That's a good man," said Mrs. Flint, "jist let's look at it."

Mr. Slick, willing to oblige, yielded to these entreaties, and soon produced the clock—a gaudy, highly varnished, trumpery looking affair. He placed it on the chimney-piece, where its beauties were pointed out and duly appreciated by Mrs. Flint, whose admiration was about ending in a proposal when Mr. Flint returned from giving his directions about the care of the horses. The Deacon praised the clock; he too thought it a hand-some one; but the Deacon was a prudent man; he had a watch; he was sorry, but he had no occasion for a clock.

"I guess you're in the wrong furrow this time, Deacon, it ain't for sale," said Mr. Slick; "and if it was, I reckon neighbour Steel's wife would have it, for she gave me no peace about it." Mrs. Flint said that Mr. Steel had enough to do, poor man, to pay his interest, without buying clocks for his wife.

"It is no consarn of mine," said Mr. Slick, "as long as he pays me what he has to do; but I guess I don't want to sell it, and besides, it comes too high; that clock can't be made at Rhode Island under forty dollars. Why, it ain't possible," said the Clock-maker, in apparent surprise, looking at his watch, "why as I'm alive it is four o'clock, and if I haven't been two hours here. How on airth shall I reach River Philip tonight? I'll tell you what, Mrs. Flint, I'll leave the clock in your care till I return, on my way to the States. I'll set it a-going and put it to the right time."

As soon as this operation was performed, he delivered the key to the Deacon with a sort of serio-comic injunction to wind up the clock every Saturday night, which Mrs. Flint said she would take care should be done, and promised to remind her husband of it, in case he should chance to forget it.

"That," said the Clockmaker, as soon as we were mounted, "that I call *'human natur'*! Now that clock is sold for forty dollars; it cost me just six dollars and fifty cents. Mrs. Flint will never let Mrs. Steel have the refusal, nor will the Deacon learn until I call for the clock, that having once indulged in the use of a superfluity, how difficult it is to give it up. We can do without any article of luxury we have never had, but when once obtained, it is not in 'human natur' ' to surrender it voluntarily. Of fifteen thousand sold by myself and partners in this Province, twelve thousand were left in this manner, and only ten clocks were ever returned; when we called for them they invariably bought them. We trust to 'soft sawder' to get them into the house, and to 'human natur',' that they never come out of it."

"Do you see them 'ere swallows," said the Clockmaker, "how low they fly? Well, I presume we shall have rain right away; and them noisy critters, them gulls, how close they keep to the water, down there in the Shubenacadie; well that's a sure sign. If we study natur', we don't want no thermometer. But I guess we shall be in time to get under cover in a shingle-maker's shed, about three miles ahead on us."

We had just reached the deserted hovel, when the rain fell in torrents.

"I reckon," said the Clockmaker, as he sat himself down on a bundle of shingles, "I reckon they are bad off for inns in this country. When a feller is too lazy to work here, he paints his name over his door, and calls it a tavern, and as like as not he makes the whole neighbourhood as lazy as himself. It is about as easy to find a good inn in Halifax, as it is to find wool on a goat's back. An inn, to be a good consarn, must be built on purpose; you can no more make a good tavern out of a common dwelling house, I expect, than a good coat out of an old pair of trousers. They are eternal lazy, you may depend. Now there might be a grand spec made there, in building a good inn and a good church."

"What a sacrilegious and unnatural union!" said I, with most unaffected surprise.

"Not at all," said Mr. Slick; "we build both on speculation in the States, and make a good deal of profit out of 'em too, I tell you. We look out a good sightly place, in a town like Halifax, that is pretty considerably well peopled, with folks that are good marks; and if there is no real right down good preacher among them, we build a handsome church, touched off like a New York liner, a real taking looking thing, and then we look out for a preacher, a crack man, a regular ten horse power chap; well, we hire him, and we have to give pretty high wages too, say twelve hundred or sixteen hundred dollars a year. We take him at first on trial for a Sabbath or two, to try his paces, and if he takes with the folks, if he goes down well, we clinch the bargain, and let and sell the pews; and I tell you it pays well, and makes a real good investment. There were few better specs among us than inns and churches, until the railroads came on the carpet; as soon as the novelty of the new preacher wears off we hire another, and that keeps up the steam."

"I trust it will be long, very long, my friend," said I, "ere the rage for speculation introduces 'the money-changers into the Temple,' with us."

Mr. Slick looked at me with a most ineffable expression of pity and surprise. "Depend on it, sir," said he, with a most philosophical air, "this Province is much behind the intelligence of the age. But if it is behind us in that respect, it is a long chalk ahead on us in others. I never seed or heerd tell of a country that had so many natural privileges as this. Why, there are twice as many harbours and water-powers here, as we have all the way from Eastport to New Or*leens*. They have all they can ax, and more than they desarve. They have iron, coal, slate, grindstone, lime, fire-stone, gypsum, free-stone, and a list as long as an auctioneer's catalogue. But they are either asleep, or stone blind to them. Their shores are crowded with fish, and their lands covered with wood. A government that lays as light on 'em as a down counterp'in, and no taxes. Then look at their dykes. The Lord seems to have made 'em on purpose for such lazy folks. If you were to tell the citizens of our country that these dykes had been cropped for a hundred years without manure, they'd say, they guessed you had seen Col. Crockett, the greatest hand at a flam in our nation. You have heerd tell of a man who couldn't see London for the houses? I tell you, if we had this country, you couldn't see the harbours for the shipping. There'd be a rush of folks to it; as there is in one of our inns, to the dinner table, when they sometimes get jammed together in the doorway, and a man has to take a running leap over their heads, afore he can get in. A little nigger boy in New York found a diamond worth two thousand dollars; well, he sold it to a watchmaker for fifty cents; the little critter didn't know no better. Your people are just like the nigger boy—they don't know the value of their diamond.

"Do you know the reason monkeys are no good? because they chatter all day long; so do the niggers, and so do the Bluenoses of Novia Scotia; it's all talk and no work. Now with us it's all work and no talk; in our shipyards, our factories, our mills, and even in our vessels, there's no talk; a man can't work and talk too. I guess if you were at the factories at Lowell we'd show you a wonder—five hundred gals at work together all in silence. I don't think our great country has such a real natural curiosity as that; I expect the world don't contain the beat of that; for a woman's tongue goes so slick of itself, without water power or steam, and moves so easy on its hinges, that it's no easy matter to put a spring-stop on it, I tell you; it comes as natural as drinkin' mint julip.

"I don't pretend to say the gals don't nullify the rule, sometimes, at intermission and arter hours, but when they do, if they don't let go, then it's a pity. You have heerd a school come out, of little boys? Lord, it's no touch to it. Or a flock of geese at it? They are no more a match for 'em than a pony is for a coachhorse. But when they are at work, all's as still as sleep and no snoring. I guess we have a right to brag o' that invention; we trained the dear critters so they don't think of striking the minutes and seconds no longer.

"Now the folks of Halifax take it all out in talking. They talk of steamboats, whalers, and railroads; but they all end where they begin—in talk. I don't think I'd be out in my latitude if I was to say they beat the womenkind at that. One fellow says, 'I talk of going to England'; another says, 'I talk of going to the country'; while a third says, 'I talk of going to sleep.' If we happen to speak of such things, we say, 'I'm right off down East,' or 'I'm away off South,' and away we go jist like a streak of lightning.

"When we want folks to talk, we pay 'em for it, such as ministers, lawyers, and members of Congress; but then we expect the use of their tongues, and not their hands; and when we pay folks to work, we expect the use of their hands, and not their tongues. I guess work don't come kind o' natural to the people of this Province, no more than it does to a full-bred horse. I expect they think they have a little too much blood in 'em for work, for they are near about as proud as they are lazy.

"Now the bees know how to sarve out such chaps, for they have their drones too. Well, they reckon it's no fun, a-making honey all summer, for these idle critters to eat all winter, so they give 'em Lynch law. They have a regular built mob of citizens, and string up the drones like the Vicksburg gamblers. Their maxim is, and not a bad one neither, I guess, 'No work, no honey.' "

It was late before we arrived at Pugnose's inn; the evening was cool, and a fire was cheering and comfortable. Mr. Slick declined any share in the bottle of wine; he said he was dyspeptic; and a glass or two soon convinced me that it was likely to produce in me something worse than dyspepsia. It was speedily removed, and we drew up to the fire. Taking a small penknife from his pocket, he began to whittle a thin piece of dry wood, which lay on the hearth; and, after musing some time, said—

"I guess you've never been in the States?" I replied that I had not, but that before I returned to England I proposed visiting that country.

"There," said he, "you'll see the great Daniel Webster; he's a great man, I tell you; King William, number four, I guess, would be no match for him as an orator—he'd talk him out of sight in half an hour. If he was in your House of Commons, I reckon he'd make some of your great folks look pretty streaked; he's a true patriot and statesman, the first in our country, and a most particular cute lawyer. There was a Quaker chap too cute for him once though. This Quaker, a pretty knowin' old shaver, had a cause down to Rhode Island; so he went to Daniel to hire him to go down and plead his case for him; so says he, 'Lawyer Webster, what's your fee?' 'Why,' says Daniel, 'let me see, I have to go down South to Washington, to plead the great insurance case of the Hartford Company—and I've got to be at Cincinnati to attend the Convention, and I don't see how I can go to Rhode Island without great loss and great fatigue; it would cost you may be more than you'd be willing to give.'

"Well, the Quaker looked pretty white about the gills, I tell you, when he heard this, for he could not do without him no how, and he did not like this preliminary talk of his at all. At last he made bold to ask him the worst of it, what he would take? 'Why,' says Daniel, 'I always liked the Quakers, they are a quiet, peaceable people, who never go to law if they can help it, and it would be better for our great country if there were more such people in it. I never seed or heerd tell of any harm in 'em except going the whole figure for Gineral Jackson, and that everlasting, almighty villain, Van Buren; yes, I love the Quakers, I hope they'll go the Webster ticket yet; and I'll go for you as low as I can any way afford, say—one thousand dollars.'

"The Quaker well nigh fainted when he heerd this, but he was pretty deep too; so says he, 'Lawyer, that's a great deal of money, but I have more causes there; if I give you the one thousand dollars will you plead the other cases I shall have to give you?' 'Yes,' says Daniel, 'I will to the best of my humble abilities.' So down they went to Rhode Island, and Daniel tried the case and carried it for the Quaker. Well, the Quaker he goes round to all the folks that had suits in court, and says he, 'What will you give me if I get the great Daniel to plead for you? It cost me one thousand dollars for a fee, but now he and I are pretty thick, and as he is on the spot, I'll get him to plead cheap for you.' So he got three hundred dollars from one, and two from another, and so on, until he got eleven hundred dollars, jist one hundred dollars more than he gave. Daniel was in a great rage when he heerd this. 'What!' said he, 'do you think I would agree to your letting me out like a horse to hire?' 'Friend Daniel,' said the Quaker, 'didst thou not undertake to plead all such cases as I should have to give thee? If thou wilt not stand to thy agreement, neither will I stand to mine.' Daniel laughed out ready to split his sides at this. 'Well,' says he, 'I guess I might as well stand still for you to put the bridle on this time, for you have fairly pinned me up in a corner of the fence anyhow.' So he went good humouredly to work and pleaded them all.

"This lazy fellow, Pugnose," continued the Clockmaker, "that keeps this inn, is going to sell off and go to the States; he says he has to work too hard here; that the markets are dull, and the winters too long; and he guesses he can live easier there; I guess he'll find his mistake afore he has been there long. Why, our country ain't to be compared to this on no account whatever; our country never made us to be the great nation we are, but we made the country. How on airth could we, if we were all like old Pugnose, as lazy, as ugly, make that cold, thin soil of New England produce what it does? Why, sir, the land between Boston and Salem would starve a flock of geese: and yet look at Salem; it has more cash than would buy Nova Scotia from the King. We rise early, live frugally, and work late; what we get we take care of. To all this we add enterprise and intelligence; a feller who finds work too hard here, had better not go to the States. I met an Irishman, one Pat Lannigan, last week, who had just returned from the States. 'Why,' says I, 'Pat, what on airth brought you back?' 'Bad luck to them,' says Pat, 'if I warn't properly bit. "What do you get a day in Nova Scotia?" says Judge Beler to me. "Four shillings, your Lordship," says I. "There are no Lords here," says he, "we are all free. Well," says he, "I'll give you as much in one day as you can earn there in two; I'll give you eight shillings." "Long life to your Lordship," says I. So next day to it I went with a party of men a-digging a piece of canal, and if it wasn't a hot day my name is not Pat Lannigan. Presently I looked up and straightened my back; says I to a comrade of mine, "Mick," says I, "I'm very dry"; with that, says the overseer, "We don't allow gentlemen to talk at their work in this country." Faith, I soon found out for my two days' pay in one, I had to do two days' work in one, and pay two weeks' board in one, and at the end of a month, I found myself no better off in pocket than in Nova Scotia; while the devil a bone in my body that didn't ache with pain, and as for my nose, it took to bleeding, and bled day and night entirely. Upon my soul, Mr. Slick,' said he, 'the poor labourer does not last long in your country; what with new rum, hard labour, and hot weather, you'll see the graves of the Irish each side of the canal, for all the world like two rows of potatoes in a field that have forgot to come up.'

"It is a land, sir," continued the Clockmaker, "of hard work. We have two kinds of slaves, the niggers and the white slaves. All European labourers and blacks, who come out to us, do our hard bodily work, while we direct it to a profitable end; neither rich nor poor, high nor low, with us, eat the bread of idleness. Our whole capital is in active operation, and our whole population is in active employment. An idle fellow, like Pugnose, who runs away to us, is clapt into harness afore he knows where he is, and is made to work; like a horse that refuses to draw, he is put into the teamboat; he finds some before him and others behind him; he must either draw, or be dragged to death."

In the morning the Clockmaker informed me that a justice's court was to be held that day at Pugnose's inn, and he guessed he could do a little business among the country folks that would be assembled there. Some of them, he said, owed him for clocks, and it would save him the world of travelling, to have the justice and constable to drive them up together. "If you want a fat wether, there's nothing like penning up the whole flock in a corner. I guess," said he, "if General Campbell knew what sort of a man that 'ere magistrate was, he'd disband him pretty quick; he's a regular suck-egg—a disgrace to the country. I guess if he acted that way in Kentucky, he'd get a breakfast of cold lead some morning, out of the small eend of a rifle, he'd find pretty difficult to digest. They tell me he issues three hundred writs a year, the cost of which, including that tarnation constable's fees, can't amount to nothing less than three thousand dollars per annum. If the Hon'ble Daniel Webster had him afore a jury, I reckon he'd turn him inside out, and slip him back again, as quick as an old stocking. He'd paint him to the life, as plain to be known as the head of Gineral Jackson. He's jist a fit feller for Lynch law, to be tried, hanged, and damned, all at once; there's more nor him in the country—there's some of the breed in every country in the Province, jist one or two to do the dirty work, as we keep niggers for jobs that would give a white man the cholera. They ought to pay his passage, as we do such critters, tell him his place is taken in the mail coach, and if he is found here after twenty-four hours, they'd make a carpenter's plumb-bob of him, and hang him outside the church steeple, to try if it was perpendicular. He almost always gives judgment for plaintiff, and if the poor defendant has an offset, he makes him sue it, so that it grinds a grist both ways for him, like the upper and lower millstone."

People soon began to assemble, some on foot, and others on horseback and in wagons. Pugnose's tavern was all bustle and confusion—plaintiffs, defendants, and witnesses all talking, quarrelling, explaining, and drinking. "Here comes the Squire," said one. "I'm thinking his horse carries more roguery than law," said another. "They must have been in proper want of timber to make a justice of," said a third, "when they took such a crooked stick as that." "Sap-headed enough too for refuse," said a stout-looking farmer. "May be so," said another, "but as hard at the heart as a log of elm." "Howsomever," said a third, "I hope it won't be long afore he has the wainy edge scored off of him, anyhow." Many more such remarks were made, all drawn from familiar objects, but all expressive of bitterness and contempt.

He carried one or two large books with him in his gig, with a considerable roll of papers. As soon as the obsequious Mr. Pugnose saw him at the door, he assisted him to alight, ushered him into the "best room," and desired the constable to attend "the Squire." The crowd immediately entered, and the constable opened the court in due form, and commanded silence.

Taking out a long list of causes, Mr. Pettifog commenced reading the names : "James Sharp versus John Slug—call John Slug." John Slug being duly called and not answering, was defaulted. In this manner he proceeded to default some twenty or thirty persons. At last he came to a cause, "William Hare versus Dennis O'Brien—call Dennis O'Brien." "Here I am," said a voice from the other room—"here I am; who has anything to say to Dennis O'Brien?"

"Make less noise, sir," said the Justice, "or I'll commit you."

"Commit me, is it?" said Dennis. "Take care then, Squire, you don't commit yourself."

"You are sued by William Hare for three pounds, for a month's board and lodging; what have you to say to it?"

"Say to it?" said Dennis. "Did you ever hear what Tim Doyle said when he was going to be hanged for stealing a pig? Says he, 'If the pig hadn't squealed in the bag, I'd never have been found out, so I wouldn't.' So I'll take warning by Tim Doyle's fate; I say nothing—let him prove it." Here Mr. Hare was called on for his proof, but taking it for granted that the board would be admitted, and the defence opened, he was not prepared with proof.

"I demand," said Dennis, "I demand an unsuit."

Here there was a consultation between the Justice and the plaintiff, when the Justice said, "I shall not nonsuit him, I shall continue the cause." "What, hang it up till next court? You had better hang me up then at once. How can a poor man come here so often? This may be the entertainment Pugnose advertises for horses, but by Jacquers, it is no entertainment for me. I admit then, sooner than come again, I admit it."

"You admit you owe him three pounds then for a month's board?"

"I admit no such thing; I say I boarded with him a month, and was like Pat Moran's cow at the end of it, at the lifting, bad luck to him." A neighbour was here called, who proved that the three pounds might be the usual price. "And do you know I taught his children to write at the school?" said Dennis. "You might," answered the witness. "And what is that worth?" "I don't know." "You don't know? Faith, I believe you're right," said Dennis, "for if the children are half as big rogues as the faither, they might leave writing alone, or they'd be like to be hanged for forgery." Here Dennis produced his account for teaching five children, two quarters, at nine shillings a quarter each, £4 10s. "I am sorry, Mr. O'Brien," said the Justice, "very sorry, but your defence will not avail you; your account is too large for one Justice; any sum over three pounds must be sued before two magistrates."

"But I only want to offset as much as will pay the board."

"It can't be done in this shape," said the magistrate; "I will consult Justice Doolittle, my neighbour, and if Mr. Hare won't settle with you, I will sue it for you."

"Well," said Dennis, "all I have to say is, that there is not so big a rogue as Hare on the whole river, save and except one scoundrel who shall be nameless," making a significant and humble bow to the Justice. Here there was a general laugh throughout the court. Dennis retired to the next room to indemnify himself by another glass of grog, and venting his abuse against Hare and the magistrate. Disgusted at the gross partiality of the Justice, I also quitted the court, fully concurring in the opinion, though not in the language, that Dennis was giving utterance to in the bar-room.

Pettifog owed his elevation to his interest at an election. It is to be hoped that his subsequent merits will be as promptly rewarded, by his dismissal from a bench which he disgraces and defiles by his presence.

As we mounted our horses to proceed to Amherst, groups of country people were to be seen standing about Pugnose's inn, talking over the events of the morning, while others were dispersing to their several homes.

"A pretty prime, superfine scoundrel, that Pettifog," said the Clockmaker; "he and his constable are well mated; and they've travelled in the same gear so long together, that they make about as nice a yoke of rascals as you'll meet in a day's ride. They pull together like one rope reeved through two blocks. That 'ere constable was e'enamost strangled t'other day; and if he hadn't had a little grain more wit than his master, I guess he'd had his windpipe stopped as tight as a bladder. There is an outlaw of a feller here, for all the world like one of our Kentucky squatters, one Bill Smith—a critter that neither fears man nor devil. Sheriff and constable can make no hand of him; they can't catch him no how; and if they do come up with him, he slips through their fingers like an eel; and then, he goes armed, and he can knock the eye out of a squirrel with a ball, at fifty yards hand running—a regular ugly customer.

"Well, Nabb, the constable, had a writ agin him, and he was ciphering a good while how he should catch him; at last he hit on a plan that he thought was pretty clever, and he schemed for a chance to try it. So one day he heerd that Bill was up at Pugnose's inn, a-settling some business, and was likely to be there all night. Nabb waits till it was considered late in the evening, and then he takes his horse and rides down to the inn, and hitches his beast behind the haystack. Then he crawls up to the window and peeps in, and watches there till Bill should go to bed, thinking the best way to catch them 'ere sort of animals is to catch them asleep. Well, he kept Nabb a-waiting outside so long, with his talking and singing, that he well nigh fell asleep first himself. At last Bill began to strip for bed. First, he takes out a long pocket pistol, examines the priming, and lays it down on the table near the head of the bed.

"When Nabb sees this, he begins to creep like all over, and

feel kinder ugly, and rather sick of his job; but when he seed him jump into bed, and heerd him snore out a noise like a man driving pigs to market, he plucked up courage, and thought he might do it easy arter all if he was to open the door softly, and make one spring on him afore he could wake. So round he goes, lifts up the latch of his door as soft as soap, and makes a jump right atop of him, as he lay on the bed. 'I guess I got you this time,' said Nabb. 'I guess so too,' said Bill, 'but I wish you wouldn't lay so plaguy heavy on me; jist turn over, that's a good fellow, will you?' With that, Bill lays his arm on him to raise him up, for he said he was squeezed as flat as a pancake; and afore Nabb knew where he was, Bill rolled him right over, and was atop of him. Then he seized him by the throat, and twisted his pipe till his eyes were as big as saucers, and his tongue grew six inches longer, while he kept making faces, for all the world like the pirate that was hanged on Monument Hill, at Boston. It was pretty near over with him, when Nabb thought of his spurs; so he just curled up both heels, and drove the spurs right into him; he let him have it just below his crupper. As Bill was naked, he had a fair chance, and he ragged him like the leaf of a book cut open with your finger. At last, Bill could stand it no longer; he let go his hold, and roared like a bull, and clapping both hands ahind him, he out of the door like a shot. If it hadn't been for them 'ere spurs, I guess Bill would have saved the hangman a job of Nabb that time."

The Clockmaker was an observing man, and equally communicative. Nothing escaped his notice; he knew everybody's genealogy, history, and means, and like a driver of an English stage-coach, was not unwilling to impart what he knew. "Do you see that snug-looking house there," said he, "with a short sarce garden afore it? That belongs to Elder Thomson. The Elder is pretty close-fisted, and holds special fast to all he gets. He is a just man and very pious; but I have observed when a man becomes near about too good, he is apt, sometimes, to slip ahead into avarice, unless he looks sharper arter his girths. A friend of mine in Connecticut, an old sea captain, who was once let in for it pretty deep by a man with a broader brim than common, said to me, 'Friend Sam,' says he, 'I don't like those folks who are too damned good.' There is, I expect, some truth in it, though he needn't have swore at all, but he was an awful hand to swear. Howsomever that may be, there is a story about the Elder that's not so coarse neither.

"It appears an old minister came there once, to hold a meetin' at his house: well, after meetin' was over, the Elder took the minister all over his farm, which is pretty tidy, I tell you; and he showed him a great ox he had, a swingeing big pig, that weighed some six or seven hundred weight, that he was plaguy proud of; but he never offered the old minister anything to eat or drink. The preacher was pretty tired of all this, and seeing no prospect of being asked to partake with the family, and tolerably sharp set, he asked one of the boys to fetch him his horse out of the barn. When he was taking leave of the Elder (there were several folks by at the time), says he, 'Elder Thomson, you have a fine farm here, a very fine farm indeed; you have a large ox too, a very large ox; and I think,' said he, 'I've seen today' (turning and looking him full in the face, for he intended to hit him pretty hard), 'I think I have seen today the greatest hog I ever saw in my life.' The neighbours snickered a good deal, and the Elder felt pretty streaked. I guess he'd give his great pig or his great ox either, if that story hadn't got wind."

WHEN we resumed our conversation, the Clockmaker said, "I guess we are the greatest nation on the face of the airth, and the most enlightened too."

This was rather too arrogant to pass unnoticed, and I was about replying, that whatever doubts there might be on that subject, there could be none whatever that they were the most modest, when he continued, "We 'go ahead'; the Nova Scotians 'go astarn.' Our ships go ahead of the ships of other folks, our steamboats beat the British in speed, and so do our stage-coaches; and I reckon a real right down New York trotter might stump the univarse for going ahead. But since we introduced the rail-roads, if we don't go ahead, it's a pity. We never fairly knew what going the whole hog was till then; we actilly went ahead of ourselves, and that's no easy matter I tell you. If they only had edication here, they might learn to do so too, but they don't know nothin'."

"You undervalue them," said I; "they have their college and academies, their grammar schools and primary institutions, and I believe there are few among them who cannot read and write."

"I guess all that's nothin'," said he. "As for Latin and Greek, we don't vally it a cent; we teach it, and so we do painting and music, because the English do, and we like to go ahead on 'em, even in them 'ere things. As for reading, it's well enough for them that has nothing to do; and writing is plaguy apt to bring a man to states-prison, particularly if he writes his name so like another man as to have it mistaken for his'n. Ciphering is the thing. If a man knows how to cipher, he is sure to grow rich. We are a 'calculating' people; we all cipher.

"A horse that won't go ahead is apt to run back, and the more you whip him the faster he goes astarn. That's jist the way with the Nova Scotians; they have been running back so fast lately, that they have tumbled over a bank or two, and nearly broke their necks; and now they've got up and shook themselves, they swear their dirty clothes and bloody noses are all owing to the banks. I guess if they won't look ahead for the future, they'll larn to look behind, and see if there's a bank near hand 'em.

"A bear always goes down a tree starn foremost. He is a cunning critter; he knows 'tain't safe to carry a heavy load over his head, and his rump is so heavy he don't like to trust it over his'n, for fear it might take a lurch, and carry him heels over head to the ground; so he lets his starn down first, and his head arter. I wish the Bluenoses would find as good an excuse in their rumps for running backwards as he has. But the bear 'ciphers'; he knows how many pounds his hams weigh, and he 'calculates' if he carried them up in the air, they might be top heavy for him.

"If we had this Province we'd go to work and 'cipher' right off. Halifax is nothing without a river or back country; add nothing to nothing, and I guess you have nothing still; add a railroad to the Bay of Fundy, and how much do you git? That requires ciphering. It will cost three hundred thousand dollars, or seventy-five thousand pounds your money; add for notions omitted in the addition column, one third, and it makes it even money, one hundred thousand pounds; interest at five per cent, five thousand pounds a year. Now turn over the slate, and count up freight. I make it upwards of twenty-five thousand pounds a year. If I had you at the desk, I'd show you a bill of items. Now comes 'subtraction'; deduct cost of engines, wear and tear and expenses, and what not, and reduce it for shortness down to five thousand pounds a year, the amount of interest. What figures have you got now? You have an investment that pays interest, I guess, and if it don't pay more, then I don't know chalk from cheese. But suppose it don't, and that it only yields two and a half per cent (and it requires good ciphering, I tell you, to say how it would act with folks that like going astern better than going ahead), what would them 'ere wise ones say then? Why, the critters would say it won't pay; but I say the sum ain't half stated. Can you count in your head?"

"Not to any extent," said I.

"Well, that's an etarnal pity," said the Clockmaker, "for I should like to show you Yankee ciphering. What is the entire real estate of Halifax worth, at a valeation?"

"I really cannot say."

"Ah," said he, "I see you don't cipher, and Latin and Greek won't do; them 'ere people had no railroad. Well, find out, and then only 'add ten per cent to it for increased value, and if it don't give the cost of a railroad, then my name is not Sam Slick. Well, the land between Halifax and Ardoise is worth—nothing;

add five per cent to that, and send the sum to the college and ax the students how much it comes to. But when you get into Hants County, I guess you have land worth coming all the way from Boston to see. His Royal Highness the King, I guess, hasn't got the like in his dominions. Well, add fifteen per cent to all them 'ere lands that border on Windsor Basin, and five per cent to what 'buts on basin of Mines, and then what do you get? A pretty considerable sum, I tell you; but it's no use to give you the *chalks*, if you can't keep the *tallies*.

"Now we will lay down the schoolmaster's assistant, and take up another book every bit and grain as good as that, although these folks affect to sneer at it—I mean human natur'."

"Ah!" said I, "a knowledge of that was of great service to you, certainly, in the sale of your clock to the old Deacon; let us see how it will assist you now."

"What does a clock want that's run down?" said he.

"Undoubtedly to be wound up," I replied.

"I guess you've hit it this time. The folks of Halifax have run down, and they'll never go, to all etarnity, till they are wound up into motion; the works are all good, and it is plaguy well cased and set; it only wants a key. Put this railroad into operation, and the activity it will inspire into business, the new life it will give the place, will surprise you. It's like lifting a child off its crawling, and putting him on his legs to run—see how the little critter goes ahead arter that. A kurnel—I don't mean a Kurnel of militia, for we don't vally that breed o' cattle nothing; they do nothing but strut about and screech all day, like peacocks—but a kurnel of grain, when sowed, will stool into several shoots, and each shoot bear many kurnels, and will multiply itself thus; four times one is four, and four times twenty-five is one hundred (you see all natur' ciphers, except the Bluenoses). Jist so, this 'ere railroad will not, perhaps, beget other railroads, but it will beget a spirit of enterprise, that will beget other useful improvements. It will enlarge the sphere and the means of trade, open new sources of traffic and supply, develop resources, and what is of more value perhaps than all, beget motion. It will teach the folks that go astarn or stand stock still, like the State House in Boston (though they do say the foundation of that has moved a little this summer), not only to 'go ahead,' but to nullify time and space."

Here his horse (who, feeling the animation of his master, had been restive of late) set off at a most prodigious rate of trotting. It was some time before he was reined up. When I overtook him, the Clockmaker said, "This old Yankee horse, you see, understands our word 'go ahead' better nor these Bluenoses.

"*What is it,*" he continued, "*what is it that 'fetters' the heels of a young country, and hangs like 'a poke' around its neck? What retards the cultivation of its soil, and the improvement of its fisheries? The high price of labour, I guess. Well, what's a railroad? The substitution of mechanical for human and animal labour, on a scale as grand as our great country. Labour is dear in America, and cheap in Europe. A railroad, therefore, is comparatively no manner of use to them, to what it is to us; it does wonders there, but it works miracles here. There it makes the old man younger, but here it makes the child a giant. To us it is river, bridge, road, and canal, all in one. It saves what we hain't got to spare, men, horses, carts, vessels, barges, and what's all in all—time.*

"Since the creation of the Universe, I guess it's the greatest invention, arter man. Now this is what I call 'ciphering' arter human natur', while figures are ciphering arter the 'assistant.' These two sorts of ciphering make edecation—and you may depend on't, Squire, there is nothing like folks ciphering if they want to 'go ahead.' "

"I GUESS," said the Clockmaker, "we know more of Nova Scotia than the Bluenoses themselves do. The Yankees see further ahead than most folks; they can e'enamost see round t'other side of a thing; indeed, some of them have hurt their eyes by it, and sometimes I think that's the reason such a sight of them wear spectacles. The first I ever heerd tell of Cumberland was from Mr. Everett of Congress; he knowed as much about it as if he had lived here all his days, and maybe a little grain more. He is a splendid man that; we class him No. 1, letter A. One night I chanced to go into General Peep's tavern at Boston. and who should I see there but the great Mr. Everett, a-studying over a map of the Province of Nova Scotia. 'Why, it ain't possible!' said I; 'if that ain't Professor Everett, as I am alive! Why, how do you do, Professor?' 'Pretty well, I give you thanks,' said he; 'how be you? but I ain't no longer Professor; I gin that up, and also the trade of preaching, and took to politics.' 'You don't say so!' said I, 'why, what on airth is the cause o' that?' 'Why,' says he, 'look here, Mr. Slick. What *is* the use of reading the Proverbs of Solomon to our free and enlightened citizens, that are every mite and morsel as wise as he was? That 'ere man undertook to say there was nothing new under the sun. I guess he'd think he spoke a little too fast, if he was to see our steamboats, railroads, and India rubber shoes—three inventions worth more nor all he knew put in a heap together.' 'Well, I don't know,' said I, 'but somehow or another I guess you'd have found preaching the best speculation in the long run; them 'ere Unitarians pay better than Uncle Sam.' (We call," said the Clockmaker, "the American public Uncle Sam, as you call the British John Bull.)

"That remark seemed to grig him a little; he felt oneasy like, and walked twice across the room, fifty fathoms deep in thought; at last he said, 'Which way are you from, Mr. Slick, this hitch?' 'Why,' says I, 'I've been away up South a-speculating in nutmegs.' 'I hope,' says the Professor, 'they were a good article, the real right down genuine thing?' 'No mistake,' says I, 'no mistake, Professor: they were all prime, first chop; but why did you ax that 'ere question?' 'Why,' says he, 'that eternal scoundrel, that Captain John Allspice of Nahant, he used to trade to Charleston, and he carried a cargo once there of fifty barrels of nutmegs: well, he put half a bushel of good ones into each eend of the barrel, and the rest he filled up with wooden ones, so like the real thing, no soul could tell the difference until *he bit one with his teeth*, and that he never thought of doing, until he was first *bit himself*. Well, it's been a standing joke with them Southerners agin us ever since.

"'It was only t'other day, at Washington, that everlasting Virginny duellist, General Cuffy, afore a number of senators, at the President's house, said to me, "Well, Everett," says he, "you know I was always dead agin your Tariff bill, but I have changed my mind since your able speech on it; I shall vote for it now." "Give me your hand," says I, "General Cuffy; the Boston folks will be dreadful glad when they hear your splendid talents are on our side. I think it will go now—we'll carry it." "Yes," says he, "your factories down East beat all natur'; they go ahead on the English a long chalk." You may depend I was glad to hear the New Englanders spoken of that way; I felt proud, I tell you. "And," says he, "there's one manufacture that might stump all Europe to produce the like." "What's that?" says I, looking as pleased all the time as a gal that's tickled. "Why," says he, "the 'facture of wooden nutmegs; that's a cap sheaf that bangs the bush; it's a real Yankee patent invention." With that all the gentlemen set up a laugh you might have heerd away down to Sandy Hook, and the General gig-gobbled like a great turkey-cock—the half nigger, half alligator-like looking villain as he is. I tell you what, Mr. Slick,' said the Professor, 'I wish with all my heart them 'ere damned nutmegs were in the bottom of the sea.' That was the first oath I ever heerd him let slip: but he was dreadful riled, and it made me feel ugly too, for it's awful to hear a minister swear; and the only match I know for it, is to hear a regular sneezer of a sinner quote Scripture. Says I, 'Mr. Everett, that's the fruit that politics bears: for my part I never seed a good graft on it yet, that bore anything good to eat, or easy to digest.'

"Well, he stood awhile looking down on the carpet, with his hands behind him, quite taken up a-ciphering in his head, and then he straightened himself up, and he put his hand upon his heart, just as he used to do in the pulpit (he looked pretty I tell you), and slowly lifting his hand off his breast, he said, 'Mr. Slick, our tree of liberty was a beautiful tree—a splendid tree;

it was a sight to look at; it was well fenced and well protected, and it grew so stately and so handsome, that strangers came from all parts of the globe to see it. They all allowed it was the most splendid thing in the world. Well, the mobs have broken in and tore down their fences, and snapped off the branches, and scattered all the leaves about, and it looks no better than a gallows tree. I am afeared,' said he, 'I tremble to think on it, but I am afeared our ways will no longer be ways of pleasantness, nor our paths paths of peace; I am, indeed, I vow, Mr. Slick.' He looked so streaked and so chop-fallen, that I felt kinder sorry for him; I actilly thought he'd a boo-hoo'd right out.

"So, to turn the conversation, says I, 'Professor, what 'ere great map is that I seed you a-studyin' over when I came in?' Says he, 'It's a map of Nova Scotia. That,' says he, 'is a valuable province, a real clever province; we hain't got the like on it, but it's most plaguily in our way.' 'Well,' says I, 'send for Sam Patch' (that 'ere man was a great diver," says the Clockmaker, "and the last dive he took was off the Falls of Niagara, and he was never heered of ag'in till t'other day, when Captain Enoch Wentworth of the *Susy Ann* whaler saw him in the South Sea. 'Why,' says Captain Enoch to him, 'why, Sam,' says he, 'how on airth did you get here? I thought you was drowned at the Canadian lines.' 'Why,' says he, 'I didn't get *on* airth here at all, but I came right slap *through* it. In that 'ere Niagara dive, I went so everlasting deep, I thought it was just as short to come up t'other side, so out I came in those parts. If I don't take the shine off the Sea Serpent, when I get back to Boston, then my name's not Sam Patch.'). 'Well,' says I, 'Professor, send for Sam Patch, the diver, and let him dive down and stick a torpedo in the bottom of the Province and blow it up; or if that won't do, send for some of our steam towboats from our great Eastern cities, and tow it out to sea; you know there's nothing our folks can't do, when they once fairly take hold on a thing in airnest.'

"Well, that made him laugh; he seemed to forget about the nutmegs, and says he, 'That's a bright scheme, but it won't do: we shall want the Province some day, and I guess we'll buy it off King William; they say he is over head and ears in debt, and owes nine hundred millions of pounds starling—we'll buy it, as we did Florida. In the meantime we must have a canal from Bay Fundy to Bay Varte, right through Cumberland Neck, by Shittyack, for our fishing vessels to go to Labradore.' 'I guess you must ax leave first,' said I. 'That's jist what I was ciphering at,' says he, 'when you came in. I believe we won't ax them at all, but jist fall to and do it; *it's a road of needcessity.* I once heard Chief Justice Marshall of Baltimore, say, "If the people's highway is dangerous, a man may take down a fence and pass through the fields as a way of *needcessity*"; and we shall do it on that principle, as the way round by Isle Sable is dangerous. I wonder the Nova Scotians don't do it for their own convenience.' Said I, 'It wouldn't make a bad speculation that.' 'The critters don't know no better,' said he. 'Well,' says I, 'the St. John's folks, why don't they? for they are pretty cute chaps, them.'

" 'They remind me,' says the Professor, 'of Jim Billings. You knew Jim Billings, didn't you, Mr. Slick?' 'Oh yes,' said I, 'I knew him. It was he that made such a talk by shipping blankets to the West Indies.' 'The same,' says he. 'Well, I went to see him the other day at Mrs. Lecain's boarding-house, and says I, "Billings, you have a nice location here." "A plaguy sight too nice," said he. "Marm Lecain makes such an etarnal touse about her carpets, that I have to go along that everlasting long entry, and down both staircases, to the street door to spit; and it keeps all the gentlemen a-running with their mouths full all day. I had a real bout with a New Yorker this morning. I run down to the street door, and afore I seed anybody a-coming, I let go, and I vow if I didn't let a chap have it all over his white waistcoat. Well, he makes a grab at me, and I shuts the door right to on his wrist, and hooks the door-chain taut, and leaves him there, and into Marm Lecain's bedroom like a shot, and hides behind the curtain. Well, he roared like a bull, till black Lucretia, one of the house helps, let him go, and they looked into all the gentlemen's rooms and found nobody; so I got out of that 'ere scrape. So, what with Marm Lecain's carpets in the house, and other folks' waistcoats in the street, it's too nice a location for me, I guess, so I shall up killock and off tomorrow to the *Tree-mont.*"

" 'Now,' says the Professor, 'the St. John's folks are jist like Billings: fifty cents would have bought him a spitbox, and saved him all them 'ere journeys to the street door; and a canal at Bay Varte would save the St. John's folks a voyage all round Nova Scotia. Why, they can't get at their own backside settlements, without a voyage most as long as one to Europe. *If we had that 'ere neck of land in Cumberland, we'd have a ship canal there, and a town at each eend of it as big as Portland.* You may talk of Solomon,' said the Professor, 'but if Solomon in all his glory was not arrayed like a lily of the field, neither was he in all his wisdom equal in knowledge to a real free American citizen.'

'Well,' said I, 'Professor, we are a most enlightened people, that's sartain, but somehow I don't like to hear you run down King Solomon neither; perhaps he warn't quite so wise as Uncle Sam, but then,' said I (drawing close to the Professor, and whispering in his ear, for fear any folks in the bar-room might hear me), 'but then,' said I, 'may be he was every bit and grain as honest.' Says he, 'Mr. Slick, there are some folks who think a good deal and say but little, and they are wise folks; and there are others ag'in, who blart right out whatever comes uppermost, and I guess they are pretty considerable superfine darned fools.'

"And with that he turned right round, and sat down to his map, and never said another word, lookin' as mad as a hatter the whole blessed time."

"DID you ever hear tell of Abernethy, a British doctor?" said the Clockmaker.

"Frequently," said I; "he was an eminent man, and had a most extensive practice."

"Well, I reckon he was a vulgar critter that," he replied; "he treated the Hon'ble Alden Gobble, Secretary to our Legation at London, dreadful bad once; and I guess if it had been me he had used that way, I'd a fixed his flint for him, so that he'd think twice afore he'd fire such another shot as that 'ere again. I'd a made him make tracks, I guess, as quick as a dog does a hog from a potato field. He'd a found his way out of the hole in the fence a plaguy sight quicker than he came in, I reckon."

"His manner," said I, "was certainly rather unceremonious at times, but he was so honest and so straightforward, that no person was, I believe, ever seriously offended at him. *It was his way.*"

"Then his way was so plaguy rough," continued the Clock-maker, "that he'd been the better if it had been hammered and mauled down smoother. I'd a levelled him flat as a flounder."

"Pray what was his offence?" said I.

"Bad enough, you may depend. The Hon'ble Alden Gobble was dyspeptic, and he suffered great oneasiness arter eatin', so he goes to Abernethy for advice. 'What's the matter with you?' said the Doctor—jist that way, without even passing the time o' day with him—'what's the matter with you?' said he. 'Why,' says Alden; 'I presume I have the dyspepsy.' 'Ah!' said he, 'I see; a Yankee swallowed more dollars and cents than he can digest.' 'I am an American citizen,' says Alden, with great dignity; 'I am Secretary to our Legation at the Court of St. James.' 'The devil you are,' said Abernethy; 'then you will soon get rid of your dyspepsy.' 'I don't see that 'ere inference,' said Alden, 'it don't follow from what you predicate at all; it ain't a natural consequence, I guess, that a man should cease to be ill because he is called by the voice of a free and enlightened people to fill an important office.' (The truth is, you could no more trap Alden than you could an Indian. He could see other folks' trail, and made none himself: he was a real diplomatist, and I believe our diplomatists are allowed to be the best in the world.) 'But I tell you it does follow,' said the Doctor; 'for in the company you'll have to keep, you'll have to eat like a Christian.'

"It was an everlasting pity Alden contradicted him, for he broke out like one ravin' distracted mad. 'I'll be damned,' said he, 'if ever I saw a Yankee that didn't bolt his food whole like a boa constrictor. How the devil can you expect to digest food, that you neither take the trouble to dissect, nor time to masticate? It's no wonder you lose your teeth, for you never use them; nor your digestion, for you overload it; nor your saliva, for you expend it on the carpets, instead of your food. It's disgusting, it's beastly. You Yankees load your stomachs as a Devonshire man does his cart, as full as it can hold, and fast as he can pitch it with a dung-fork, and drive off; and then you complain that such a load of compost is too heavy for you. Dyspepsy, eh! infernal guzzling, you mean. I'll tell you what, Mr. Secretary of Legation, take half the time to eat that you do to drawl out your words, chew your food half as much as you do your filthy tobacco, and you'll be well in a month.'

"'I don't understand such language,' said Alden (for he was fairly riled and got his dander up, and when he shows clear grit, he looks wicked ugly, I tell you), 'I don't understand such language, sir; I came here to consult you professionally, and not to be——' 'Don't understand!' said the Doctor, 'why it's plain English; but here, read my book!' and he shoved a book into his hands and left him in an instant, standing alone in the middle of the room.

"If the Hon'ble Alden Gobble had gone right away and demanded his passport, and returned home with the legation in one of our first-class frigates (I guess the English would as soon see p'ison as one o' them 'ere Serpents) to Washington, the President and the people would have sustained him in it, I guess, until an apology was offered for the insult to the nation. I guess if it had been me," said Mr. Slick, "I'd a headed him afore he slipt out o' the door, and pinned him up agin the wall, and make him bolt his words ag'in, as quick as he throw'd 'em up, for I never seed an Englishman that didn't cut his words as short as he does his horse's tail, close up to the stump."

"It certainly was very coarse and vulgar language, and I think," said I, "that your Secretary had just cause to be offended at such an ungentlemanlike attack, although he showed his good sense in treating it with the contempt it deserved."

"It was plaguy lucky for the Doctor, I tell you, that he cut his stick as he did, and made himself scarce, for Alden was an ugly customer; he'd a gi'n him a proper scalding; he'd a taken the bristles off his hide, as clean as the skin of a spring shote of a pig killed at Christmas."

The Clockmaker was evidently excited by his own story, and to indemnify himself for these remarks on his countrymen, he indulged for some time in ridiculing the Nova Scotians.

"Do you see that 'ere flock of colts?" said he, as we passed one of those beautiful prairies that render the valleys of Nova Scotia so verdant and so fertile. "Well, I guess they keep too much of that 'ere stock. I heerd an Indian one day ax a tavern-keeper for some rum. 'Why, Joe Spawdeeck,' said he, 'I reckon you have got too much already.' 'Too much of anything,' said Joe, 'is not good; but too much rum is jist enough.' I guess these Bluenoses think so about their horses; they are fairly eat up by them, out of house and home, and they are no good neither. They bean't good saddle horses, and they bean't good draft beasts; they are jist neither one thing nor t'other. They are like the drink of our Connecticut folks. At mowing time they use molasses and water—nasty stuff, only fit to catch flies; it spiles good water and makes bad beer. No wonder the folks are poor. Look at them 'ere great dykes; well, they all go to feed horses; and look at their grain fields on the upland; well, they are all sowed with oats to feed horses, and they buy their bread from us : so we feed the asses, and they feed the horses. If I had them critters on that 'ere marsh, on a location of mine, I'd jist take my rifle and shoot every one on 'em—the nasty, yo-necked, cat-hammed, heavy-headed, flat-eared, crooked-shanked, long-legged, narrow-chested, good-for-nothin' brutes; they ain't worth their keep one winter. I vow, I wish one of these Bluenoses, with his go-to-meetin' clothes on, coat-tails pinned up behind like a leather blind of a shay, an old spur on one heel, and pipe stuck through his hat-band, mounted on one of these limber-timbered critters, that moves its hind legs like a hen scratchin' gravel, was sot down in Broadway, in New York, for a sight. Lord! I think I hear the West Point cadets a-larfin' at him. 'Who brought that 'ere scare-crow out of standin' corn and stuck him here?' 'I guess that 'ere citizen came from away down East, out of the Notch of the White Mountains.' 'Here comes the cholera doctor, from Canada —not from Canada, I guess, neither, for he don't look as if he had ever been among the rapids.' If they wouldn't poke fun at him, it's a pity.

"If they'd keep less horses, and more sheep, they'd have food and clothing, too, instead of buying both. I vow I've larfed afore now till I have fairly wet myself a-cryin', to see one of these folks catch a horse: may be he has to go two or three miles of an arrand. Well, down he goes on the dyke, with a bridle in one hand, and an old tin pan in another, full of oats, to catch his beast. First, he goes to one flock of horses, and then to another, to see if he can find his own critter. At last he gets sight of him, and goes softly up to him, shakin' of his oats, and a-coaxin' him, and jist as he goes to put his hand upon him, away he starts, all head and tail, and the rest with him; that starts another flock, and they set a third off, and at last every troop on 'em goes, as if Old Nick was arter them, till they amount to two or three hundred in a drove. Well, he chases them clear across the Tantramer Marsh, seven miles good, over ditches, creeks, mire holes, and flag ponds, and then they turn and take a fair chase for it back again, seven miles more. By this time, I presume, they are all pretty considerably well tired, and Bluenose, he goes and gets up all the men folks in the neighbourhood, and catches his beast, as they do a moose arter he is fairly run down; so he runs fourteen miles, to ride two, because he is in a tarnation hurry. It's e'enamost equal to eatin' soup with a fork, when you are short of time. It puts me in mind of catching birds by sprinkling salt on their tails; it's only one horse a man can ride out of half a dozen, arter all. One has no shoes, t'other has a colt, one ain't broke, another has a sore back, while a fifth is so etarnal cunnin', all Cumberland couldn't catch him, till winter drives him up to the barn for food.

"Most of them 'ere dyke marshes have what they call '*honey pots*' in 'em; that is, à deep hole all full of squash, where you can't find no bottom. Well, every now and then, when a feller goes to look for his horse, he sees his tail a-stickin' right out on eend, from one of these honey pots, and wavin' like a head of broom corn; and sometimes you see two or three trapped there, e'enamost smothered, everlastin' tired, half swimmin', half wadin', like rats in a molasses cask. When they find 'em in that 'ere pickle, they go and get ropes, and tie 'em tight round their necks, and half hang 'em to make 'em float, and then haul 'em out. Awful looking critters they be, you may depend, when they do come out; for all the world like half-drowned kittens—all slinkey slimey, with their great long tails glued up like a swab

of oakum dipped in tar. If they don't look foolish, it's a pity!
Well, they have to nurse these critters all winter, with hot
mashes, warm covering, and what not, and when spring comes,
they mostly die, and if they don't, they are never no good arter.
I wish with all my heart half the horses in the country were
barrelled up in these here honey pots, and then there'd be near
about one-half too many left for profit. Jist look at one of these
barnyards in the spring—half a dozen half-starved colts, with
their hair looking a thousand ways for Sunday, and their coats
hangin' in tatters, and half a dozen good-for-nothin' old horses,
a-crowdin' out the cows and sheep.

"*Can you wonder that people who keep such an unprofitable
stock, come out of the small eend of the horn in the long run?*"

As we approached the inn at Amherst, the Clockmaker grew uneasy.

"It's pretty well on in the evening, I guess," said he, "and Marm Pugwash is as onsartain in her temper as a mornin' in April; it's all sunshine or all clouds with her, and if she's in one of her tantrums, she'll stretch out her neck and hiss, like a goose with a flock of goslins. I wonder what on airth Pugwash was a-thinkin' on, when he signed articles of partnership with that 'ere woman; she's not a bad-lookin' piece of furniture neither, and it's a proper pity sich a clever woman should carry sich a stiff upper lip. She reminds me of our old minister Joshua Hopewell's apple trees.

"The old minister had an orchard of most particular good fruit, for he was a great hand at buddin', graftin', and what not, and the orchard (it was on the south side of the house) stretched right up to the road. Well, there were some trees hung over the fence; I never seed such bearers; the apples hung in ropes—for all the world like strings of onions—and the fruit was beautiful. Nobody touched the minister's apples, and when other folks lost their'n from the boys, his'n always hung there like bait to a hook, but there never was so much as a nibble at 'em. So I said to him one day, 'Minister,' said I, 'how on airth do you manage to keep your fruit that's so exposed, when no one else can't do it nohow?' 'Why,' says he, 'they are dreadful pretty fruit, ain't they?' 'I guess,' said I, 'there ain't the like on 'em in all Connecticut.' 'Well,' says he, 'I'll tell you the secret, but you needn't let on to no one about it. That 'ere row next the fence, I grafted it myself; I took great pains to get the right kind; I sent clean up to Roxberry and away down to Squaw-neck Creek'—I was afeared he was a-goin' to give me day and date for every graft, being a terrible long-winded man in his stories, so says I, 'I know that, Minister, but how do you preserve them?' 'Why, I was a-goin' to tell you,' said he, 'when you stopped me. That 'ere outward row I grafted myself with the choicest kind I could find, and I succeeded. They are beautiful, but so eternal sour, no human soul can eat them. Well, the boys think the old minister's graftin' has all succeeded about as well as that row, and they sarch no farther. They snicker at my graftin', and I laugh in my sleeve, I guess, at their penetration.'

"Now, Marm Pugwash is like the minister's apples—very temptin' fruit to look at, but desperate sour. If Pugwash had a watery mouth when he married, I guess it's pretty puckery by this time. However, if she goes to act ugly, I'll give her a dose of 'soft sawder,' that will take the frown out of her frontispiece, and make her dial-plate as smooth as a lick of copal varnish. It's a pity she's such a kickin' devil, too, for she has good points: good eye—good foot—neat pastern—fine chest—a clean set of limbs, and carries a good—— But here we are; now you'll see what 'soft sawder' will do."

When we entered the house, the traveller's room was all in darkness, and on opening the opposite door into the sitting-room, we found the female part of the family extinguishing the fire for the night. Mrs. Pugwash had a broom in her hand, and was in the act (the last act of female housewifery) of sweeping the hearth. The strong flickering light of the fire, as it fell upon her tall fine figure and beautiful face, revealed a creature worthy of the Clockmaker's comments.

"Good evening, marm," said Mr. Slick, "how do you do, and how's Mr. Pugwash?"

"He," said she, "why he's been abed this hour; you don't expect to disturb him this time of night, I hope?"

"O no," said Mr. Slick, "certainly not; and I am sorry to have disturbed you, but we got detained longer than we expected; I am sorry that——"

"So am I," said she, "but if Mr. Pugwash will keep an inn when he has no occasion to, his family can't expect no rest."

Here the Clockmaker, seeing the storm gathering, stooped down suddenly, and staring intently, held out his hand and exclaimed, "Well, if that ain't a beautiful child! Come here, my little man, and shake hands along with me; well, I declare, if that 'ere little feller ain't the finest child I ever seed! What, not abed yet? Ah, you rogue, where did you get them 'ere pretty rosy cheeks; stole them from mamma, eh? Well, I wish my old mother could see that child, it is such a treat. In our country," said he, turning to me, "the children are all as pale as chalk, or as yaller as an orange. Lord! that 'ere little feller would be a show in our country; come to me, my man." Here the "soft sawder" began to operate. Mrs. Pugwash said in a milder tone than we had yet heard, "Go, my dear, to the gentleman; go, dear." Mr. Slick kissed him, asked him if he would go to the States along with him, and told him all the little girls there would fall in love with him, for they didn't see such a beautiful face once in a month of Sundays. "Black eyes—let me see—ah, mamma's eyes too, and black hair also, as I am alive; why, you are mamma's own boy—the very image of mamma."

"Do be seated, gentlemen," said Mrs. Pugwash. "Sally, make a fire in the next room."

"She ought to be proud of you," he continued. "Well, if I live to return here, I must paint your face, and have it put on my clocks, and our folks will buy the clocks for the sake of the face. Did you ever see," said he, again addressing me, "such a likeness between one human and another, as between this beautiful little boy and his mother?"

"I am sure you have had no supper," said Mrs. Pugwash to me; "you must be hungry, and weary too. I will get you a cup of tea."

"I am sorry to give you so much trouble," said I.

"Not the least trouble in the world," she replied, "on the contrary, a pleasure."

We were then shown into the next room, where the fire was now blazing up, but Mr. Slick protested he could not proceed without the little boy, and lingered behind me to ascertain his age, and concluded by asking the child if he had any aunts that looked like mamma.

As the door closed, Mr. Slick said, "It's a pity she don't go well in gear. The difficulty with those critters is to get them to start; arter that there is no trouble with them if you don't check 'em too short. If you do, they'll stop again, run back, and kick like mad, and then Old Nick himself wouldn't start 'em. Pugwash, I guess, don't understand the natur' of the critter; she'll never go kind in harness for him. *When I see a child*," said the Clockmaker, "*I always feel safe with these women folk, for I have always found that the road to a woman's heart lies through her child.*"

"You seem," said I, "to understand the female heart so well, I make no doubt you are a general favourite among the fair sex."

"Any man," he replied, "that understands horses, has a pretty considerable fair knowledge of women; for they are jist alike in temper, and require the very identical same treatment. En-

courage the timid ones, be gentle and steady with the fractious,
but lather the sulky ones like blazes.

"People talk an everlasting sight of nonsense about wine,
women, and horses. I've bought and sold 'em all, I've traded in
all of them, and I tell you, there ain't one in a thousand that
knows a grain about either on 'em. You hear folks say, O, such
a man is an ugly-grained critter, he'll break his wife's heart; jist
as if a woman's heart was as brittle as a pipe stalk. The female
heart, as far as my experience goes, is just like a new India rubber
shoe; you may pull and pull at it, till it stretches out a yard long,
and then let go, and it will fly right back to its old shape. Their
hearts are made of stout leather, I tell you; there's a plaguy sight
of wear in 'em.

"I never knowed but one case of a broken heart, and that was
in t'other sex, one Washington Banks. He was a sneezer. He was
tall enough to spit down on the heads of your grenadiers, and
near about high enough to wade across Charlestown River, and
as strong as a towboat. I guess he was somewhat less than a foot
longer than the moral law and catechism too. He was a perfect
pictur' of a man; you couldn't fault him in no particular; he was
so just a made critter, folks used to run to the winder when he
passed, and say, 'There goes Washington Banks, bean't he
lovely?' I do believe there wasn't a gal in the Lowell factories
that warn't in love with him. Sometimes, at intermission, on
Sabbath days, when they all came out together (an amazin'
handsum sight too, near about a whole congregation of young
gals), Banks used to say, 'I vow, young ladies, I wish I had five
hundred arms to reciprocate one with each of you; but I reckon
I have a heart big enough for you all; it's a whapper, you may
depend, and every mite and morsel of it at your service.' 'Well,
how you do act, Mr Banks,' half a thousand little clipper-clapper
tongues would say, all at the same time, and their dear little eyes
sparklin', like so many stars twinklin' of a frosty night.

"Well, when I last seed him, he was all skin and bone, like a
horse turned out to die. He was teetotally defleshed, a mere
walkin' skeleton. 'I am dreadful sorry,' says I, 'to see you, Banks,
lookin' so peeked; why, you look like a sick turkey hen, all
legs; what on airth ails you?' 'I am dyin',' says he, 'of a broken
heart.' 'What,' says I, 'have the gals been jiltin' you?' 'No, no,'
says he, 'I bean't such a fool as that neither.' 'Well,' says I, 'have
you made a bad speculation?' 'No,' says he, shakin' his head, 'I
hope I have too much clear grit in me to take on so bad for
that.' 'What under the sun is it, then?' 'Why,' says he, 'I made

a bet the fore part of summer with Leftenant Oby Knowles, that I could shoulder the best bower of the *Constitution* frigate. I won my bet, but the anchor was so etarnal heavy it broke my heart.' Sure enough, he did die that very fall; and he was the only instance I ever heerd tell of a broken heart."

CUMBERLAND OYSTERS PRODUCE MELANCHOLY FOREBODINGS

THE soft sawder of the Clockmaker had operated effectually on the beauty of Amherst, our lovely hostess of Pugwash's inn: indeed, I am inclined to think with Mr. Slick, that "The road to a woman's heart lies through her child," from the effect produced upon her by the praises bestowed on her infant boy.

I was musing on this feminine susceptibility to flattery, when the door opened, and Mrs. Pugwash entered, dressed in her sweetest smiles and her best cap, an auxiliary by no means required by her charms, which, like an Italian sky, when unclouded, are unrivalled in splendour. Approaching me, she said, with an irresistible smile, "Would you like, Mr.——" Here there was a pause, a hiatus, evidently intended for me to fill up with my name; but that no person knows, nor do I intend they shall; at Medley's Hotel, in Halifax, I was known as the Stranger in No. 1. The attention that incognito procured for me, the importance it gave me in the eyes of the master of the house, its lodgers and servants, is indescribable. It is only great people who travel incog. State travelling is inconvenient and slow; the constant weight of form and etiquette oppresses at once the strength and the spirits. It is pleasant to travel unobserved, to stand at ease, or exchange the full suit for the undress coat and fatigue jacket. Wherever, too, there is mystery there is importance; there is no knowing for whom I may be mistaken; but let me once give my humble cognomen and occupation, and I sink immediately to my own level, to a plebeian station, and a vulgar name; not even my beautiful hostess, nor my inquisitive friend, the Clockmaker, who calls me "Squire," shall extract that secret! "Would you like, Mr.——"

"Indeed, I would," said I, "Mrs. Pugwash; pray be seated, and tell me what it is."

"Would you like a dish of superior Shittyacks for supper?"

"Indeed I would," said I, again, laughing: "but pray tell me what it is?"

"Laws me!" said she with a stare. "Where have you been all

your days, that you never heerd of our Shittyack oysters? I thought everybody had heerd of them."

"I beg pardon," said I, "but I understood at Halifax, that the only oysters in this part of the world were found on the shores of Prince Edward Island."

"O! dear, no," said our hostess, "they are found all along the coast from Shittyack, through Bay of Vartes, away to Ramshag. The latter we seldom get, though the best; there is no regular conveyance, and when they do come, they are generally shelled and in kegs, and never in good order. I have not had a real good Ramshag in my house these two years, since Governor Maitland was here; he was amazing fond of them, and Lawyer Talkem-deaf sent his carriage there on purpose to procure them fresh for him. Now we can't get them, but we have the Shittyacks in perfection; say the word, and they shall be served up imme-diately."

A good dish and an unexpected dish is most acceptable, and certainly my American friend and myself did ample justice to the oysters, which, if they have not so classical a name, have quite as good a flavour as their far-famed brethren of Milton. Mr. Slick ate so heartily, that when he resumed his conversation, he indulged in the most melancholy forebodings.

"Did you see that 'ere nigger," said he, "that removed the oyster shells? Well, he's one of our Chesapickers, one of General Cuffy's slaves. I wish Admiral Cockburn had a taken them all off our hands at the same time. We made a pretty good sale of them 'ere black cattle, I guess, to the British; I wish we were well rid of 'em all. The Blacks and the Whites in the States show their teeth and snarl; they are jist ready to fall to. The Protestants and Catholics begin to lay back their ears, and turn tail for kickin'. The Abolitionists and Planters are at it like two bulls in a pastur'. Mob-law and Lynch-law are working like yeast in a barrel, and frothing at the bung-hole. Nullification and Tariff are like a charcoal pit, all covered up, but burning inside, and sending out smoke at every crack, enough to stifle a horse. General Govern-ment and State Government every now and then square off and spar, and the first blow given will bring a genuine set-to. Surplus Revenue is another bone of contention; like a shin of beef thrown among a pack of dogs, it will set the whole on 'em by the ears.

"You have heerd tell of cotton rags dipped in turpentine, haven't you, how they produce combustion? Well, I guess we have the elements of spontaneous combustion among us in abundance; when it does break out, if you don't see an eruption of human gore worse than Etna lava, then I'm mistaken. There'll be the very devil to pay, that's a fact. I expect the blacks will butcher the Southern whites, and the Northerners will have to turn out and butcher them again; and all this shoot, hang, cut, stab, and burn business will sweeten our folks' temper, as raw meat does that of a dog; it fairly makes me sick to think on it. The explosion may clear the air again, and all be tranquil once more, but it's an even chance if it don't leave us the three steamboat options—to be blown sky-high, to be scalded to death, or drowned."

"If this sad picture you have drawn be indeed true to nature, how does your country," said I, "appear so attractive as to draw to it so large a portion of our population?"

"It ain't its attraction," said the Clockmaker; "it's nothin' but its power of suction; it is a great whirlpool—a great vortex : it drags all the straw and chips, and floating sticks, drift-wood, and trash into it. The small crafts are sucked in, and whirl round and round like a squirrel in the cage—they'll never come out. Bigger ones pass through at certain times of tide, and can come in and out with good pilotage, as they do at Hell Gate up the Sound."

"You astonish me," said I, "beyond measure; both your previous conversation with me, and the concurrent testimony of all my friends who have visited the States, give a different view of it."

"*Your friends!*" said the Clockmaker, with such a tone of ineffable contempt that I felt a strong inclination to knock him down for his insolence, "your friends! Ensigns and leftenants, I guess, from the British marchin' regiments in the Colonies, that run over five thousand miles of country in five weeks, on leave of absence, and then return, lookin' as wise as the monkey that had seen the world. When they get back they are so chock full of knowledge of the Yankees that it runs over of itself; like a hogshead of molasses rolled about in hot weather, a white froth and scum bubbles out of the bung—wishy-washy trash they call tours, sketches, travels, letters, and what not; vapid stuff, jist sweet enough to catch flies, cockroaches, and half-fledged gals. It puts me in mind of my French. I larnt French at night school, one winter, of our minister, Joshua Hopewell (he was the most larned man of the age, for he taught himself e'enamost every language in Europe); well, next spring, when I went to Boston, I met a Frenchman, and I began to jabber away French to him : 'Polly woes a french shay,' says I. 'I don't understand Yankee

yet,' says he. 'You don't understand?' says I, 'why, it's French.
I guess you didn't expect to hear such good French, did you,
away down East here? But we speak it real well, and it's generally allowed we speak English, too, better than the British.' 'O,'
says he, 'you one very droll Yankee; dat very good joke, sare:
you talk Indian, and call it French.' 'But,' says I, 'Mister Mount-
shear, it is French, I vow; real merchantable, without wainy edge
or shakes—all clear stuff; it will pass survey in any market; it's
ready stuck and seasoned.' 'O, very like,' says he, bowin' as
polite as a black waiter at New Orleens, 'very like, only I never
heerd it afore; O, very good French dat—clear stuff, no doubt,
but I no understand; it's all my fault, I dare say, sare.'

"Thinks I to myself, a nod is as good as a wink to a blind
horse. I see how the cat jumps: minister knows so many lan-
guages he hain't been particular enough to keep 'em in separate
parcels, and mark 'em on the back, and they've got mixed; and
sure enough, I found my French was so overrun with other sorts,
that it was better to lose the whole crop than go to weedin', for
as fast as I pulled up any strange seedlin' it would grow right up
ag'in as quick as wink, if there was the least bit of root in the
world left in the ground; so I left it all to rot on the field.

"There is no way so good to larn French as to live among 'em,
and if you want to understand us, you must live among us, too;
your Halls, Hamiltons, and De Rouses, and such critters, what
can they know of us? Can a chap catch a likeness flying along
the railroad? Can he even see the featur's? Old Admiral Anson
once axed one of our folks afore our glorious Revolution (if the
British had a known us a little grain better at that time, they
wouldn't have got whipped like a sack as they did then) where
he came. 'From the Chesapeake,' said he. 'Aye, aye,' said
the Admiral, 'from the West Indies.' 'I guess,' said the Southerner,
'you may have been clean round the world, Admiral, but you
have been plaguy little in it, not to know better nor that.'

"I shot a wild goose at River Philip last year, with the rice of
Varginny fresh in his crop; he must have cracked on near about
as fast as them other geese, the British travellers. Which knowed
the most of the country they passed over, do you suppose? I
guess it was much of a muchness—near about six of one, and
a half-dozen of t'other; two eyes ain't much better than one, if
they are both blind.

"No, if you want to know all about us and the Bluenoses (a
pretty considerable share of Yankee blood in them too, I tell
you; the old stock comes from New England, and the breed is

tolerable pure yet, near about one half apple sarce, and t'other half molasses, all except to the East'ard, where there is a cross of the Scotch), jist ax me, and I'll tell you candidly. I'm not one of them that can't see no good points in my neighbour's critter, and no bad ones in my own; I've seen too much of the world for that, I guess. Indeed, in a general way, I praise other folks' beasts, and keep dark about my own. Says I, when I meet Blue-nose mounted, 'That's a real smart horse of your'n; put him out, I guess he'll trot like mad.' Well, he lets him have the spur, and the critter does his best, and then I pass him like a streak of lightning with mine. The feller looks all taken aback at that. 'Why,' says he, 'that's a real clipper of your'n, I vow.' 'Middlin',' says I (quite cool, as if I had heard that 'ere same thing a thousand times), 'he's good enough for me, jist a fair trotter, and nothin' to brag of.' That goes near about as far ag'in in a general way, as a crackin' and a boastin' does. Never *tell* folks you can go ahead on 'em, but *do* it; it spares a great deal of talk, and helps them to save their breath to cool their broth.

"No, if you want to know the ins and the outs of the Yankees —I've wintered them and summered them; I know all their points, shape, make, and breed; I've tried 'em alongside of other folks, and I know where they fall short, where they mate 'em, and where they have the advantage, about as well as some who think they know a plaguy sight more. It ain't them that stare the most, that see the best always, I guess. Our folks have their faults, and I know them (I warn't born blind, I reckon), but your friends, the tour writers, are a little grain too hard on us. Our old nigger wench had several dirty, ugly-lookin' children, and was proper cross to 'em. Mother used to say, '*Juno, it's better never to wipe a child's nose at all, I guess, than to wring it off.*' "

"JIST look out of the door," said the Clockmaker, "and see what a beautiful night it is, how calm, how still, how clear it is; bean't it lovely? I like to look up at them 'ere stars, when I am away from home; they put me in mind of our national flag, and it is generally allowed to be the first flag in the univarse now. The British can whip all the world, and we can whip the British. It's near about the prettiest sight I know of, is one of our first-class frigates, manned with our free and enlightened citizens, all ready for sea; it is like the great American Eagle, on its perch, balancing itself for a start on the broad expanse of blue sky, afeared of nothin' of its kind, and president of all it surveys. It was a good emblem that we chose, warn't it?"

There was no evading so direct, and at the same time so conceited an appeal as this. "Certainly," said I, "the emblem was well chosen. I was particularly struck with it on observing the device on your naval buttons during the last war—an eagle with an anchor in its claws. That was a natural idea, taken from an ordinary occurrence: a bird purloining the anchor of a frigate —an article so useful and necessary for the food of its young. It was well chosen, and exhibited great taste and judgment in the artist. The emblem is more appropriate than you are aware of: boasting of what you cannot perform; grasping at what you cannot attain; an emblem of arrogance and weakness; of ill-directed ambition and vulgar pretension."

"It's a common phrase," said he with great composure, "among seamen, to say 'Damn your buttons,' and I guess it's natural for you to say so of the buttons of our navals; I guess you have a right to that 'ere oath. It's a sore subject, that, I reckon, and I believe I hadn't ought to have spoken of it to you at all. Brag is a good dog, but Holdfast is a better one."

He was evidently annoyed, and with his usual dexterity gave vent to his feelings by a sally upon the Bluenoses, who, he says, are a cross of English and Yankee, and therefore first cousins to us both. "Perhaps," said he, "that 'ere Eagle might with more propriety have been taken off as perched on an anchor, instead of holding it in his claws, and I think it would have been more natural; but I suppose it was some stupid foreign artist that made that 'ere blunder—I never seed one yet that was equal to our'n. If that Eagle is represented as trying what he can't do, it's an honourable ambition arter all; but these Bluenoses won't try what they can do. They put me in mind of a great big hulk of a horse in a cart, that won't put his shoulder to the collar at all for all the lambastin' in the world, but turns his head round and looks at you, as much as to say, 'What an everlastin' heavy thing an empty cart is, isn't it?' *An Owl should be their emblem, and the motto, 'He sleeps all the days of his life.'* The whole country is like this night; beautiful to look at, but silent as the grave—still as death, asleep, becalmed.

"If the sea was always calm," said he, "it would p'ison the univarse; no soul could breathe the air, it would be so uncommon bad. Stagnant water is always onpleasant, but salt water when it gets tainted beats all natur'; motion keeps it sweet and wholesome, and that our minister used to say is one of the 'wonders of the great deep.' This province is stagnant; it ain't deep like still water neither, for it's shaller enough, gracious knows, but it is motionless, noiseless, lifeless. If you have ever been to sea in a calm, you'd know what a plaguy tiresome thing it is for a man that's in a hurry. An everlastin' flappin' of the sails, and a creakin' of the booms, and an onsteady pitchin' of the ship, and folks lyin' about dozin' away their time, and the sea a-heavin' a long heavy swell, like the breathin' of the chist of some great monster asleep. A passenger wonders the sailors are so plaguy easy about it, and he goes a-lookin' out east, and a-spyin' out west, to see if there's any chance of a breeze, and says to himself, 'Well, if this ain't dull music, it's a pity.' Then how streaked he feels when he sees a steamboat a-clippin' it by him like mad, and the folks on board pokin' fun at him, and askin' him if he has any word to send to home. 'Well,' he says, 'if any soul ever catches me on board a sail vessel again, when I can go by steam, I'll give him leave to tell me of it, that's a fact.'

"That's partly the case here. They are becalmed, and they see us going ahead on them, till we are e'enamost out of sight; yet they hain't got a steamboat, and they hain't got a railroad; indeed, I doubt if one half on 'em ever seed or heerd tell of one or t'other of them. I never seed any folks like 'em except the Indians, and they won't even so much as look; they haven't the least morsel of curiosity in the world; from which one of our Unitarian preachers (they are dreadful hands at *doubtin'*, them—I don't doubt but some day or another, they will doubt whether everything ain't a *doubt*), in a very learned work, doubts whether they were ever descended from Eve at all. Old marm Eve's children, he says, are all lost, it is said, in consequence of too much curiosity, while these copper-coloured folks are lost from havin' too little. How can they be the same? Thinks I, that may be logic, old Dubersome, but it ain't sense: don't extremes meet? Now, these Bluenoses have no motion in 'em, no enterprise, no spirit, and if any critter shows any symptoms of activity, they say he is a man of no judgment, he's speculative, he's a schemer, in short, he's mad. They vegetate like a lettuce plant in a sarce garden—they grow tall and spindlin', run to seed right off, grow as bitter as gall, and die.

"A gal once came to our minister to hire as a house help; says she, 'Minister, I suppose you don't want a young lady to do chamber business and breed worms, do you?—for I've half a mind to take a spell at livin' out.' She meant," said the Clockmaker, "housework and rearing silk-worms. 'My pretty maiden,' says he, a-pattin' her on the cheek (for I've often observed old men always talk kinder pleasant to women), 'my pretty maiden, where was you brought up?' 'Why,' says she, 'I guess I warn't brought at all, I growed up.' 'Under what platform,' says he (for he was very particular that all his house helps should go to his meetin'), 'under what church platform?' 'Church platform!' says she, with a toss of her head, like a young colt that got a check of the curb, 'I guess I warn't raised under a platform at all, but in as good a house as your'n, grand as you be.' 'You said well,' said the old minister, quite shocked, 'when you said you growed up, dear, for you have grown up in great ignorance.' 'Then I guess you had better get a lady that knows more than me,' says she, 'that's flat. I reckon I am every bit and grain as good as you be. If I don't understand a bum-byx (silk-worm), both feedin', breedin', and rearin', then I want to know who does, that's all; church platform, indeed!' says she; 'I guess you were raised under a glass frame in March, and transplanted on Independence Day, warn't you?' And off she sot, lookin' as scorney as a London lady, and leavin' the poor minister standin' starin' like a stuck pig. 'Well, well,' says he, liftin' up both hands, and turnin' up the whites of his eyes like a duck in thunder, 'if that don't bang the bush! It fearly beats sheep shearin' after the blackberry bushes have got the wool. It does, I vow; them are the tares them Unitarians sow in our grain fields at night; I guess they'll ruinate the crops yet, and make the ground so everlasting foul, we'll have to pare the sod and burn it, to kill the roots. Our fathers sowed the right seed here in the wilderness, and watered it with their tears, and watched over it with fastin' and prayer, and now it's fairly run out, that's a fact, I snore.. It's got choked up with all sorts of trash in natur', I declare. Dear, dear, I vow I never seed the beat o' that in all my born days.'

"Now the Bluenoses are like that 'ere gal; they have grown up, and grown up in ignorance of many things they hadn't ought not to know; and it's as hard to teach grown-up folks as it is to break a six-year-old horse; and they do rile one's temper so— they act so ugly, that it tempts one sometimes to break their confounded necks; it's near about as much trouble as it's worth."

"What remedy is there for all this supineness?" said I; "how can these people be awakened out of their ignorant slothfulness, into active exertion?"

"The remedy," said Mr. Slick, "is at hand; it is already workin' its own cure. They must recede before our free and enlightened citizens, like the Indians; our folks will buy them out, and they must give place to a more intelligent and ac-*tive* people. They must go to the lands of Labrador, or be located back of Canada; they can hold on there a few years, until the wave of civilization reaches them, and then they must move again as the savages do. It is decreed; I hear the bugle of destiny a-soundin' of their retreat, as plain as anything. Congress will give them a concession of land, if they petition, away to Alleghany's backside territory, and grant them relief for a few years; for we are out of debt, and don't know what to do with our surplus revenue. The only way to shame them, that I know, would be to sarve them as Uncle Enoch sarved a neighbour of his in Varginny.

"There was a lady that had a plantation near hand to his'n, and there was only a small river atwixt the two houses, so that folks could hear each other talk across it. Well, she was a dreadful cross-grained woman, a real catamount, as savage as a she-bear that has cubs; an old farrow critter, as ugly as sin, and one that both hooked and kicked too—a most particular onmarciful she-devil, that's a fact. She used to have some of her niggers tied up every day, and flogged uncommon severe, and their screams and screeches were horrid—no soul could stand it; nothin' was heerd all day but 'O Lord Missus! O Lord Missus!' Enoch was fairly sick of the sound, for he was a tender-hearted man, and says he to her one day, 'Now do, marm, find out some other place to give your cattle the cowskin, for it worries me to hear 'em take on so dreadful bad; I can't stand it, I vow; they are flesh and blood as well as we be, though the meat is a different colour.' But it was no good; she jist up and told him to mind his own business, and she guessed she'd mind her'n. He was determined to shame her out of it; so one mornin' arter breakfast he goes into the cane field, and says he to Lavender, one of the black overseers, 'Muster up the whole gang of slaves, every soul, and bring 'em down to the whippin' post, the whole stock of them, bulls, cows, and calves.' Well, away goes Lavender, and drives up all the niggers. 'Now you catch it,' says he, 'you lazy villains; I tole you so many a time—I tole you massa he lose all patience wid you, you good-for-nothin' rascals. I grad, upon my soul, I werry grad; you mind now what old Lavender say anoder time.' The black overseers are always the most cruel," said the Clockmaker; "they have no sort of feeling for their own people.

"Well, when they were gathered there according to orders, they looked streaked enough you may depend, thinkin' they were going to get it all round; and the wenches they fell to a-cryin', wringin' their hands, and boo-hooing like mad. Lavender was there with his cowskin, grinnin' like a chessy cat, and crackin' it about, ready for business. 'Pick me out,' says Enoch, 'four that have the loudest voices.' 'Hard matter dat,' says Lavender, 'hard matter dat, massa; dey all talk loud, dey all lub talk more better nor work—de idle villains; better gib 'em all a little tickle, jist to teach 'em to larf on t'other side of de mouf; dat side bran' new, dey never use it yet.' 'Do as I order you, sir,' said Uncle, 'or I'll have you triced up, you cruel old rascal you.' When they were picked out and sot by themselves, they hanged their heads, and looked like sheep going to the shambles. 'Now,' says Uncle Enoch, 'my pickaninnies, do you sing out as loud as Niagara, at the very tip eend of your voice—

> ' "Don't kill a nigger, pray,
>   Let him lib anoder day.
>   O Lord Missus—O Lord Missus!

> ' "My back be very sore,
>   No stand it any more.
>   O Lord Missus—O Lord Missus!"

And all the rest of you join chorus, as loud as you can bawl, "O Lord Missus." ' The black rascals understood the joke real well. They larfed ready to split their sides; they fairly lay down on the ground, and rolled over and over with lafter. Well, when they came to the chorus, 'O Lord Missus,' if they didn't let go, it's a pity. They made the river ring ag'in—they were heerd clean out to sea. All the folks ran out of the lady's house, to see what on airth was the matter on Uncle Enoch's plantation. They thought there was actilly a rebellion there; but when they listened awhile, and heerd it over and over again, they took the hint, and returned a-larfin' in their sleeves. Says they, 'Master Enoch Slick, he upsides with Missus this hitch anyhow.' Uncle never heerd anything more of 'O Lord Missus,' after that. Yes, they ought to be shamed out of it, those Bluenoses. When reason fails to convince, there is nothin' left but ridicule. If they have no ambition, apply to their feelings, clap a blister on their pride, and it will do the business. It's like a-puttin' ginger under a horse's tail; it makes him carry up real hand*sum*, I tell you. When I was a boy, I was always late to school; well, father's preachin' I didn't mind much, but I never could bear to hear my mother say, 'Why Sam, are you actilly up for all day? Well, I hope your airly risin' won't hurt you, I declare. What on airth is a-goin' to happen now? Well, wonders will never cease.' It raised my dander; at last says I, 'Now, mother, don't say that 'ere any more for gracious' sake, for it makes me feel ugly, and I'll get up as airly as any on you'; and so I did, and I soon found what's worth knowin' in this life—*An early start makes easy stages.*"

THE next morning was warmer than several that had preceded it. It was one of those uncommonly fine days that distinguish an American autumn.

"I guess," said Mr. Slick, "the heat today is like a glass of mint julip, with a lump of ice in it; it tastes cool, and feels warm; it's real good, I tell you. I love such a day as this, dearly. It's generally allowed the finest weather in the world is in America; there ain't the beat of it to be found anywhere." He then lighted a cigar, and throwing himself back on his chair, put both feet out of the window, and sat with his arms folded, a perfect picture of happiness.

"You appear," said I, "to have travelled over the whole of this Province, and to have observed the country and the people with much attention; pray what is your opinion of the present state and future prospects of Halifax?"

"If you will tell me," said he, "when the folks there will wake up, then I can answer you; but they are fast asleep. As to the Province, it's a splendid Province, and calculated to go ahead. It will grow as fast as a Varginny gal; and they grow so amazin' fast, if you put your arm round one of their necks to kiss them, by the time you're done, they've grown up into women. It's a pretty Province I tell you, good above and better below; surface covered with pastures, meadows, woods, and a 'nation sight of water privileges, and under the ground full of mines. It puts me in mind of the soup at the *Tree*-mont House.

"One day I was a-walkin' in the Mall, and who should I meet but Major Bradford, a gentleman from Connecticut, that traded in calves and pumpkins for the Boston market. Says he, 'Slick, where do you get your grub today?' 'At General Peep's tavern,' says I. 'Only fit for niggers,' says he; 'why don't you come to the *Tree*-mont House? That's the most splendid thing, it's generally allowed, in all the world.' 'Why,' says I, 'that's a notch above my mark; I guess it's too plaguy dear for me; I can't afford it nohow.' 'Well,' says he, 'it's dear in one sense, but it's dog cheap in another: it's a grand place for speculation. There's so many rich Southerners and strangers there that have more money than wit, that you might do a pretty good business there without goin' out of the street door. I made two hundred dollars this mornin' in little less than half no time. There's a Carolina lawyer there as rich as a bank, and says he to me arter breakfast, "Major," says he, "I wish I knew where to get a real slapping trotter of a horse, one that could trot with a flash of lightning for a mile, and beat it by a whole neck or so." Says I, "My Lord," for you must know, he says he's the nearest male heir to a Scotch dormant peerage, "my Lord," says I, "I have one, a proper sneezer, a chap that can go ahead of a railroad steamer, a real natural traveller, one that can trot with the ball out of the small eend of a rifle, and never break into a gallop." Says he, "Major, I wish you wouldn't give me that 'ere nickname, I don't like it," though he looked as tickled all the time as possible; "I never knew," says he, "a lord that warn't a fool, that's a fact, and that's the reason I don't go ahead and claim the title." "Well," says I, "my Lord, I don't know, but somehow I can't help a-thinkin' if you have a good claim, you'd be more like a fool not to go ahead with it." "Well," says he, "lord or no lord, let's look at your horse." So away I went to Joe Brown's livery stable, at t'other eend of the city, and picked out the best trotter he had, and no great stick to brag on either; says I, "Joe Brown, what do you ax for that 'ere horse?" "Two hundred dollars," says he. "Well," says I, "I will take him out and try him, and if I like him I will keep him." So I shows our Carolina lord the horse, and when he gets on him, says I, "Don't let him trot as fast as he can, resarve that for a heat; if folks find out how everlastin' fast he is, they'd be afeared to stump you for a start." When he returned, he said he liked the horse amazingly, and axed the price. "Four hundred dollars," says I; "you can't get nothin' special without a good price; pewter cases never hold good watches." "I know it," says he; "the horse is mine." Thinks I to myself, that's more than ever I could say of him then, anyhow.'

'"Well, I was goin' to tell you about the soup: says the Major, 'It's near about dinner time; jist come and see how you like the location.' There was a sight of folks there, gentlemen and ladies in the public room—I never seed so many afore except at Commencement Day—all ready for a start, and when the gong sounded, off we sot like a flock of sheep. Well, if there warn't a jam you may depend; some one give me a pull, and I nearabouts went heels up over head; so I reached out both hands, and caught hold of the first thing I could, and what should it be but a lady's dress. Well, as I'm alive, rip went the frock, and tear goes the petticoat, and when I righted myself from my beam-eends away they all came home to me, and there she was, the pretty critter, with all her upper riggin' standin' as far as her waist, and nothin' left below but a short linen under-garment. If she didn't scream, it's a pity; and the more she screamed, the more folks larfed, for no soul could help larfin', till one of the waiters folded her up in a tablecloth.

" 'What an awkward devil you be, Slick,' says the Major; 'now that comes of not falling in first; they should have formed four deep, rear rank in open order, and marched in to our splendid national air, and filed off to their seats, right and left, shoulders forward. I feel kinder sorry, too,' says he, 'for that 'ere young heifer; but she showed a proper pretty leg though, Slick, didn't she? I guess you don't often get such a chance as that 'ere.' Well, I gets near the Major at table, and afore me stood a china utensil with two handles, full of soup, about the size of a foot-tub, with a large silver scoop in it, near about as big as a ladle of a maple sugar kettle. I was jist about bailing out some soup into my dish, when the Major said, 'Fish it up from the bottom, Slick.' Well, sure enough, I gives it a drag from the bottom, and up come the fat pieces of turtle, and the thick rich soup, and a sight of little forced meat balls, of the size of sheep's dung. No soul could tell how good it was; it was near about as handsum as father's old genuine particular cider, and that you could feel tingle clean away down to the tip eends of your toes. 'Now,' says the Major, 'I'll give you, Slick, a new wrinkle on your horn. Folks ain't thought nothin' of, unless they live at Treemont: it's all the go. Do you dine at Peep's tavern every day, and then off hot foot to Treemont, and pick your teeth on the street steps there, and folks will think you dine there. I do it often, and it saves two dollars a day.' Then he put his finger on his nose, and says he, 'Mum is the word.'

"Now, this Province is jist like that 'ere soup—good enough at top, but dip down and you have the riches: the coal, the iron ore, the gypsum, and what not. As for Halifax, it's well enough in itself, though no great shakes neither—a few sizeable houses, with a proper sight of small ones, like half a dozen old hens with their broods of young chickens; but the people, the strange critters, they are all asleep. They walk in their sleep, and talk in their sleep, and what they say one day they forget the next; they say they were dreaming. You know where Governor Camp-bell lives, don't you, in a large stone house, with a great wall round it, that looks like a state prison? Well, near hand there is a nasty, dirty, horrid-lookin' buryin' ground there; it's filled with large grave rats as big as kittens, and the springs of black water there go through the chinks of the rocks and flow into all the wells, and fairly p'ison the folks; it's a dismal place, I tell you; I wonder the air from it don't turn all the silver in the Governor's house of a brass colour—and folks say he has four cart-loads of it—it's so everlastin' bad; it's near about as nosey as a slave ship of niggers. Well, you may go there and shake the folks to all etarnity, and you won't wake 'em, I guess; and yet there ain't much difference atween their sleep and the folks at Halifax, only they lie still there and are quiet, and don't walk and talk in their sleep, like them above ground.

"Halifax reminds me of a Russian officer I once seed at Warsaw; he had lost both arms in battle—but I guess I must tell you first why I went there, 'cause that will show you how we speculate. One Sabbath day, after bell ringin', when most of the women had gone to meetin'—for they were great hands for pretty sarmons, and our Unitarian ministers all preach poetry, only they leave the rhyme out; it sparkles like perry—I goes down to East India wharf to see Captain Zeek Hancock, of Nantucket, to inquire how oil was, and if it would bear doing anything in; when who should come along but Jabish Green. 'Slick,' says he, 'how do you do? Isn't this as pretty a day as you'll see between this and Norfolk? It whips English weather by a long chalk'; and then he looked down at my watch seals, and looked and looked as if he thought I'd stole 'em. At last he looks up, and says he, 'Slick, I suppose you wouldn't go to Warsaw, would you, if it was made worth your while?' 'Which Warsaw?' says I, for I believe in my heart we have a hundred of them. 'None of our'n at all,' says he; 'Warsaw in Poland.' 'Well, I don't know,' says I; 'what do you call worth while?' 'Six dollars a day, expenses paid, and a bonus of one thousand dollars, if speculation turns out well.' 'I am off,' says I, 'whenever you say go.' 'Tuesday,' says he, 'in the Hamburg packet. Now,' says he, 'I'm in a tarnation hurry; I'm goin' a-pleasurin' today in the Custom House boat, along with Josiah Bradford's gals down to Nahant. But I'll tell you what I am at: the Emperor of Russia has ordered the Poles to cut off their queues on the 1st of January; you must buy them all up, and ship them off to London for the wig makers. Human hair is scarce, and risin'. 'Lord a massy!' says I, 'how queer they will look, won't they? Well, I vow, that's what the sea folks call sailing under bare Poles, come true, ain't it?' 'I guess it will turn out a good spec,' says he; and a good one it did turn out—he cleared ten thousand dollars by it.

"When I was at Warsaw, as I was a-sayin', there was a Russian officer there who had lost both his arms in battle, a good-natured, contented critter, as I e'enamost ever seed, and he was fed with spoons by his neighbours; but arter a while they grew tired of it, and I guess he near about starved to death at last. Now Halifax is like that 'ere *Spooney*, as I used to call him; it is fed by the outports, and they begin to have enough to do to feed themselves; it must larn to live without 'em. They have no river, and no country about them; let them make a railroad to Minas Basin, and they will have arms of their own to feed themselves with. If they don't do it, and do it soon, I guess they'll get into a decline that no human skill will cure. They are proper thin now; you can count their ribs e'enamost as far as you can see them. *The only thing that will either make or save Halifax, is a railroad across the country to Bay of Fundy.*

" 'It will do to talk of,' says one. 'You'll see it some day,' says another. 'Yes,' says a third, 'it will come, but we are too young yet.'

"Our old minister had a darter, a real clever-looking gal as you'd see in a day's ride, and she had two or three offers of marriage from 'sponsible men, most particular good specs; but minister always said, "Phœbe, you are too young; the day will come, but you are too young yet, dear.' Well, Phœbe didn't think so at all; she said she guessed she knew better nor that; so next offer she had, she said she had no notion to lose another chance; off she shot to Rhode Island, and got married. Says she, 'Father's too old, he don't know.' That's jist the case at Halifax. The old folks say the country is too young, the time will come, and so on; and in the meantime the young folks won't wait, *and run off to the States, where the maxim is, 'Youth is the time for improvement; a new country is never too young for exertion; push on—keep movin'—go ahead.'*

"Darn it all," said the Clockmaker, rising with great animation, clinching his fist, and extending his arm, "darn it all, it fairly makes my dander rise, to see the nasty, idle, loungin', good-for-nothing, do-little critters; they ain't fit to tend a bear trap, I vow. They ought to be quilted round and round a room, like a lady's lap-dog, the matter of two hours a day, to keep them from dyin' of apoplexy."

"Hush, hush!" said I, "Mr. Slick, you forget."

"Well," said he, resuming his usual composure, "well, it's enough to make one vexed though, I declare—isn't it?"

Mr. Slick has often alluded to this subject, and always in a most decided manner. I am inclined to think he is right. Mr. Howe's papers on the railroad I read, till I came to his calculations, but I never could read figures; "I can't cipher," and there I paused; it is a barrier; I retreated a few paces, took a running leap, and cleared the whole of them. Mr. Slick says he has *under* and not *over* rated its advantages. He appears to be such a shrewd, observing, intelligent man, and so perfectly at home on these subjects, that I confess I have more faith in this humble but eccentric Clockmaker, than in any other man I have met with in this Province. I therefore pronounce, *"There will be a railroad."*

"I RECKON," said the Clockmaker, as we strolled through Amherst, "you have read Hook's story of the boy that one day asked one of his father's guests who his next-door neighbour was, and when he heerd his name, asked him if he warn't a fool. 'No, my little feller,' said he, 'he bean't a fool, he is a most particular sensible man : but why did you ax that 'ere question?' 'Why,' said the little boy, 'mother said t'other day you were next door to a fool, and I wanted to know who lived next door to you.' His mother felt pretty ugly, I guess, when she heerd him run right slap on that 'ere breaker.

"Now these Cumberland folks have curious next-door neighbours, too; they are placed by their location right atwixt fire and water; they have New Brunswick politics on one side, and Nova Scotia politics on t'other side of them, and Bay Fundy and Bay Varte on t'other two sides; they are actilly in hot water; they are up to their cruppers in politics, and great hands for talking of House of Assembly political Unions, and what not. Like all folks who wade so deep, they can't always tell the natur' of the ford. Sometimes they strike their shins agin a snag of a rock; at other times, they go whap into a quicksand, and if they don't take special care they are apt to go souse over head and ears into deep water. I guess if they'd talk more of *rotation*, and less of *elections*, more of them 'ere *dykes*, and less of *banks*, and attend more to *top dressing*, and less to *re-dressing*, it'd be better for 'em."

"Now you mention the subject, I think I have observed," said I. "that there is a great change in your countrymen in that respect. Formerly, whenever you met an American, you had a dish of politics set before you, whether you had an appetite for it or not; but lately I have remarked they seldom allude to it. Pray, to what is this attributable?"

"I guess," said he, "they have enough of it to home, and are sick of the subject. They are cured the way our pastry cooks cure their 'prentices of stealing sweet notions out of their shops When they get a new 'prentice they tell him he must never so much as look at all them 'ere nice things; and if he dares to lay the weight of his finger upon one of them, they'll have him up for it before a justice; they tell him it's every bit and grain as bad as stealing from a till. Well, that's sure to set him at it, just as a high fence does a breachy ox, first to look over it, and then push it down with its rump; it's human natur'. Well, the boy eats and eats till he can't eat no longer, and then he gets sick at his stomach, and hates the very sight of sweetmeats arterwards.

"We've had politics with us till we're dog sick of 'em, I tell you. Besides, I guess we are as far from perfection as when we set out a-rowin' for it. You may get purity of Election, but how are you to get purity of Members? It would take a great deal of ciphering to tell that. I never heerd tell of one who had seed it.

"The best member I e'enamost ever seed was John Adams. Well, John Adams could no more plough a straight furrow in politics than he could haul the plough himself. He might set out straight at beginnin' for a little way, but he was sure to get crooked afore he got to the eend of the ridge, and sometimes he would have two or three crooks in it. I used to say to him, 'How on airth is it, Mr. Adams'—for he was no way proud like, though he was President of our great nation, and it is allowed to be the greatest nation in the world, too; for you might see him sometimes of an arternoon a-swimmin' along with the boys in the Potomac; I do believe that's the way he larned to give the folks the dodge so spry—well I used to say to him, 'How on airth is it, Mr. Adams, you can't make straight work on it?' He was a grand hand at an excuse, though minister used to say that folks that were good at an excuse were seldom good for nothin' else; sometimes he said the ground was so tarnation stony, it throwed the plough out; at other times he said the off ox was such an ugly, wilful-tempered critter, there was no doin' nothin' with him; or that there was so much machinery about the plough, it made it plaguy hard to steer; or maybe it was the fault of them that went afore him, that they laid it down so bad—unless he was hired for another term of four years the work wouldn't look well; and if all them 'ere excuses wouldn't do, why, he would take to scolding the nigger that drove the team, throw all the blame on him, and order him to have an everlastin' lacin' with the cowskin. You might as well catch a weasel asleep as catch him. He had somethin' the matter with one eye; well, he knew I know'd that when I was a boy; so one day a feller presented a petition to him, and he told him it was very affectin'. Says he, 'It fairly draws tears from me,' and his weak eye took to lettin' off its water like statiee; so as soon as the chap went, he winks to me with t'other one, quite knowin', as much as to say, 'You see it's all in my eye, Slick, but don't let on to anyone about it, that I said so.' That eye was a regular cheat, a complete New England wooden nutmeg. Folks said Mr. Adams was a very tender-hearted man. Perhaps he was, but I guess that eye didn't pump its water out o' that place.

"Members in general ain't to be depended on, I tell you. Politics makes a man as crooked as a pack does a peddler; not that they are so awful heavy neither, but *it teaches a man to stoop in the long run.* Arter all, there's not that difference in 'em—at least there ain't in Congress—one would think; for if one of them is clear of one vice, why, as like as not, he has another fault just as bad. An honest farmer, like one of these Cumberland folks, when he goes to choose atwixt two that offers for votes, is jist like the flying-fish. That 'ere little critter is not content to stay to home in the water, and mind its business, but he must try his hand at flyin', and he is no great dab at flyin', neither. Well, the moment he's out of water, and takes to flyin', the sea fowl are arter him, and let him have it; and if he has the good luck to escape them, and dive into the sea, the dolphin, as like as not, has a dig at him, that knocks more wind out of him than he got while aping the birds, a plaguy sight. I guess the Bluenoses know jist about as much about politics as this foolish fish knows about flying. *All critters in nature are better in their own element.*

"It beats cock-fightin', I tell you, to hear the Bluenoses, when they get together, talk politics. They have got three or four evil spirits, like the Irish Banshees, that they say cause all the mischief in the Province: the Council, the Banks, the House of Assembly, and the Lawyers. If a man places a higher valiation on himself than his neighbours do, and wants to be a magistrate before he is fit to carry the inkhorn for one, and finds himself safely delivered of a mistake, he says it is all owing to the Council. The members are cunnin' critters, too; they know this feelin', and when they come home from Assembly, and people ax 'em, 'Where are all them 'ere fine things you promised us?' 'Why,' they say, 'we'd a had 'em all for you, but for that eternal Council; they nullified all we did.' The country will come to no good till them chaps show their respect for it, by covering their bottoms with homespun. If a man is so tarnation lazy he won't work, and in course has no money, why he says it's all owin' to the banks, they won't discount, there's no money, they've ruined the Province. If there bean't a road made up to every citizen's door, away back to the woods—who as like as not has squatted there—why, he says the House of Assembly have voted all the money to pay great men's salaries, and there's nothin' left for poor settlers, and cross roads. Well, the lawyers come in for their share of cake and ale, too; if they don't catch it, it's a pity.

"There was one Jim Munroe, of Onion County, Connecticut, a desperate idle fellow, a great hand at singin' songs, a-skatin', drivin' about with the gals, and so on. Well, if anybody's windows were broke, it was Jim Munroe; and if there were any youngsters in want of a father they were sure to be poor Jim's. Jist so it is with the lawyers here; they stand godfathers for every misfortune that happens in the country. When there is a mad dog a-goin' about, every dog that barks is said to be bit by the mad one, so he gets credit for all the mischief that every dog does for three months to come. So every feller that goes yelpin' home from a courthouse smartin' from the law, swears he is bit by a lawyer. Now there may be something wrong in all these things—and it can't be otherwise in natur'—in Council, Banks, House of Assembly, and Lawyers: but change them all, and it's an even chance if you don't get worse ones in their room. It is in politics as in horses: when a man has a beast that's near about up to the notch, he'd better not swap him; if he does, he's e'enamost sure to get one not so good as his own. *My rule is, I'd rather keep a critter whose faults I do know, than change him for a beast whose faults I don't know.*"

THE DANCING MASTER ABROAD

"I wish that 'ere black heifer in the kitchen would give over singing that 'ere everlastin' dismal tune," said the Clockmaker; "it makes my head ache. You've heerd a song afore now," said he, "haven't you, till you was fairly sick of it? for I have, I vow. The last time I was in Rhode Island—all the gals sing there, and it's generally allowed there's no such singers anywhere; they beat the *Eye*-talians a long chalk; they sing so high, some on 'em, they go clear out o' hearin' sometimes, like a lark—well, you heerd nothin' but 'O no, we never mention her'; well, I grew so plaguy tired of it, I used to say to myself, I'd sooner see it than hear tell of it, I vow; I wish to gracious you would 'never mention her,' for it makes me feel ugly to hear that same thing for ever and ever and amen that way. Well, they've got a cant phrase here, 'The schoolmaster is abroad,' and every feller tells you that fifty times a day.

"There was a chap said to me not long ago at Truro, 'Mr. Slick, this country is rapidly improving; "the schoolmaster is abroad now," ' and he looked as knowin' as though he had found a mare's nest. 'So I should think,' said I, 'and it would jist be about as well, I guess, if he'd stay to home and mind his business; for your folks are so consoomedly ignorant, I reckon he's abroad e'enamost all his time. I hope when he returns, he'll be the better of his travels, and that's more nor many of our young folks are who go "abroad," for they import more airs and nonsense than they dispose of one while, I tell you; some of the stock remains on hand all the rest of their lives.' There's nothin' I hate so much as cant, of all kinds; it's a sure sign of a tricky disposition. If you see a feller cant in religion, clap your hand into your pocket, and lay right hold of your puss, or he'll steal it, as sure as you're alive; and if a man cants in politics, he'll sell you if he gets a chance, you may depend. Law and physic are jist the same, and every mite and morsel as bad. If a lawyer takes to cantin', it's like the fox preachin' to the geese; he'll eat up his whole con-gregation: and if a doctor takes to it, he's a quack as sure as rates. The Lord have massy on you, for he won't. I'd sooner trust my chance with a naked hook any time, than one that's half-covered with bad bait. The fish will sometimes swallow the one, without thinkin', but they get frightened at t'other, turn tail, and off like a shot.

"Now, to change the tune, I'll give the Bluenoses a new phrase. They'll have an election most likely next year, and then 'the Dancin' Master will be abroad.' A candidate is a most particular polite man, a-noddin' here, and a-bowin' there, and a-shakin' hands all round. Nothin' improves a man's manners like an election. 'The Dancin' Master's abroad then'; nothin' gives the paces equal to that; it makes them as squirmy as an eel; they cross hands and back ag'in, set to their partners, and right and left in great style, and slick it off at the eend, with a real complete bow, and a smile for all the world as sweet as a cat makes at a pan of new milk. Then they get as full of compliments as a dog is full of fleas—inquirin' how the old lady is to home, and the little boy that made such a wonderful smart answer, they never can forget it till next time; a-praisin' a man's farm to the nines, and a-tellin' of him how scandalous the road that leads to his location has been neglected, and how much he wants to find a real complete hand that can build a bridge over his brook, and axin' him if *he* ever built one. When he gets the hook baited with the right fly, and the simple critter begins to jump out of water arter it, all mouth and gills, he winds up the reel, and takes leave, a-thinkin' to himself, 'Now you see what's to the eend of my line, I guess I'll know where to find you when I want you.'

"There's no sort of fishin' requires so much practice as this. When bait is scarce, one worm must answer for several fish. A handful of oats in a pan, arter it brings one horse up in a pastur' for the bridle, serves for another; a-shakin' of it is better than a-givin' of it—it saves the grain for another time. It's a poor business arter all, is electioneering, and when 'the Dancin' Master is abroad,' he's as apt to teach a man to cut capers and get larfed at as anything else. It ain't everyone that's soople enough to dance real complete. Politics take a great deal of time, and grind away a man's honesty near about as fast as cleaning a knife with brick dust. '*It takes its steel out.*' What does a critter get arter all for it in this country? Why, nothin' but expense and disappointment. As King Solomon says—and that 'ere man was up to a thing or two, you may depend, though our Professor did say he warn't so knowin' as Uncle Sam—it's all vanity and vexation of spirit.

"I raised a four-year-old colt once, half blood, a perfect pictur' of a horse, and a genuine clipper; could gallop like the wind; a real daisy, a perfect doll; had an eye like a weasel, and nostril like Commodore Rogers' speakin' trumpet. Well, I took it down to the races at New York, and father he went along with me; for says he, 'Sam, you don't know everything, I guess; you hain't cut your wisdom teeth yet, and you are goin' among them that's had 'em through their gums this while past.' Well, when we gets to the races, father gets colt and puts him in an old wagon, with a worn-out Dutch harness and breast-band; he looked like Old Nick, that's a fact. Then he fastened a head martingale on, and buckled it to the girths atwixt his fore legs. Says I, 'Father, what on airth are you at? I vow, i feel ashamed to be seen with such a catamaran as that, and colt looks like old Satan himself—no soul would know him.' 'I guess I warn't born yesterday,' says he; 'let me be, I know what I am at. I guess I'll slip it into 'em afore I've done, as slick as a whistle. I guess I can see as far into a millstone as the best on 'em.'

"Well, father never entered the horse at all, but stood by and seed the races, and the winnin' horse was followed about by the matter of two or three thousand people a-praisin' of him and admirin' him. They seemed as if they never had seed a horse afore. The owner of him was all up on eend a-boastin' of him, and a-stumpin' the course to produce a horse to run agin him for four hundred dollars. Father goes up to him, lookin' as soft as dough, and as meechin' as you please, and says he, 'Friend, it ain't everyone that has four hundred dollars; it's a plaguy sight of money, I tell you; would you run for one hundred dollars, and give me a little start? If you would, I'd try my colt out of my old wagon agin you, I vow.' 'Let's look at your horse,' says he; so away they went, and a proper sight of people arter them to look at colt, and when they seed him they sot up such a larf, I felt e'enamost ready to cry for spite. Says I to myself, 'What can possess the old man to act arter that fashion? I do believe he has taken leave of his senses.' 'You needn't larf,' says father, 'he's smarter than he looks; our minister's old horse, Captain Jack, is reckoned as quick a beast of his age as any in our location, and that 'ere colt can beat him for a lick of a quarter of a mile quite easy; I seed it myself.' Well, they larfed ag'in louder than before, and says father, 'If you dispute my word, try me; what odds will you give?' 'Two to one,' says the owner, 'eight hundred to four hundred dollars.' 'Well, that's a great deal of money, ain't it?' says father; 'if I was to lose it I'd look pretty foolish, wouldn't I? How folks would pass their jokes at me when I went home again. You wouldn't take that 'ere wagon and harness for fifty dollars of it, would you?' says he. 'Well,' says the other, 'sooner than disappoint you, as you seem to have set your mind on losing your money, I don't care if I do.'

"As soon as it was settled, father drives off to the stables, and then returns mounted, with a red silk pocket handkerchief tied round his head, and colt a-looking like himself, as proud as a nabob, chock full of spring, like the wire eend of a bran' new pair of trouser gallusses. One said, 'That's a plaguy nice-lookin' colt that old feller has, arter all.' 'That horse will show play for it yet,' says a third; and I heard one feller say, 'I guess that's a regular Yankee trick, a complete take in.' They had a fair start for it, and off they sot; father took the lead and kept it, and won the race, though it was a pretty tight scratch, for father was too old to ride colt; he was near about the matter of seventy years old.

"Well, when the colt was walked round after the race, there was an amazin' crowd arter him, and several wanted to buy him; but says father, 'How am I to get home without him, and what shall I do with that 'ere wagon and harness, so far as I be from Slickville?' So he kept them in talk, till he felt their pulses pretty well, and at last he closed with a Southerner for seven hundred dollars, and we returned, having made a considerable good spec of colt. Says father to me, 'Sam,' says he, 'you seed the crowd a-follerin' the winnin' horse, when we came there, didn't you?' 'Yes, sir,' said I, 'I did.' 'Well, when colt beat him, no one follered him at all, but come a-crowdin' about *him*. That's popularity,' said he, 'soon won, soon lost—cried up sky high one minute, and deserted the next, or run down; colt will share the same fate. He'll get beat afore long, and then he's done for. The multitude are always fickle-minded. Our great Washington found that out, and the British officer that beat Bonaparte; the bread they gave him turned sour afore he got half through the loaf. His soap had hardly stiffened afore it ran right back to lye and grease ag'in.

" 'I was sarved the same way. I like to have missed my pension; the Committee said I warn't at Bunker's Hill at all, the villains. That was a glo—' Thinks I, old boy, if you once get into that 'ere field you'll race longer than colt, a plaguy sight; you'll run clear away to the fence to the far eend afore you stop; so I jist cut in and took a hand myself. 'Yes,' says I, 'you did 'em, father, properly; that old wagon was a bright scheme; it led 'em on till you got 'em on the right spot, didn't it?' Says father, 'There's a moral, Sam, in everything in natur'. Never have nothin' to do with elections; you see the vally of popularity in the case of that 'ere horse: sarve the public nine hundred and ninety-nine times, and the thousandth, if they don't agree with you, they desart and abuse you. See how they sarved old John Adams; see how they let Jefferson starve in his old age; see how good old Munroe like to have got right into jail, after his term of President was up. They may talk of independence,' says father, 'but Sam, I'll tell you what independence is'—and he gave his hands a slap agin his trousers pocket, and made the gold eagles he won at the race all jingle ag'in—'That!' says he, giving them another wipe with his fist, and winkin', as much as to say, Do you hear that, my boy! 'that I call independence.' He was in great spirits, the old man; he was so proud of winnin' the race, and puttin' the leake into the New Yorkers, he looked all dander. 'Let them great hungry, ill-favoured, long-legged bitterns,' says he (only he called them by another name that don't sound quite pretty), 'from the outlandish States to Congress, talk about independence; but Sam,' said he, hitting the shiners ag'in till he made them dance right up on eend in his pocket, 'I like to feel it.'

" 'No, Sam,' said he, 'line the pocket well first, make that independent, and then the spirit will be like a horse turned out to grass in the spring for the first time; he's all head and tail, a-snortin' and kickin' and racin' and carrying on like mad; it soon gets independent too. While it's in the stall it may hold up, and paw, and whinny, and feel as spry as anything, but the leather strap keeps it to the manger, and the lead weight to the eend of it makes it hold down its head at last. No,' says he, 'here's independence!' and he gave the eagles such a drive with his fist, he bust his pocket, and sent a whole raft of them a-spinnin' down his leg to the ground. Says I, 'Father,' and I swear I could hardly keep from larfin', he looked so peskily vexed—'Father,' says I, 'I guess there's a moral in that 'ere too: Extremes nary way are none o' the best.' 'Well, well,' says he, kinder snappishly, 'I suppose you're half right, Sam, but we've said enough about it; let's drop the subject; and see if I have picked 'em all up for my eyes are none of the best, now I'm near hand to seventy.' "

"WHAT success had you," said I, "in the sale of your clocks among the Scotch in the eastern part of the Province? Do you find them as gullible as the Bluenoses?"

"Well," said he, "you have heerd tell that a Yankee never answers one question, without axing another, haven't you? Did you ever see an English stage-driver make a bow? because if you hain't obsarved it, I have, and a queer one it is, I swan. He brings his right arm up, jist across his face, and passes on, with a knowin' nod of his head, as much as to say, How do you do? but keep clear o' my wheels, or I'll fetch your horses a lick in the mouth as sure as you're born: jist as a bear puts up his paw to fend off the blow of a stick from his nose. Well, that's the way I pass them 'ere bare-breeched Scotchmen. Lord, if they were located down in these here Cumberland marshes, how the mosquitoes would tickle them up, wouldn't they? They'd set 'em scratchin' thereabouts, as an Irishman does his head, when he's in sarch of a lie. Them 'ere fellers cut their eye-teeth afore they ever sot foot in this country, I expect. When they get a bawbee, they know what to do with it, that's a fact; they open their pouch and drop it in, and it's got a spring like a fox-trap; it holds fast to all it gets, like grim death to a dead nigger. They are proper skinflints, you may depend. Oatmeal is no great shakes at best; it ain't even as good for a horse as real yaller Varginny corn; but I guess I warn't long in finding out that the grits hardly pay for the riddlin'. No, a Yankee has as little chance among them as a Jew has in New England; the sooner he clears out the better. You can no more put a leake into them, than you can send a chisel into teak wood; it turns the edge of the tool the first drive. If the Bluenoses knew the value of money as well as they do, they'd have more cash, and fewer clocks and tin reflectors, I reckon.

"Now, it's different with the Irish; they never carry a puss, for they never have a cent to put in it. They are always in love or in liquor, or else in a row; they are the merriest shavers I ever seed. Judge Beler—I dare say you have heerd tell of him; he's a funny feller—he put a notice over his factory gate at Lowell, 'No cigars or Irishmen admitted within these walls'; for, said he, 'The one will set a flame a-goin' among my cottons, and t'other among my gals. I won't have no such inflammable and dangerous things about me on no account.' When the British wanted our folks to join in the treaty to chock the wheels of the slave-trade, I recollect hearin' old John Adams say we had ought to humour them; for, says he, 'They supply us with labour on easier terms, by shippin' out the Irish.' Says he, 'They work better, and they work cheaper, and they don't live so long. The blacks, when they are past work, hang on forever, and a proper bill of expense they be; but hot weather and new rum rub out the poor rates for t'other ones.'

"The English are the boys for tradin' with; they shell out their cash like a sheaf of wheat in frosty weather; it flies all over the thrashin' floor: but then they are a cross-grained, ungainly, kickin' breed of cattle, as I e'enamost ever seed. Whoever gave them the name of John Bull, knew what he was about, I tell you; for they are all bull-necked, bull-headed folks, I vow; sulky, ugly tempered, vicious critters, a-pawin' and a-roarin' the whole time, and plaguy onsafe unless well watched. They are as headstrong as mules, and as conceited as peacocks."

The astonishment with which I heard this tirade against my countrymen absorbed every feeling of resentment. I listened with amazement at the perfect composure with which he uttered it. He treated it as one of those self-evident truths that need neither proof nor apology, but as a thing well known and admitted by all mankind.

"There's no richer sight that I know of," said he, "than to see one on 'em when he first lands in one of our great cities. He swells out as big as a balloon; his skin is ready to burst with wind—a regular walking bag of gas; and he prances over the pavement like a bear over hot iron; a great awkward hulk of a feller—for they ain't to be compared to the French in manners—a-smirkin' at you, as much as to say, 'Look here, Jonathan, here's an Englishman; here's a boy that's got blood as pure as a Norman pirate, and lots of the blunt of both kinds, a pocket full of one, and a mouthful of t'other: bean't he lovely?' and then he looks as fierce as a tiger, as much as to say, 'Say boo to a goose, if you dare.'

"No, I believe we may stump the univarse; we improve on everything, and we have improved on our own species. You'll search one while, I tell you, afore you'll find a man that, take him by and large, is equal to one of our free and enlightened citizens. He's the chap that has both speed, wind, and bottom; he's clear grit—ginger to the backbone, you may depend. It's generally allowed there ain't the beat of them to be found anywhere. Spry as a fox, supple as an eel, and cute as a weasel. Though I say it, that shouldn't say it, they fairly take the shine off creation; they are actilly equal to cash."

He looked like a man who felt that he had expressed himself so aptly and so well, that anything additional would only weaken its effect; he therefore changed the conversation immediately, by pointing to a tree at some little distance from the house, and remarking that it was the rock maple or sugar tree.

"It's a pretty tree," said he, "and a profitable one too to raise. It will bear tapping for many years, though it gets exhausted at last. This Province is like that 'ere tree : it is tapped till it begins to die at the top, and if they don't drive in a spile and stop the everlastin' flow of the sap, it will perish altogether. All the money that's made here, all the interest that's paid in it, and a pretty considerable portion of rent too, all goes abroad for investment, and the rest is sent to us to buy bread. It's drained like a bog; it has opened and covered trenches all through it, and then there's others to the foot of the upland to cut off the springs.

"Now you may make even a bog too dry; you may take the moisture out to that degree that the very sile becomes dust, and blows away. The English funds, and our banks, railroads, and canals, are all absorbing your capital like a sponge, and will lick it up as fast as you can make it. That very bridge we heerd of at Windsor is owned in New Brunswick, and will pay toll to that Province. The capitalists of Nova Scotia treat it like a hired house : they won't keep it in repair; they neither paint it to preserve the boards, nor stop a leak to keep the frame from rottin' : but let it go to wrack, sooner than drive a nail or put in a pane of glass. 'It will sarve our turn out,' they say.

"There's neither spirit, enterprise, nor patriotism here; but the whole country is as inactive as a bear in winter, that does nothin' but scrouch up in his den, a-thinkin' to himself, 'Well, if I ain't an unfortunate devil, it's a pity; I have a most splendid warm coat as e'er a gentleman in these here woods, let him be who he will; but I got no socks to my feet, and have to sit for ever-lastingly a-suckin' of my paws to keep 'em warm; if it warn't for that, I guess I'd make some o' them chaps that have hoofs to their feet and horns to their heads, look about them pretty sharp

I know.' It's dismal, now ain't it? If I had the framin' of the Governor's message, if I wouldn't show 'em how to put timber together you may depend; I'd make them scratch their heads and stare, I know.

"I went down to Matanzas in the Fulton steamboat once; well, it was the first of the kind they ever seed, and proper scared they were to see a vessel without sails or oars, goin' right straight ahead, nine knots an hour, in the very wind's eye, and a great streak of smoke arter her as long as the tail of a comet. I believe they thought it was Old Nick alive, a-treatin' himself to a swim. You could see the niggers a-clippin' it away from the shore, for dear life, and the soldiers a-movin' about as if they thought that we were a-goin' to take the whole country. Presently a little, half-starved, orange-coloured looking Spanish officer, all dressed off in his livery, as fine as a fiddle, came off with two men in a boat to board us. Well, we yawed once or twice, and motioned to him to keep off for fear he should get hurt; but he came right on afore the wheel, and I hope I may be shot if the paddle didn't strike the bow of the boat with that force, it knocked up the starn like a plank tilt, when one of the boys playing on it is heavier than t'other, and chucked him right atop of the wheel-house. You never seed a fellow in such a dunderment in your life. He had picked up a little English from seein' our folks there so much, and when he got up, the first thing he said was, 'Damn all sheenery, I say; where's my boat?' and he looked round as if he thought it had jumped on board too. 'Your boat?' said the captain, 'why I expect it's gone to the bottom, and your men have gone down to look arter it'; for we never seed or heerd tell of one or t'other of them arter the boat was struck. Yes, I'd make 'em stare like that 'ere Spanish officer, as if they had seed out of their eyes for the first time. Governor Campbell didn't expect to see such a country as this when he came here, I reckon; I know he didn't.

"When I was a little boy, about knee high or so, and lived down Connecticut River, mother used to say, 'Sam, if you don't give over acting so like Old Scratch, I'll send you off to Nova Scotia, as sure as you are born; I will, I vow.' Well, Lord, how that 'ere used to frighten me; it made my hair stand right up on eend, like a cat's back when she's wrathy; it made me drop it as quick as wink; like a tin nightcap put on a dipped candle a-goin' to bed, it put the fun right out. Neighbour Dearborne's darter married a gentleman to Yarmouth, that speculates in the smuggling line. Well, when she went on board to sail down to Nova

Scotia, all her folks took on as if it was a funeral; they said she was goin' to be buried alive, like the nuns in Portengale that get a-frolickin', break out of the pastur' and race off, and get catched and brought back ag'in. Says the old Colonel, her father, 'Deliverance, my dear, I would sooner foller you to your grave, for that would be an eend to your troubles, than to see you go off to that dismal country, that's nothin' but an iceberg aground'; and he howled as loud as an Irishman that tries to wake his wife when she is dead. Awful accounts we have of the country, that's a fact; but if the Province is not so bad as they make it out, the folks are a thousand times worse.

"You've seen a flock of partridges of a frosty mornin' in the fall, a crowdin' out of the shade to a sunny spot, and huddlin' up there in the warmth? Well, the Bluenoses have nothin' else to do half the time but sun themselves. Whose fault is that? Why, it's the fault of the legislature. *They don't encourage internal improvement, nor the investment of capital in the country; and the result is apathy, inaction, and poverty.* They spend three months in Halifax, and what do they do? Father gave me a dollar once, to go to the fair at Hartford, and when I came back, says he, 'Sam, what have you got to show for it?' Now I ax what have they to show for their three months' setting? They mislead folks; they make 'em believe all the use of the Assembly is to bark at Councillors, Judges, Bankers, and such cattle, to keep 'em from eatin' up the crops; and it actilly costs more to feed them when they are watchin', than all the others could eat if they did break a fence, and get in. Indeed, some folks say they are the most breachy of the two, and ought to go to pound themselves. If their fences are good, them hungry cattle couldn't break through; and if they ain't, they ought to stake 'em up, and withe them well; *but it's no use to make fences unless the land is cultivated.* If I see a farm all gone to wrack, I say, Here's bad husbandry and bad management; and if I see a Province like this, of great capacity, and great natural resources, poverty-stricken, I say, There's bad legislation.

"No," said he, with an air of more seriousness than I had yet observed; "*how much it is to be regretted, that, laying aside personal attacks and petty jealousies, they would not unite as one man, and with one mind and one heart apply themselves sedulously to the internal improvement and development of this beautiful Province. Its value is utterly unknown, either to the general or local government, and the only persons who duly appreciate it are the Yankees.*"

"I MET a man this mornin'," said the Clockmaker, "from Halifax, a real conceited lookin' critter as you e'enamost ever seed, all shines and didoes. He looked as if he had picked up his airs arter some officer of the regilars had worn 'em out and cast 'em off. They sot on him like second-hand clothes, as if they hadn't been made for him and didn't exactly fit. He looked fine, but awkward, like a captain of militia when he gets his uniform on, to play sodger; a-thinkin' himself mighty hand*sum*, and that all the world is a-lookin' at him. He marched up and down afore the street door like a peacock, as large as life and twice as natural; he had a riding-whip in his hand, and every now and then struck it agin his thigh, as much as to say, 'Ain't that a splendid leg for a boot, now? Won't I astonish the Amherst folks, that's all?' Thinks I, 'You are a pretty blade, ain't you? I'd like to fit a Yankee handle on to you, that's a fact.' When I came up, he held up his head near about as high as a shot factory, and stood with his fists on his hips, and eyed me from head to foot, as a shakin' Quaker does a town lady; as much as to say, What a queer critter you be! that's toggery I never seed afore; you're some carnal minded maiden, that's sartain.

" 'Well,' says he to me, with the air of a man that chucks a cent into a beggar's hat, 'a fine day this, sir.' 'Do you actilly think so?' said I, and I gave it the real Connecticut drawl. 'Why,' said he, quite short, 'if I didn't think so, I wouldn't say so.' 'Well,' says I, 'I don't know, but if I did think so, I guess I wouldn't say so.' 'Why not?' says he. 'Because, I expect,' says I, 'any fool could see that as well as me'; and then I stared at him, as much as to say, 'Now if you like that 'ere swap, I am ready to trade with you ag'in as soon as you like.' Well, he turned right round on his heel and walked off, a-whistlin' Yankee Doodle to himself. He looked jist like a man that finds whistlin' a plaguy sight easier than thinkin'.

"Presently I heerd him ax the groom who that 'ere Yankee lookin' feller was. 'That?' said the groom, 'why, I guess it's Mr. Slick.' 'Sho!' said he, 'how you talk! What! Slick the Clockmaker? Why, it ain't possible; I wish I had a known that 'ere afore, I declare, for I have a great curiosity to see him; folks say he is amazin' clever feller that'; and he turned and stared, as if it was old Hickory himself. Then he walked round and about like a pig round the fence of a potato field, a-watchin' for a chance to cut in; so, thinks I, I'll jist give him something to talk about when he gets back to the city; I'll fix a Yankee handle on him in no time.

" 'How's times to Halifax, sir,' said I. 'Better,' says he, 'much better : business is done on a surer bottom than it was, and things look bright ag'in.' 'So does a candle,' says I, 'jist afore it goes out; it burns up ever so high, and then sinks right down, and leaves nothin' behind but grease, and an everlastin' bad smell. I guess they don't know how to feed their lamp, and it can't burn long on nothin'. No, sir, the jig is up with Halifax, and it's all their own fault. If a man sits at his door and sees stray cattle in his field, a-eatin' up of his crop, and his neighbours a-eatin' off his grain, and won't so much as go and drive 'em out, why, I should say it sarves him right.'

" 'I don't exactly understand, sir,' said he. Thinks I, it would be strange if you did, for I never see one of your folks yet that could understand a hawk from a handsaw. 'Well,' said I, 'I will tell you what I mean : draw a line from Cape Sable to Cape Cansoo, right through the Province, and it will split it into two, this way'; and I cut an apple into two halves; 'now,' says I, 'the worst half, like the rotten half of the apple, belongs to Halifax, and the other sound half belongs to St. John. Your side of the Province on the seacoast is all stone; I never seed such a proper sight of rocks in my life; it's enough to starve a rabbit. Well, t'other side, on the Bay of Fundy, is a superfine country; there ain't the beat of it to be found anywhere. Now, wouldn't the folks living away up to the Bay be pretty fools to go to Halifax, when they can go to St. John with half the trouble? St. John is the natural capital of the Bay of Fundy; it will be the largest city in America, next to New York. It has an immense back country as big as Great Britain, a first chop river, and amazin' sharp folks, most as cute as the Yankees; it's a splendid location for business. Well, they draw all the produce of the Bay shores, and where the produce goes, the supplies return; it will take the whole trade of the Province. I guess your rich folks will find they've burnt their fingers; they've put their foot in it, that's a fact. Houses without tenants, wharves without shipping, a town without people—what a grand investment! If you have any loose dollars, let 'em out on mortgage in Halifax, that's a security; keep clear of the country for your life; the people may run, but the town can't. No, take away the troops, and you're done; you'll sing the dead march folks did at Louisburg and Shelburne. Why you hain't got a single thing worth havin', but a good harbour, and as for that the coast is full of 'em. You haven't a pine log, a spruce board, or a refuse shingle; you neither raise wheat, oats, or hay, nor never can; you have no staples on airth, unless it be them iron ones for the padlocks in Bridewell. You've sowed pride and reaped poverty; take care of your crop, for it's worth harvestin'. You have no river and no country; what in the name of fortin' have you to trade on?'

" 'But,' said he (and he showed the whites of his eyes like a wall-eyed horse), 'but,' said he, 'Mr. Slick, how is it, then, Halifax ever grew at all! Hasn't it got what it always had? It's no worse than it was.' 'I guess,' said I, 'that pole ain't strong enough to bear you, neither; if you trust to that, you'll be into the brook as sure as you are born; you once had the trade of the whole Province, but St. John has run off with that now; you've lost all but your trade in blueberries and rabbits with the niggers at Hammond Plains. *You've lost your customers; your rivals have a better stand for business—they've got the corner store; four great streets meet there, and it's near the market slip.*'

"Well, he stared; says he, 'I believe you're right, but I never thought of that afore.' Thinks I, nobody'd ever suspect you of the trick of thinkin' that ever I heerd tell of. 'Some of our great men,' said he, 'laid it all to your folks' selling so many clocks and Polyglot Bibles; they say you have taken off a horrid sight of money.' 'Did they, indeed?' said I; 'well, I guess it ain't pins and needles that's the expense of housekeepin', it is something more costly than that.' 'Well, some folks say it's the banks,' says he. 'Better still,' says I; 'perhaps you've hearn tell, too, that greasin' the axle makes a gig harder to draw, for there's jist about as much sense in that.' 'Well, then,' says he, 'others say it's smugglin' has made us so poor.' 'That guess,' said I, 'is most as good as t'other one; whoever found out that secret ought to get a patent for it, for it's worth knowin'. Then the country has grown poorer, hasn't it, because it has bought cheaper this year than it did the year before? Why, your folks are cute chaps, I vow; they'd puzzle a Philadelphia lawyer, they are so amazin' knowin'.' 'Ah,' said he, and he rubbed his hands and smiled, like a young doctor when he gets his first patient; 'ah,' said he, 'if the timber duties are altered, down comes St. John, body and breeches; it's built on a poor foundation—it's all show; they are speculatin' like mad; they'll ruin themselves.' Says I, 'If you wait till they're dead for your fortin', it will be one while, I tell you, afore you pocket the shiners. It's no joke waitin' for a dead man's shoes. Suppose an old feller of eighty was to say, "When that 'ere young feller dies, I'm to inherit his property," what would you think? Why, I guess you'd think he was an old fool. *No, sir, if the English don't want their timber, we do want it all; we have used our'n up; we hain't got a stick even to whittle.* If the British don't offer we will, and St. John, like a dear little weeping widow, will dry up her tears and take to frolickin' ag'in, and accept it right off.

" 'There isn't at this moment such a location hardly in America, as St. John; for besides all its other advantages it has this great one: its only rival, Halifax, has got a dose of opium that will send it snoring out of the world, like a feller who falls asleep on the ice of a winter's night. It has been asleep so long, I actilly think it never will wake. It's an easy death, too: you may rouse them up, if you like, but I vow I won't. I once brought a feller to that was drowned, and one night he got drunk and quilted me; I couldn't walk for a week. Says I, "You're the last chap I'll ever save from drowning in all my born days, if that's all the thanks I get for it." No, sir, Halifax has lost the run of its custom. Who does Yarmouth trade with? St. John. Who does Annapolis County trade with? St. John. Who do all the folks on the Basin of Mines, and Bay Shore, trade with? St. John. Who does Cumberland trade with? St. John. Well, Pictou, Lunenburg, and Liverpool supply themselves, and the rest, that ain't worth havin', trade with Halifax. They take down a few half-starved pigs, old viteran geese, and long-legged fowls, some ram mutton and tough beef, and swap them for tea, sugar, and such little notions for their old women to home; while the railroads and canals of St. John are goin' to cut off your Gulf Shore trade to Miramichi, and along there. Flies live in the summer and die in winter: you're jist as noisy in war as those little critters, but you sing small in peace.

" 'No, you're done for; you are up a tree, you may depend; pride must fall. Your town is like a ballroom arter a dance. The folks have eat, drank, and frolicked, and left an empty house, the lamps and hangings are left, but the people are gone.'

" 'Is there no remedy for this?' said he; and he looked as wild as a Cherokee Indian. Thinks I, the handle is fitted on proper tight now. 'Well,' says I, 'when a man has a cold, he had ought to look out pretty sharp, afore it gets seated on his lungs; if he don't, he gets into a gallopin' consumption, and it's a gone goose with him. There is a remedy, if applied in time : *make a railroad to Minas Basin, and you have a way for your customers to get to you, and a conveyance for your goods to them.* When I was in New York last, a cousin of mine, Hezekiah Slick, said to me, "I do believe, Sam, I shall be ruined : I've lost all my custom; they are widening and improving the streets, and there's so many carts and people to work in it, folks can't come to my shop to trade; what on airth shall I do? and I'm payin' a dreadful high rent too." "Stop, Ki," said I, "when the street is all finished off and slicked up, they'll all come back ag'in, and a whole raft more on 'em too; you'll sell twice as much as ever you did; you'll put off a proper swad of goods next year, you may depend"; and so he did, he made money hand over hand. A railroad will bring back your customers, if done right off; but wait till trade has made new channels, and fairly gets settled in them, and you'll never divart it ag'in to all eternity. When a feller waits till a gal gets married, I guess it will be too late to pop the question then.

" 'St. John *must* go ahead, at any rate; you *may*, if you choose, but you must exert yourselves, I tell you. If a man has only one leg, and wants to walk, he must get an artificial one. If you have no river, make a railroad, and that will supply its place.'

" 'But,' says he, 'Mr. Slick, people say it never will pay in the world; they say it's as mad a scheme as the canal.' 'Do they, indeed?' says I; 'send them to me, then, and I'll fit the handle on to them in tu tu's. I say it will pay, and the best proof is, our folks will take tu thirds of the stock. Did you ever hear anyone else but your folks ax whether a dose of medicine would pay when it was given to save life? If that everlastin' long Erie Canal can secure to New York the supply of that far-off country, most t'other side of creation, surely a railroad of forty-five miles can give you the trade of the Bay of Fundy. A railroad will go from Halifax to Windsor, and make them one town, easier to send goods from one to t'other than from Governor Campbell's house to Admiral Cockburn's. A bridge makes a town, a river makes a town, a canal makes a town; but a railroad is bridge, river, thoroughfare, canal, all in one : what a whappin' large place that would make, wouldn't it? It would be the dandy, that's a fact. No, when you go back, take a piece of chalk, and the first dark night, write on every door in Halifax, in large letters—*a railroad*; and if they don't know the meanin' of it, says you, "It's a Yankee word; if you'll go to Sam Click, the Clockmaker" (the chap that fixed a Yankee handle on to a Halifax blade'—and I made him a scrape of my leg, as much as to say That's you!) ' "every man that buys a Clock shall hear all about a Railroad." ' "

"I THINK," said I, "this is a happy country, Mr. Slick. The people are fortunately all of one origin; there are no national jealousies to divide, and no very violent politics to agitate them. They appear to be cheerful and contented, and are a civil, good-natured, hospitable race. Considering the unsettled state of almost every part of the world, I think I would as soon cast my lot in Nova Scotia as in any part I know of."

"It's a clever country, you may depend," said he, "a very clever country; full of mineral wealth, aboundin' in superior water privileges and noble harbours, a large part of it prime land, and it is in the very heart of the fisheries. But the folks put me in mind of a sect in our country they call the Grahamites: they eat no meat, and no exciting food, and drink nothin' stronger than water. They call it Philosophy (and that is such a pretty word it has made fools of more folks than them afore now), but I call it tarnation nonsense. I once travelled all through the State of Maine with one of them 'ere chaps. He was as thin as a whippin' post. His skin looked like a blown bladder arter some of the air had leaked out, kinder wrinkled and rumpled like, and his eye as dim as a lamp that's livin' on a short allowance of ile. He put me in mind of a pair of kitchen tongs, all legs, shaft, and head, and no belly; a real gander-gutted lookin' critter, as holler as a bamboo walkin' cane, and twice as yaller. He actilly looked as if he had been picked off a rack at sea, and dragged through a gimlet-hole. He was a lawyer. Thinks I, the Lord a massy on your clients, you hungry, half-starved lookin' critter you, you'll eat 'em up alive as sure as the Lord made Moses. You are just the chap to strain at a gnat and swallow a camel, tank, shank, and flank, all at a gulp.

"Well, when we came to an inn, and a beefsteak was sot afore us for dinner, he'd say, 'O, that is too good for me, it's too exciting; all fat meat is diseased meat: give me some bread and cheese.' 'Well,' I'd say, 'I don't know what you call too good, but it ain't good enough for me, for I call it as tough as laushong, and that will bear chawing all day. When I liquidate for my dinner, I like to get about the best that's goin', and I ain't a bit too well pleased if I don't.' Exciting, indeed! thinks I. Lord, I should like to see you excited, if it was only for the fun of the thing. What a temptin' lookin' critter you'd be among the gals, wouldn't you? Why, you look like a subject the doctor boys had dropped on the road arter they had dug you up, and had cut stick and run for it.

"Well, when tea came, he said the same thing: 'It's too exciting; give me some water, do; that's follerin' the law of natur'.' 'Well,' says I, 'if that's the case, you ought to eat beef.' 'Why,' says he, 'how do you make out that 'ere proposition?' 'Why,' says I, 'if drinking water, instead of tea, is natur', so is eatin' grass according to natur'; now all flesh is grass, we are told, so you had better eat that and call it vegetable; like a man I once seed, who fasted on fish on a Friday, and when he had done, whipped a leg o' mutton into the oven, and took it out fish. Says he, "It's 'changed *plaice*,' that's all"; and "*plaice*" ain't a bad fish. The Catholics fast enough, gracious knows, but then they fast on a great rousin' big salmon, at two dollars and forty cents a pound, and lots of old Madeira to make it float light on the stomach; there's some sense in mortifying the appetite arter that fashion, but plaguy little in your way. No,' says I, 'friend, you may talk about natur' as you please; I've studied natur' all my life, and I vow if your natur' could speak out, it would tell you it don't over half like to be starved arter that plan. If you knowed as much about the marks of the mouth as I do, you'd know that you have carniverous as well as graniverous teeth, and that natur' meant by that, you should eat most anything that 'ere doorkeeper, your nose, would give a ticket to, to pass into your mouth. Father rode a race at New York course, when he was near hand to seventy—and that's more nor you'll do, I guess—and he eats as hearty as a turkey-cock; and he never confined himself to water neither, when he could get anything convened him better. Says he, "Sam, grandfather Slick used to say there was an old proverb in Yorkshire, 'A full belly makes a strong back,' and I guess if you try it, natur' will tell you so too." If ever you go to Connecticut, jist call into father's, and he'll give you a real right down genuine New England breakfast, and if that don't happify your heart, then my name's not Sam Slick. It will make you feel about among the stiffest, I tell you. It will blow your jacket out like a pig at sea. You'll have to shake a reef or two out of your waistban's and make good stowage, I guess, to carry it all under hatches. There's nothin' like a good pastur' to cover the ribs, and make the hide shine, depend on't.'

"Now this Province is like that 'ere Grahamite lawyer's beef
—it's too good for the folks that's in it; they either don't avail
its value or won't use it, because work ain't arter their 'law of
natur'.' As you say, they are quiet enough (there's worse folks
than the Bluenoses, too, if you come to that), and so they had
ought to be quiet, for they have nothin' to fight about. As for
politics, they have nothin' to desarve the name; but they talk
about it, and a plaguy sight of nonsense they do talk, too.

"Now with us the country is divided into two parties, of the
mammoth breed—the *ins* and the *outs*, the *administration* and
the *opposition*. But where's the administration here? Where's
the War Office, the Foreign Office, and the Home Office? Where's
the Secretary of the Navy? Where's the State Bank? Where's
the Ambassadors and Diplomatists (them are the boys to wind off
a snarl of ravellins as slick as if it were on a reel), and where's
that Ship of State, fitted up all the way from the forecastle clean
up to the starn-post, chock full of good snug berths, handsomely
found and furnished, tier over tier, one above another, as thick
as it can hold? That's a helm worth handlin', I tell you; I don't
wonder that folks mutiny below, and fight on the decks above
for it; it makes a plaguy uproar the whole time, and keeps the
passengers for everlastingly in a state of alarm for fear they'd
do mischief by bustin' the b'iler, a-runnin' aground, or gettin'
foul of some other craft.

"This Province is better as it is, quieter and happier far; they
have berths enough and big enough; they should be careful not
to increase 'em; and if they were to do it over ag'in, perhaps
they'd be as well with fewer. They have two parties here, the
Tory party and the Opposition party, and both on 'em run to
extremes. Them radicals, says one, are for levellin' all down to
their own level, though not a peg lower; that's their gauge, jist
down to their own notch and no further; and they'd agitate the
whole country to obtain that object, for if a man can't grow
to be as tall as his neighbour, if he cuts a few inches off him,
why, then they are both of one heighth. They are a most dangerous, disaffected people; they are eternally appealin' to the
worst passions of the mob. Well, says t'other, them aristocrats,
they'll ruinate the country; they spend the whole revenue on
themselves. What with Bankers, Councillors, Judges, Bishops,
and Public Officers, and a whole tribe of Lawyers, as hungry as
hawks, and jist about as marciful, the country is devoured, as if
there was a flock of locusts a-feedin' on it. There's nothin' left

for roads and bridges. When a chap sets out to canvass, he's got to antagonize one side or t'other. If he hangs on to the powers that be, then he's a Council-man; he's for votin' large salaries, for doin' as the great people at Halifax tell him. He is a fool. If he is on t'other side, a railin' at Banks, Judges, Lawyers, and such cattle, and bawlin' for what he knows he can't get, then he is a rogue. So that, if you were to listen to the weak and noisy critters on both sides, you'd believe the House of Assembly was one half rogues and t'other half fools. All this arises from ignorance. *If they knew more of each other, I guess they'd lay aside one half their fears and all their abuse. The upper classes don't know one half the virtue that's in the middlin' and lower classes; and they don't know one half the integrity and good feelin' that's in the others; and both are fooled and gulled by their own noisy and designin' champions.* Take any two men that are by the ears, they opinionate all they hear of each other, impute all sorts of onworthy motives, and misconstrue every act; let them see more of each other, and they'll find out to their surprise that they had not only been lookin' through a magnifying glass that warn't very true, but a coloured one also, that changed the complexion, and distorted the features; and each one will think t'other a very good kind of chap, and like as not a plaguy pleasant one too.

"If it was axed which side was farthest from the mark in this Province, I vow I should be puzzled to say. As I don't belong to the country, and don't care a snap of my finger for either of 'em, I suppose I can judge better than any man in it; but I snore I don't think there's much difference. The popular side—I won't say patriotic, for we find in our steamboats a man who has a plaguy sight of property in his portmanter is quite as anxious for its safety as him that's only one pair of yarn stockings and a clean shirt, is for his'n—the popular side are not so well informed as t'other, and they have the misfortin' of havin' their passions addressed more than their reason, therefore they are often out of the way, or rather led out of it, and put astray by bad guides; well, t'other side have the prejudices of birth and education to dim their vision, and are alarmed to undertake a thing, from the dread of ambush, or open foes, that their guides are etarnally descrying in the mist; *and besides, power has a natural tendency to corpulency.* As for them guides, I'd make short work of 'em, if it was me.

"In the last war with Britain, the *Constitution* frigate was close in once on the shores of Ireland, a-lookin' arter some marchant ships, and she took on board a pilot; well, he was a deep, sly, twistical lookin' chap, as you e'enamost ever seed. He had a sort of dark, down look about him, and a leer out of the corner of one eye, like a horse that's goin' to kick. The captain guessed he read in his face, 'Well, now, if I was to run this here Yankee right slap on a rock and bilge her, the King would make a man of me for ever.' So says he to the first leftenant, 'Reeve a rope through that 'ere block at the tip eend of the fore yard and clap a runnin' noose in it.' The leftenant did it as quick as wink, and came back, and says he, 'I guess it's done.' 'Now,' says the captain, 'look here, pilot; here's a rope you hain't seed yet; I'll jist explain the use of it to you in case you want the loan of it. If this here frigate, manned with our free and enlightened citizens, gets aground, I'll give you a ride on the slack of that 'ere rope, right up to that yard by the neck, by gum.' Well, it rubbed all the writin' out of his face as quick as spittin' on a slate takes a sum out, you may depend. Now, they should rig up a crane over the street door of the State House at Halifax, and when any of the pilots at either eend of the buildin' run 'em on the breakers on purpose, string 'em up like an onsafe dog. A sign of that 'ere kind, with 'A house of public entertainment' painted under it, would do the business in less than no time. If it wouldn't keep the hawks out of the poultry yard, it's a pity; it would scare them out of a year's growth, that's a fact; if they used it once, I guess they wouldn't have occasion for it ag'in in a hurry; it would be like the aloe tree, that bears fruit only once in a hundred years.

"If you want to know how to act any time, Squire, never go to books, leave them to gals and schoolboys; but go right off and cipher it out of natur', that's a sure guide; it will never deceive you, you may depend. For instance, 'What's that to me?' is a phrase so common that it shows it's a natural one, when people have no particular interest in a thing. Well, when a feller gets so warm on either side as never to use that phrase at all, watch him, that's all! keep your eye on him, or he'll walk right into you afore you know where you be. If a man runs to me and says, 'Your fence is down,' 'Thank you,' says I, 'that's kind.' If he comes ag'in and says, 'I guess some stray cattle have broke into your short sarce garden,' I thank him again; says I, 'Come now, this is neighbourly'; but when he keeps etarnally tellin' me this thing of one sarvant, and that thing of another sarvant, hints that my friend ain't true, that my neighbours are inclined to take advantage of me, and that suspicious folks are seen about my place, I say to myself, What on airth makes this critter take such a wonderful interest in my affairs? I don't like to hear such tales; he's arter somethin' as sure as the world, if he warn't he'd say, 'What's that to me?' I never believe much what I hear said by a man's violent friend, or violent enemy. I want to hear what a disinterested man has to say. *Now, as a disinterested man, I say if the members of the House of Assembly, instead of raisin' up ghosts and hobgoblins to frighten folks with, and to show what swordsmen they be, a-cuttin' and a-thrustin' at phantoms that only exist in their own brains, would turn to, heart and hand, and develop the resources of this fine country, facilitate the means of transport, promote its internal improvement, and encourage its foreign trade, they would make it the richest and greatest, as it now is one of the happiest sections of all America. I hope I may be skinned if they wouldn't—they would, I swan."*

THE descendants of Eve have profited little by her example. The curiosity of the fair sex is still insatiable, and, as it is often ill directed, it frequently terminates in error. In the country this feminine propensity is troublesome to a traveller, and he who would avoid importunities would do well to announce at once, on his arrival at a Cumberland inn, his name and his business, the place of his abode, and the length of his visit.

Our beautiful hostess, Mrs. Pugwash, as she took her seat at the breakfast table this morning, exhibited the example that suggested these reflections. She was struck with horror at our conversation, the latter part only of which she heard, and of course misapplied and misunderstood.

"She was run down by the *President*," said I, "and has been laid up for some time. Gulard's people have stripped her, in consequence of her making water so fast."

"Stripped whom?" said Mrs. Pugwash, as she suddenly dropped the teapot from her hand; "stripped whom—for heaven's sake tell me who it is?"

"The *Lady Ogle*," said I.

"Lady Ogle?" said she, "how horrid!"

"Two of her ribs were so broken as to require to be replaced with new ones."

"Two new ribs!" said she, "well I never heerd the beat of that in all my born days; poor critter, how she must have suffered."

"On examining her below the waist they found——"

"Examining her still lower," said she (all the pride of her sex revolting at the idea of such an indecent exhibition), "you don't pretend to say they stripped her below the waist! What did the Admiral say? Did he stand by and see her handled in that way?"

"The Admiral, madam," said I, "did not trouble his head about it. They found her extremely unsound there, and much worm-eaten."

"Worm-eaten," she continued, "how awful! It must have been them nasty jiggers that got in there; they tell me they are dreadful thick in the West Indies; Joe Crow had them in his feet, and lost two of his toes. Worm-eaten, dear, dear! but still that ain't so bad as having them great he-fellows strip one. I promise you if them Gulards had undertaken to strip me, I'd taught them different guess manners; I'd died first before I'd submitted to it. I always heerd tell the English quality ladies were awful bold, but I never heerd the like o' that."

"What on airth are you drivin' at?" said Mr. Slick. "I never seed you so much out in your latitude afore, marm, I vow. We were talkin' of repairin' a vessel, not strippin' a woman : what under the sun could have put that 'ere crotchet into your head?" She looked mortified and humbled at the result of her own absurd curiosity, and soon quitted the room. "I thought I should have snorted right out two or three times," said the Clockmaker; "I had to pucker up my mouth like the upper eend of a silk puss, to keep from yawhawin' in her face, to hear the critter let her clapper run that fashion. She is not the first hand that has caught a lobster, by puttin' in her oar afore her turn, I guess. She'll mind her stops next hitch, I reckon." This was our last breakfast at Amherst.

An early frost that smote the potato fields, and changed the beautiful green colour of the Indian corn into shades of light yellow and dark brown, reminded me of the presence of autumn, of the season of short days and bad roads. I determined to proceed at once to Parrsboro', and thence by the Windsor and Kentville route to Annapolis, Yarmouth, and Shelburne, and to return by the shore road, through Liverpool and Lunenburg, to Halifax. I therefore took leave (though not without much reluctance) of the Clockmaker, whose intention had been to go to Fort Lawrence.

"Well," said he, "I vow I am sorry to part company along with you; a considerable long journey like our'n, is like sitting up late with the gals : a body knows it's getting on pretty well towards mornin', and yet feels loth to go to bed, for it's just the time folks grow sociable. I got a scheme in my head," said he, "that I think will answer both on us; I got debts due to me in all them 'ere places for clocks sold by the consarn; now suppose you leave your horse on these marshes this fall; he'll get as fat as a fool, he won't be able to see out of his eyes in a month; and I'll put 'Old Clay' (I call him Clay arter our senator, who is a prime bit of stuff) into a Yankee wagon I have here, and drive you all round the coast."

This was too good an offer to be declined. A run at grass for my horse, an easy and comfortable wagon, and a guide so original and amusing as Mr. Slick, were either of them enough to induce my acquiescence.

As soon as we had taken our seats in the wagon, he observed—

"We shall progress real handsum now; that 'ere horse goes etarnal fast; he near about set my axle on fire twice. He's a spanker, you may depend. I had him when he was a two-year-old, all legs and tail, like a devil's darnin' needle, and had him broke on purpose by father's old nigger, January Snow. He knows English real well, and can do near about anything but speak it. He helped me once to gin a Bluenose a proper handsum quiltin'."

"He must have stood a poor chance indeed," said I, "a horse kicking, and a man striking him at the same time."

"O! not arter that pattern at all," said he; "Lord, if Old Clay had kicked him, he'd a smashed him like that 'ere saucer you broke at Pugnose's inn, into ten hundred thousand million flinders. O! no, if I didn't fix his flint for him in fair play, it's a pity. I'll tell you how it was. I was up to Truro, at Ezra Whitter's inn. There was an arbitration there atween Deacon Text and Deacon Faithful. Well, there was a 'nation sight of folks there, for they said it was a biter bit, and they came to witness the sport, and to see which critter would get the earmark.

"Well, I'd been doin' a little business there among the folks, and had jist sot off for the river, mounted on Old Clay, arter takin' a glass of Ezra's most particular handsum Jamaiky, and was trottin' off pretty slick, when who should I run agin but Tim Bradley. He is a dreadful ugly, cross-grained critter, as you e'enamost ever seed, when he is about half-shaved. Well, I stopped short, and says I, 'Mr. Bradley, I hope you bean't hurt; I'm proper sorry I run agin you; you can't feel uglier than I do about it, I do assure you.' He called me a Yankee peddler, a cheatin' vagabond, a wooden nutmeg, and threw a good deal of assorted hardware of that kind at me; and the crowd of folks cried out, 'Down with the Yankee!' 'Let him have it, Tim!' 'Teach him better manners!' and they carried on pretty high, I tell you. Well, I got my dander up too, I felt all up on eend like· and thinks I to myself, My lad, if I get a clever chance, I'll give you such a quiltin' as you never had since you were raised from a seedlin', I vow. So says I, 'Mr. Bradley, I guess you had better let me be; you know I can't fight no more than a cow; I never was brought up to wranglin', I don't like it.' 'Haul off the cowardly rascal!' they all bawled out, 'haul him off and lay it into him!' So he lays right hold of me by the collar, and gives

me a pull, and I lets on as if I'd lost my balance, and falls right
down. Then I jumps up on eend, and says I, 'Go ahead, Clay,'
and the old horse he sets off ahead, so I knew I had him when I
wanted him. 'Then,' says I, 'I hope you are satisfied now, Mr.
Bradley, with that 'ere ungenteel fall you gin me.' Well, he
makes a blow at me, and I dodged it. 'Now,' says I, 'you'll be
sorry for this, I tell you; I won't be treated this way for nothin',
I'll go right off and swear my life agin you; I'm most afeerd
you'll murder me.' Well, he strikes at me ag'in, thinkin' he had
a genuine soft horn to deal with, and hits me in the shoulder.
'Now,' says I, 'I won't stand here to be lathered like a dog all
day long this fashion, it ain't pretty at all; I guess I'll give you a
chase for it.' Off I sets arter my horse like mad, and he arter me
(I did that to get clear of the crowd, so that I might have fair
play at him). Well, I soon found I had the heels of him, and
could play him as I liked. Then I slackened up a little, and when
he came close up to me, so as nearly to lay his hand upon me, I
squatted right whap down, all short, and he pitched over me
near about a rod or so, I guess, on his head, and ploughed up the
ground with his nose the matter of a foot or two. If he didn't
polish up the coulter, and both mouldboards of his face, it's a
pity. 'Now,' says I, 'you had better lay where you be and let me
go, for I am proper tired; I blow like a horse that's got the
heaves; and besides,' says I, 'I guess you had better wash your
face, for I am most afeared you hurt yourself.' That riled him
properly; I meant that it should; so he ups and at me awful spite-
ful, like a bull; then I lets him have it, right, left, right, jist three
corkers, beginning with the right hand, shifting to the left, and
then with the right hand ag'in. This way I did it,'' said the Clockmaker (and he showed me the manner in which it was done);
"it's a beautiful way of hitting, and always does the business—
a blow for each eye, and one for the mouth. It sounds like ten
pounds ten on a blacksmith's anvil; I bunged up both eyes for
him, and put in the dead lights in tu tu's, and drew three of his
teeth, quicker a plaguy sight than the Truro doctor could, to
save his soul alive. 'Now,' says I, 'my friend, when you recover
your eyesight I guess you'll see your mistake; I warn't born in
the woods to be scared by an owl. The next time you feel in a
most particular elegant good humour, come to me, and I'll play
you the second part of that identical same tune, that's a fact.'

"With that I whistled for Old Clay, and back he comes, and
I mounted and off, jist as the crowd came up. The folks looked
staggered, and wondered a little grain how it was done so

cleverly in short metre. If I didn't quilt him in no time, you may depend; I went right slap into him, like a flash of lightning into a gooseberry bush. He found his suit ready made and fitted afore he thought he was half measured. Thinks I, Friend Bradley, I hope you know yourself now, for I vow no livin' soul would; you swallowed your soup without singin' out scaldins, and you're near about a pint and a half nearer cryin' than larfin'.

"Yes, as I was sayin', this Old Clay is a real knowin' one; he's as spry as a colt yet, clear grit, ginger to the backbone; I can't help a-thinkin' sometimes the breed must have come from old Kentuck, half horse, half alligator, with a cross of the airthquake.

"I hope I may be teetotally ruinated, if I'd take eight hundred dollars for him. Go ahead, you old clinker-built villain," says he, "and show the gentleman how wonderful hand*sum* you can travel. Give him the real Connecticut quickstep. That's it! that's the way to carry the President's message to Congress from Washington to New York in no time! that's the go to carry a gal from Boston to Rhode Island, and trice her up to a Justice to be married, afore her father's out of bed of a summer's mornin'. Ain't he a beauty? a real doll? none of your Cumberland critters, that the more you quilt them, the more they won't go; but a proper one, that will go free gratis for nothin', all out of his own head volun*terrily*. Yes, a horse like Old Clay is worth the whole seed, breed, and generation of the Amherst beasts put together. He's a horse every inch of him, stock, lock, and barrel, is Old Clay."

"THERE goes one of them 'ere everlastin' rottin' poles in that bridge; they are no better than a trap for a critter's leg," said the Clockmaker. "They remind me of a trap Jim Munroe put his foot in one night, that near about made one leg half a yard longer than t'other. I believe I told you of him, what a desperate idle feller he was; he came from Onion County in Connecticut. Well, he was courtin' Sister Sall. She was a real handsum-looking gal; you scarce ever seed a more out-and-out complete critter than she was; a fine figur' head, and a beautiful model of a craft as any in the State, a real clipper, and as full of fun and frolic as a kitten. Well, he fairly turned Sall's head; the more we wanted her to give him up, the more she wouldn't, and we got plaguy oneasy about it, for his character was none of the best. He was a universal favourite with the gals, though he didn't behave very pretty neither, forgetting to marry where he promised, and where he hadn't ought to have forgot, too; yet so it was, he had such an uncommon winnin' way with him, he could talk them over in no time. Sall was fairly bewitched.

"At last, father said to him one evening when he came a-courtin', 'Jim,' says he, 'you'll never come to no good, if you act like Old Scratch as you do; you ain't fit to come into no decent man's house at all, and your absence would be ten times more agreeable than your company, I tell you. I won't consent to Sall's goin' to them 'ere huskin' parties and quiltin' frolics along with you no more, on no account, for you know how Polly Brown and Nancy White——' 'Now don't,' says he, 'now don't, Uncle Sam, say no more about that; if you know'd all, you wouldn't say it was my fault; and besides, I have turned right about; I am on t'other tack now, and the long leg, too; I am as steady as a pump bolt, now. I intend to settle myself and take a farm.' 'Yes, yes; and you could stock it, too, by all accounts, pretty well, unless you are much misreported,' says father, 'but it won't do. I knew your father, he was our sargeant; a proper clever and brave man he was, too; he was one of the heroes of our glorious Revolution. I had a great respect for him, and I am sorry, for his sake, you will act as you do; but I tell you once for all you must give up all thoughts of Sall, now and for ever-lastin'.' When Sall heerd this, she began to knit away like mad, in a desperate hurry; she looked foolish enough, that's a fact. First she tried to bite in her breath, and look as if there was nothin' particular in the wind; then she blushed all over like scarlet fever, but she recovered that pretty soon; and then her colour went and came, and came and went, till at last she grew as white as chalk, and down she fell slap off her seat on the floor, in a faintin' fit. 'I see,' says father, 'I see it now, you etarnal villain,' and he made a pull at the old-fashioned sword, that always hung over the fireplace (we used to call it Old Bunker, for his stories always begun, 'When I was at Bunker's Hill'), and drawing it out he made a clip at him as wicked as if he was stabbing a rat with a hayfork; but Jim, he outs of the door like a shot, and draws it to arter him, and father sends Old Bunker right through the panel. 'I'll chop you up as fine as mince-meat, you villain,' said he, 'if ever I catch you inside my door ag'in; mind what I tell you, *you'll swing for it yet*.' Well, he made himself considerable scarce arter that; he never sot foot inside the door ag'in, and I thought he had gin up all hopes of Sall, and she of him; when one night, a most particular uncommon dark night, as I was a-comin' home from neighbour Dearborne's, I heerd someone a-talkin' under Sall's window. Well, I stops and listens, and who should be near the ash saplin' but Jim Munroe, a-tryin' to persuade Sall to run off with him to Rhode Island to be mar-ried. It was all settled he should come with a horse and shay to the gate, and then help her out of the window, jist at nine o'clock, about the time she commonly went to bed. Then he axes her to reach down her hand for him to kiss (for he was proper clever at soft sawder), and she stretched it down, and he kisses it; and says he, 'I believe I must have the whole of you out arter all,' and gives her a jerk that kinder startled her; it came so sudden like it made her scream; so off he sot, hot foot, and over the gate in no time.

"Well, I ciphered over this all night, a-calculatin' how I should reciprocate that trick with him, and at last I hit on a scheme. I recollected father's words at partin', '*Mind what I tell you, you'll swing for it yet*'; and thinks I, Friend Jim, I'll make that prophecy come true yet, I guess. So the next night, jist at dark, I gives January Snow, the old nigger, a nidge with my elbow, and as soon as he looks up, I winks and walks out, and he arter me. Says I, 'January, can you keep your tongue within your teeth, you old nigger, you?' 'Why massa, why you ax that 'ere question? My Gor A'mity, you tink old Snow he don't know that 'ere yet? My tongue he got plenty room now, debil a tooth left; he can stretch out ever so far; like a little leg in a big bed, he lay quiet enough, massa, neber fear.' 'Well, then,' says I, 'bend down that 'ere ash sapling softly, you old Snowball, and make no noise.' The saplin' was no sooner bent than secured to the ground by a notched peg and a noose, and a slip-knot was suspended from the tree, jist over the track that led from the pathway to the house. 'Why my Gor, massa, that's a——' 'Hold your mug, you old nigger,' says I, 'or I'll send your tongue a-sarchin' arter your teeth; keep quiet, and follow me in presently.'

"Well, jist as it struck nine o'clock, says I, 'Sally, hold this here hank of twine for a minute, till I wind a trifle on it off; that's a dear critter.' She sot down her candle, and I put the twine on her hands, and then I begins to wind and wind away ever so slow, and drops the ball every now and then, so as to keep her downstairs. 'Sam,' says she, 'I do believe you won't wind that 'ere twine off all night; do give it to January; I won't stay no longer; I'm e'enamost dead asleep.' 'The old feller's arm is so plaguy onsteady,' says I, 'it won't do; but hark! what's that? I'm sure I heerd something in the ash saplin', didn't you, Sall?' 'I heerd the geese there, that's all,' says she; 'they always come under the windows at night'; but she looked scared enough, and says she, 'I vow, I'm tired holdin' out of my arms this way, and I won't do it no longer'; and down she throwed the hank on the floor. 'Well,' says I, 'stop one minute, dear, till I send old January out to see if anybody is there; perhaps some o' neighbour Dearborne's cattle have broke into the sarce garden. January went out, though Sall said it was no use, for she knew the noise of the geese; they always kept close to the house at night, for fear of the varmin. Presently in runs old Snow, with his hair standin' up on eend, and the whites of his eyes lookin' as big as the rims of a soup-plate. 'O! Gor A'mity,' said he, 'O massa, O Miss Sally, O!' 'What on airth is the matter with you?' said Sally; 'how you do frighten me; I vow, I believe you're mad.' 'O my Gor,' said he, 'O! massa, Jim Munroe he hang himself on the ash saplin' under Miss Sally's window—O my Gor!' That shot was a settler, it struck poor Sall right atwixt wind and water; she gave a lurch ahead, then heeled over, and sunk right down in another faintin' fit; and Juno, old Snow's wife, carried her off and laid her down on the bed. Poor thing, she felt ugly enough, I do suppose.

"Well, father, I thought he'd a-fainted too; he was so struck up all of a heap, he was completely bung fungered. 'Dear, dear!' said he, 'I didn't think it would come to pass so soon, but I knew it would come; I foretold it; says I, the last time I seed him "Jim," says I, "mind what I say, *you'll swing for it yet*." Give me the sword I wore when I was at Bunker's Hill—maybe there is life yet—I'll cut him down.' The lantern was soon made ready, and out we went to the ash saplin'. 'Cut me down, Sam! that's a good fellow,' said Jim; 'all the blood in my body has swashed into my head, and's a-runnin' out o' my nose; I'm e'enamost smothered; be quick, for Heaven's sake.' 'The Lord be praised,' said father, 'the poor sinner is not quite dead yet. Why, as I'm alive—well if that don't beat all natur'! Why he has hanged himself by one leg, and's a-swingin' like a rabbit, upside down, that's a fact. Why, if he ain't snared, Sam; he is properly wired I declare; I vow this is some o' your doin's, Sam. Well, it was a clever scheme too, but a little grain too dangerous, I guess. 'Don't stand starin' and jawin' there all night,' said Jim, 'cut me down, I tell you—or cut my throat, and be damned to you, for I am chokin' with blood.' 'Roll over that 'ere hogshead, old Snow,' said I, 'till I get atop on it and cut him down.' So I soon released him, but he couldn't walk a bit. His ankle was swelled and sprained like vengeance, and he swore one leg was near about six inches longer than t'other. 'Jim Munroe,' says father, 'little did I think I should ever see you inside my door ag'in, but I bid you enter now; we owe you that kindness, anyhow.'

"Well, to make a long story short, Jim was so chop-fallen, and so down in the mouth, he begged for Heaven's sake it might be kept a secret; he said he would run the State if ever it got wind, he was sure he couldn't stand it. 'It will be one while, I guess,' said father, 'afore you are able to run or stand either; but if you will give me your hand, Jim, and promise to give over your evil ways, I will not only keep it secret, but you shall be a welcome guest at old Sam Slick's once more, for the sake of your father. He was a brave man, one of the heroes of Bunker's Hill; he was our sergeant and——' 'He promises,' says I, 'father' (for the old man had stuck his right foot out, the way he always stood when he told about the old war; and as Jim couldn't stir a peg, it was a grand chance, and he was a-goin' to give him the whole Revolution from General Gage up to Independence), 'he promises,' says I, 'father.' Well, it was all settled, and things soon grew as calm as a pan of milk two days old; and afore a year was over, Jim was as steady a-goin' man as Minister Joshua Hopewell, and was married to our Sall. Nothin' was ever said about the snare till arter the weddin'. When the minister had finished axin' a blessin', father goes up to Jim, and says he, 'Jim Munroe, my boy,' givin' him a rousin' slap on the shoulder that sot him a-coughin' for the matter of five minutes (for he was a mortal powerful man, was father), 'Jim Munroe, my boy,' says he, 'you've got the snare round your neck, I guess now, instead of your leg; the saplin' has been a father to you; you may be the father of many saplin's.'

"We had a most special time of it, you may depend, all except the minister; father got him into a corner, and gave him chapter and verse for the whole war. Every now and then as I come near them, I heard Bunker's Hill, Brandywine, Clinton, Gates, and so on. It was broad day when we parted, and the last that went was poor minister. Father followed him clean down to the gate, and says he, 'Minister, we hadn't time this hitch, or I'd a told you all about the *Evakyation* of New York, but I'll tell you that the next time we meet.' "

"I NEVER see one of them queer little old-fashioned teapots, like that 'ere in the cupboard of Marm Pugwash," said the Clock-maker, "that I don't think of Lawyer Crowningshield and his wife. When I was down to Rhode Island last, I spent an evening with them. After I had been there awhile, the black house-help brought in a little home-made dipped candle, stuck in a turnip sliced in two, to make it stand straight, and sot it down on the table. 'Why,' says the Lawyer to his wife, 'Increase, my dear, what on earth is the meanin' o' that? What does little Viney mean by bringin' in such a light as this, that ain't fit for even a log hut of one of our free and enlightened citizens away down East; where's the lamp?' 'My dear,' says she, 'I ordered it—you know they are a-goin' to set you up for Governor next year, and I allot we must economize or we will be ruined; the salary is only four hundred dollars a year, you know, and you'll have to give up your practice; we can't afford nothin' now.'

"Well, when tea was brought in, there was a little wee china teapot, that held about the matter of half a pint or so, and cups and sarcers about the bigness of children's toys. When he seed that, he grew most peskily riled, his under lip curled down like a peach leaf that's got a worm in it, and he stripped his teeth and showed his grinders, like a bull-dog. 'What foolery is this?' said he. 'My dear,' said she, 'it's the foolery of being Governor; if you choose to sacrifice all your comfort to being the first rung in the ladder, don't blame me for it. I didn't nominate you; I had no art nor part in it. It was cooked up at that 'ere Convention, at Town Hall.' Well, he sot for some time without sayin' a word, lookin' as black as a thunder-cloud, just ready to make all natur' crack ag'in. At last he gets up, and walks round behind his wife's chair, and takin' her face between his two hands, he turns it up and give her a buss that went off like a pistol; it fairly made my mouth water to see him; thinks I, Them lips ain't a bad bank to deposit one's spare kisses in, neither. 'Increase, my dear,' said he, 'I believe you are half right; I'll decline tomorrow I'll have nothin' to do with it. *I won't be a Governor, on no account.'*

"Well, she had to haw and gee like, both a little, afore she could get her head out of his hands; and then she said, 'Zachariah,' says she, 'how you do act! Ain't you ashamed? Do for gracious' sake behave yourself!' and she coloured up all over like a crimson piany; 'if you haven't foozled all my hair too, that's a fact,' says she; and she put her curls to rights, and looked as pleased as fun, though poutin' all the time, and walked right out of the room. Presently in come two well-dressed house-helps, one with a splendid gilt lamp, a real London touch, and another with a tea tray, with a large solid silver coffee-pot, and teapot, and a cream jug, and sugar bowl, of the same genuine metal, and a most elegant set of real gilt china. Then in came Marm Crowningshield herself, lookin' as proud as if she would not call the President her cousin; and she gave the Lawyer a look, as much as to say, I guess when Mr. Slick is gone, I'll pay you off that 'ere kiss with interest, you dear, you; I'll answer a bill at sight for it, I will, you may depend. 'I believe,' said he ag'in, 'you are right, Increase, my dear, it's an expensive kind of honour that, bein' Governor, and no great thanks neither; great cry and little wool; all talk and no cider. It's enough, I guess, for a man to govern his own family, ain't it, dear?' 'Sartin, my love,' said she, 'sartin, a man is never so much in his own proper sphere as there; and besides,' said she, 'his will is supreme to home; there is no danger of any one non-concurring him there'; and she gave me a sly look, as much as to say, I let him think he is master in his own house, for when ladies wear the breeches, their petticoats ought to be long enough to hide them; but I allot, Mr. Slick, you can see with half an eye that the 'grey mare is the better horse' here.

"What a pity it is," continued the Clockmaker, "that the Bluenoses would not take a leaf out of Marm Crowningshield's book—talk more of their own affairs and less of politics. I'm sick of everlastin' sound of 'House of Assembly,' and 'Council,' and 'great folks.' They never alleviate talking about them from July to eternity.

"I had a curious conversation about politics once, away up to the right here. Do you see that 'ere house," said he, "in the field, that's got a lurch to leeward, like a North River sloop struck with a squall off West Point, lopsided like? It looks like Seth Pine, a tailor down to Hartford, that had one leg shorter than t'other, when he stood at ease at militia trainin', a-restin' on the littlest one. Well, I had a special frolic there the last time I passed this way. I lost the linch-pin out of my forrard axle, and I turned up there to get it sot to rights. Just as I drove through the gate, I saw the eldest gal a-makin' for the house for dear life. She had a short petticoat on that looked like a kilt, and her bare legs put me in mind of the long shanks of a bittern down in a rush swamp, a-drivin' away like mad full chisel arter a frog. I could not think what on airth was the matter. Thinks I, She wants to make herself look decent like afore I get in; she don't like to pull her stockings on afore me. So I pulls up the old horse and let her have a fair start. Well, when I came to the door, I heard a proper scuddin'; there was a regular flight into Egypt, jist such a noise as little children make when the mistress comes suddenly into school, all a-huddlin' and scroudgin' into their seats, as quick as wink. 'Dear me!' says the old woman, as she put her head out of a broken window to avail who it was, 'is it you, Mr. Slick? I sniggers, if you didn't frighten us properly; we actilly thought it was the sheriff; do come in.'

"Poor thing, she looked half starved and half savage; hunger and temper had made proper strong lines in her face, like water furrows in a ploughed field; she looked bony and thin, like a horse that has had more work than oats, and had a wicked expression, as though it warn't over safe to come too near her heels—an everlastin' kicker. 'You may come out, John,' said she to her husband, 'it's only Mr. Slick'; and out came John from under the bed backwards, on all fours, like an ox out of the shoein' frame, or a lobster skullin' wrong eend foremost; he looked as wild as a hawk. Well, I swan, I thought I should have split—I could hardly keep from bursting right out with larfter; he was all covered with feathers, lint, and dust, the savin's of all the sweepin's since the house was built, shoved under there for tidiness. He actilly sneezed for the matter of ten minutes; he seemed half choked with the flaff and stuff, that came out with him like a cloud. Lord, he looked like a goose half picked, as if all the quills were gone, but the pin-feathers and down were left, jist ready for singein' and stuffin'. He put me in mind of a sick Adjutant, a great tall hulkin' bird, that comes from the East Indgies, a'most as high as a man, and most as knowin' as a Blue-nose. I'd a gin a hundred dollars to have had that chap as a show at a fair; tar and feathers warn't half as nateral. You've seen a gal both larf and cry at the same time, hain't you? Well, I hope I may be shot if I couldn't have done the same. To see that critter come like a turkey out of a bag at Christmas, to be fired at for ten cents a shot, was as good as a play; but to look round and see the poverty—the half-naked children, the old pine stumps for chairs; a small bin of poor, watery, yaller potatoes in the corner; daylight through the sides and roof of the house, looking like the tarred seams of a ship, all black where the smoke got out; no utensils for cookin' or eatin', and starvation wrote as plain as a handbill on their holler cheeks, skinny fingers, and sunk eyes—went right straight to the heart. I do declare I believe I should have cried, only they didn't seem to mind it themselves. They had been used to it; like a man that's married to a thunderin' ugly wife, he gets so accustomed to the look of her everlastin' dismal mug, that he don't think her ugly at all.

"Well, there was another chap a-settin' by the fire, and he *did* look as if he saw it, and felt it too; he didn't seem over half pleased, you may depend. He was the district schoolmaster, and he told me he was takin' a spell at boardin' there, for it was their turn to keep him. Thinks I to myself, Poor devil, you've brought your pigs to a pretty market, that's a fact. I see how it is, the Bluenoses can't cipher. The cat's out of the bag now; it's no wonder they don't go ahead, for they don't know nothin'; the 'schoolmaster is abroad,' with the devil to it, for he has no home at all. Why Squire, you might jist as well expect a horse to go right off in gear, before he is halter broke, as a Bluenose to get on in the world, when he has got no schoolin'.

"But to get back to my story. 'Well,' says I, 'how's times with you, Mrs. Spry?' 'Dull,' says she, 'very dull; there's no markets now, things don't fetch nothin'.' Thinks I, Some folks hadn't ought to complain of markets, for they don't raise nothin' to sell, but I didn't say so; *for poverty is keen enough, without sharpening its edge by pokin' fun at it.* 'Potatoes,' says I, 'will fetch a good price this fall, for it's a short crop, in a general way; how's your'n?' 'Grand,' says she, 'as complete as ever you seed; our tops were small and didn't look well; but we have the handsomest bottoms, it's generally allowed, in all our place; you never seed the beat of them; they are actilly worth lookin' at.' I vow I had to take a chaw of tobaccy to keep from snorting right out, it sounded so queer like. Thinks I to myself, Old lady, it's a pity you couldn't be changed eend for eend then, as some folks do their stockings: it would improve the look of your dial-plate amazin'ly then, that's a fact.

"Now there was human natur', Squire," said the Clockmaker, "there was pride even in that hovel. It is found in rags as well as kings' robes—where butter is spread with the thumb as well as the silver knife; *natur' is natur' wherever you find it.*

"Jist then, in came one or two neighbours to see the sport, for they took me for a sheriff, or constable, or something of that breed, and when they saw it was me they sot down to hear the news; they fell right to at politics as keen as anything, as if it had been a dish of real Connecticut slapjacks, or hominy; or what is better still, a glass of real genuine splendid mint julep; whe-eu-up, it fairly makes my mouth water to think of it. 'I wonder,' says one, 'what they will do for us this winter in the House of Assembly?' 'Nothin',' says the other, 'they never do nothin' but what the great people at Halifax tell 'em. Squire Yeoman is the man; he'll pay up the great folks this hitch; he'll let 'em have their own; he's jist the boy that can do it.' Says I, 'I wish I could say all men were as honest then, for I am afeard there are a great many won't pay me up this winter; I should like to trade with your friend; who is he?' 'Why,' says he, 'he is the member for Isle Sable County, and if he don't let the great folks have it, it's a pity.' 'Who do you call great folks? for,' said I, 'I vow I haven't seed one since I came here. The only one that I know that comes near hand to one is Nicholas Overknocker, that lives all along shore, about Margaret's Bay, and he is a great man—it takes a yoke of oxen to drag him. When I first seed him, says I, "What on airth is the matter o' that man? Has he the dropsy? For he is actilly the greatest man I ever seed; he must weigh the matter of five hundredweight; he'd cut three inches on the rib; he must have a proper sight of lard, that chap." No,' says I, 'don't call 'em great men, for there ain't a great man in the country, that's a fact; there ain't one that desarves the name; folks will only larf at you if you talk that way. There may be some rich men, and I believe there be, and it's a pity there warn't more on 'em, and a still greater pity they have so little spirit or enterprise among 'em; but a country is none the worse having rich men in it, you may depend. Great folks! Well, come, that's a good joke, that bangs the bush. No, my friend,' says I, '*the meat that's at the top of the barrel, is sometimes not so good as that that's a little grain lower down: the upper and lower eends are plaguy apt to have a little taint in em, but the middle is always good.*'

" 'Well,' says the Bluenose, 'perhaps they bean't great men, exactly in that sense, but they are great men compared to us poor folks; and they eat up all the revenue; there's nothin' left for roads and bridges; they want to ruin the country, that's a

fact.' 'Want to ruin your granny,' says I (for it raised my dander
to hear the critter talk such nonsense); 'I did hear of one chap,'
says I, 'that sot fire to his own house once, up to Squantum, but
the cunnin' rascal insured it first; now how can your great folks
ruin the country without ruinin' themselves, unless they have
insured the Province? Our folks will insure all creation for half
nothin', but I never heerd tell of a country being insured agin
rich men. Now if you ever go to Wall Street to get such a policy,
leave the door open behind you, that's all; or they'll grab right
hold of you, shave your head and blister it, clap a strait-jacket
on you, and whip you right into a madhouse, afore you can say
Jack Robinson. No, your great men are nothin' but rich men,
and I can tell you for your comfort, there's nothin' to hinder
you from bein' rich too, if you will take the same means as they
did. They were once all as poor folks as you be, or their fathers
afore them; for I know their whole breed, seed, and generation,
and they wouldn't thank you to tell them that you knew their
fathers and grandfathers, I tell you. If ever you want the loan of
a hundred pounds from any of them, keep dark about that; see
as far ahead as you please, but it ain't always pleasant to have
folks see too far back. Perhaps they be a little proud or so, but
that's nateral; all folks that grow up right off, like a mushroom
in one night, are apt to think no small beer of themselves. A
cabbage has plaguy large leaves to the bottom, and spreads them
out as wide as an old woman's petticoats, to hide the ground it
sprung from, and conceal its extraction, but what's that to you?
If they get too large salaries, dock 'em down at once, but don't
keep talkin' about it for everlastinly. If you have too many
sarvants, pay some on 'em off, or when they quit your sarvice
don't hire others in their room, that's all; but you miss your mark
when you keep firin' away the whole blessed time that way.

"'I went out a-gunnin' when I was a boy, and father went
with me to teach me. Well, the first flock of plover I seed I let
slip at 'em, and missed 'em. Says father, says he, "What a block-
head you be, Sam! that's your own fault; they were too far off;
you hadn't ought to have fired so soon. At Bunker's Hill we let
the British come right on till we seed the whites of their eyes,
and then we let them have it slap bang." Well, I felt kinder
grigged at missin' my shot, and I didn't over half like to be
scolded too; so says I, "Yes, father; but recollect you had a mud
bank to hide behind, where you were proper safe, and you had
a rest for your guns too; but as soon as you seed a little more
than the whites of their eyes, you run for your dear life, full

split; and so I don't see much to brag on in that arter all, so come now." "I'll teach you to talk that way, you puppy you," said he, "of that glorious day"; and he fetched me a wipe that I do believe, if I hadn't a dodged, would have spoiled my gunnin' for that hitch; so I gave him a wide berth arter that all day. Well, the next time I missed, says I, "She hung fire so ever-lastinly, it's no wonder"; and the next miss, says I, "The powder is no good, I vow." Well, I missed every shot, and I had an excuse for every one on 'em: the flint was bad, or she flashed in the pan, or the shot scaled, or something or another; and when all wouldn't do, I swore the gun was no good at all. "Now," says father (and he edged up all the time, to pay me off for that hit at his Bunker's Hill story, which was the only shot I didn't miss), "you hain't got the right reason arter all. It was your own fault, Sam."

" 'Now that's jist the case with you; you may blame Banks, and Council, and House of Assembly, and "the great men," till you are tired, but it's all your own fault; *you've no spirit and no enterprise; you want industry and economy; use them, and you'll soon be as rich as the people at Halifax you call great folks.* They didn't grow rich by talkin', but by workin'; instead of lookin' arter other folks' business, they looked about the keenest arter their own. You are like the machinery of one of our boats—good enough, and strong enough, but of no airthly use till you get the steam up; you want to be set in motion, and then you'll go ahead like anything, you may depend. *Give up politics. It's a barren field, and well watched too; where one critter jumps a fence into a good field and gets fat, more nor twenty are chased round and round, by a whole pack of yelpin' curs, till they are fairly beat out, and eend by bein' half starved, and are at the liftin' at last. Look to your farms, your water powers, your fisheries, and factories. In short,'* says I, puttin' on my hat and startin', *'look to yourselves, and don't look to others.'* "

"IT'S a most curious, unaccountable thing, but it's a fact," said the Clockmaker, "the Bluenoses are so conceited, they think they know everything; and yet there ain't a livin' soul in Nova Scotia knows his own business real complete, farmer or fisherman, lawyer or doctor, or any other folk. A farmer said to me one day, up to Pugnose's inn, at River Philip, 'Mr. Slick,' says he, 'I allot this ain't *"a bread country"*; I intend to sell off the house I improve, and go to the States.' 'If it ain't a bread country,' said I, 'I never seed one that was. There is more bread used here, made of best superfine flour, and No. 1 Genesee, than in any other place of the same population in the univarse. You might as well say it ain't a clock country, when to my sartin knowledge, there are more clocks than Bibles in it. I guess you expect to raise your bread ready made, don't you? Well, there's only one class of our free and enlightened citizens that can do that, and that's them that are born with silver spoons in their mouths. It's a pity you wasn't availed of this truth, afore you up killoch and off; take my advice and bide where you be.'

"Well, the fishermen are jist as bad. The next time you go into the fish-market at Halifax, stump some of the old hands; says you, 'How many fins has a cod, at a word?' and I'll liquidate the bet if you lose it. When I've been along-shore afore now, a-vendin' of my clocks, and they began to raise my dander, by belittling the Yankees, I always brought them up by a round turn by that requirement, 'How many fins has a cod, at a word?' Well, they never could answer it; and then, says I, 'When you larn your own business, I guess it will be time enough to teach other folks their'n.'

"How different it is with our men folk. If they can't get through a question, how beautifully they can go round it, can't they? Nothin' never stops them; I had two brothers, Josiah and Eldad, one was a lawyer, and the other a doctor. They were a-talkin' about their examinations one night, at a huskin' frolic, up to Governor Ball's big stone barn at Slickville. Says Josy, 'When I was examined, the Judge axed me all about real estate;

and, says he, "Josiah," says he, "what's a fee?" "Why," says I, "Judge, it depends on the natur' of the case. In a common one," says I, "I call six dollars a pretty fair one; but lawyer Webster has got afore now, I've heerd tell, one thousand dollars, and that *I do call* a fee." Well, the Judge he larfed ready to split his sides (thinks I, Old chap, you'll bust like a steam b'iler, if you hain't got a safety valve somewhere or another), and says he, "I vow, that's superfine; I'll indorse your certificate for you, young man; there's no fear of you; you'll pass the inspection brand anyhow."

" 'Well,' says Eldad, 'I hope I may be skinned if the same thing didn't e'enamost happen to me at my examination. They axed me a 'nation sight of questions. Some on 'em I could answer, and some on 'em no soul could, right off the reel at a word, without a little cipherin'; at last they axed me, "How would you calculate to put a patient into a sweat when common modes wouldn't work nohow?" "Why," says I, "I'd do as Dr. Comfort Payne sarved father." "And how was that?" said they. "Why," says I, "he put him into such a sweat as I never seed him in afore, in all my born days, since I was raised, by sending him in his bill, and if that didn't sweat him it's a pity; it was an ac*tive* dose you may depend." "I guess that 'ere chap has cut his eye-teeth," said the President; "let him pass as approbated." ' '

"They both knowed well enough; they only made as if they didn't, to poke a little fun at them, for the Slick family were counted in a general way to be pretty considerable cute.

"They reckon themselves here a chalk above us Yankees, but I guess they have a wrinkle or two to grow afore they progress ahead on us yet. If they hain't got a full cargo of conceit here, then I never seed a load, that's all. They have the hold chock full, deck piled up to the pump handles, and scuppers under water. They larnt that of the British, who are actilly so full of it, they remind me of Commodore Trip. When he was about half shaved he thought everybody drunk but himself. I never liked the last war; I thought it unnateral, and that we hadn't ought to have taken hold of it at all, and so most of our New England folks thought; and I wasn't sorry to hear Gineral Dearborne was beat, seein' we had no call to go into Canada. But when the *Guerriere* was captivated by our old ironsides, the *Constitution*, I did feel lifted up a'most as high as a stalk of Varginny corn among Connecticut middlins; I grew two inches taller, I vow, the night I heerd that news. Brag, says I, is a good dog, but Holdfast is better. The British navals had been a-braggin' and a-hectorin' so long, that when they landed in our cities they swaggered

e'enamost as much as Uncle Peleg (big Peleg as he was called);
and when he walked up the centre of one of our narrow Boston
streets, he used to swing his arms on each side of him, so that
folks had to clear out of both footpaths; he's cut, afore now, the
fingers of both hands agin the shop windows on each side of
the street. Many the poor feller's crupper bone he's smashed,
with his great thick boots, a-throwin' out his feet afore him
e'enamost out of sight, when he was in full rig a-swigglin' away
at the top of his gait. Well, they cut as many shines as Uncle
Peleg. One frigate they guessed would captivate, sink, or burn
our whole navy. Says a naval, one day, to the skipper of a
fishing boat that he took, says he, 'Is it true, Commodore Deca-
tur's sword is made of an old iron hoop?' 'Well,' says the
skipper, 'I'm not quite certified as to that, seein' as I never sot
eyes on it; but I guess if he gets a chance he'll show you the
temper of it some of these days, anyhow.'

"I mind once a British man-o'-war took one of our Boston
vessels, and ordered all hands on board, and sent a party to
scuttle her; well, they scuttled the fowls and the old particular
genuine rum, but they obliviated their arrand and left her. Well,
next day another frigate (for they were as thick as toads arter a
rain) comes near her, and fires a shot for her to bring to. No
answer was made, there bein' no livin' soul on board, and
another shot fired, still no answer. 'Why, what on airth is the
meanin' of this?' said the captain; 'why don't they haul down
that damn goose and gridiron?' (That's what he called our eagle
and stars on the flag.) 'Why,' says the first leftenant, 'I guess
they are all dead men; that shot frightened them to death.' 'They
are afeared to show their noses,' says another, 'lest they should
be shaved off by our shots.' 'They are all down below
"a-calculatin'"' their loss, I guess,' says a third. 'I'll take my
'davy,' says the captain, 'it's some Yankee trick—a torpedo in
her bottom, or some such trap; we'll let her be'; and sure
enough, next day, back she came to shore of herself. 'I'll give
you a quarter of an hour,' says the captain of the *Guerriere* to
his men, 'to take that 'ere Yankee frigate, the *Constitution*.' I
guess he found his mistake where he didn't expect it, without
any great sarch for it either. Yes (to eventuate my story), it did
me good; I felt dreadful nice, I promise you. It was as lovely as
bitters of a cold mornin'. Our folks beat 'em arter that so often,
they got a little grain too much conceit also. They got their heels
too high for their boots, and began to walk like Uncle Peleg too,
so that when the *Chesapeake* got whipped I warn't sorry. We

could spare that one, and it made our navals look round, like a feller who gets a hoist, to see who's a-larfin' at him. It made 'em brush the dust off, and walk on rather sheepish. It cut their combs, that's a fact. The war did us a plaguy sight of good in more ways than one, and it did the British some good, too. It taught 'em not to carry their chins too high, for fear they shouldn't see the gutters—a mistake that's spoiled many a bran' new coat and trousers afore now.

"Well, these Bluenoses have caught this disease, as folks do the Scotch fiddle, by shakin' hands along with the British. Conceit has become here, as Doctor Rush says (you have heerd tell of him? he's the first man of the age; and it's generally allowed our doctors take the shine off of all the world), acclimated; it is citizenized among 'em; and the only cure is a real good quiltin'. I met a first chop Colchester gag this summer, a-goin' to the races to Halifax, and he knowed as much about racin', I do suppose, as a Choctaw Ingian does of a railroad. Well he was a-praisin' of his horse, and runnin' on like statiee. He was begot, he said, by Roncesvalles, which was better than any horse that ever was seen, because he was once in a duke's stable in England. It was only a man that had blood like a lord, said he, that knew what blood in a horse was. Captain Currycomb, an officer at Halifax, had seen his horse, and praised him; and that was enough—that stamped him—that fixed his value. It was like the President's name to a bank-note—it makes it pass current. 'Well,' says I, 'I hain't got a drop of blood in me, nothin' stronger than molasses and water, I vow; but I guess I know a horse when I see him for all that, and I don't think any great shakes of your beast, any-how. What start will you give me,' says I, 'and I will run Old Clay agin you, for a mile lick right on eend.' 'Ten rods,' said he, 'for twenty dollars.' Well, we run, and I made Old Clay bite in his breath, and only beat him by half a neck. 'A tight scratch,' says I, 'that, and it would have sarved me right if I had been beat. I had no business to run an old roadster so everlastin' fast; it ain't fair on him, is it?' Says he, 'I will double the bet and start even, and run you ag'in if you dare.' 'Well,' says I, 'since I won the last, it wouldn't be pretty not to give you a chance; I do suppose I oughtn't to refuse, but I don't love to abuse my beast by knockin' him about this way.'

As soon as the money was staked, I said, 'Hadn't we better,' says I, 'draw stakes? That 'ere blood horse of your'n has such uncommon particular bottom, he'll perhaps leave me clean out of sight.' 'No fear of that,' said he, larfin', 'but he'll beat you

easy, anyhow. No flinchin',' says he, 'I'll not let you go back of
the bargain. It's run or forfeit.' 'Well,' says I, 'friend, there is
fear of it; your horse will leave me out of sight, to a sartainty,
that's a fact, for he *can't keep up to me no time*. I'll drop him,
hull down, in tu tu's.' If Old Clay didn't make a fool of him, it's
a pity. Didn't he gallop pretty, that's all? He walked away from
him, jist as the *Chancellor Livingston* steamboat passes a sloop
at anchor in the North River. Says I, 'I told you your horse would
beat me clean out of sight, but you wouldn't believe me; now,'
says I, 'I will tell you something else. That 'ere horse will help
you to lose more money to Halifax than you are a-thinkin' on;
for there ain't a beast gone down there that won't beat him. He
can't run a bit, and you may tell the British captain I say so.
*Take him home and sell him; buy a good yoke of oxen, they are
fast enough for a farmer; and give up blood horses to them that
can afford to keep stable-helps to tend 'em, and leave bettin'
alone to them as has more money nor wit, and can afford to
lose their cash, without thinkin' ag'in of their loss.*' 'When I
want your advice,' said he, 'I will ask it,' most peskily sulky.
'You might have got it before you axed for it,' said I, 'but not
afore you wanted it, you may depend on it. But stop,' said I,
'let's see that all's right afore we part'; so I counts over the
fifteen pounds I won of him, note by note, as slow as anything,
on purpose to rile him; then I mounts Old Clay ag'in, and says
I, 'Friend, you have considerably the advantage of me this hitch,
anyhow.' 'Possible!' says he, 'how's that?' 'Why,' says I, 'I guess
you'll return rather lighter than you came, and that's more nor
I can say, anyhow'; and then I gave him a wink and a jupe of
the head, as much as to say, 'Do you take?' and rode on and
left him starin' and scratchin' his head like a feller who's lost
his road. If that citizen ain't a born fool, or too far gone in the
disease, depend on't, he found '*a cure for conceit*.' "

THE long, rambling dissertation on conceit, to which I had just listened, from the Clockmaker, forcibly reminded me of the celebrated aphorism *"gnothi seauton,"* know thyself, which, both from its great antiquity and wisdom, has been by many attributed to an oracle.

With all his shrewdness to discover, and his humour to ridicule the foibles of others, Mr. Slick was blind to the many defects of his own character; and while prescribing "a cure for conceit," exhibited in all he said, and all he did, the most overweening conceit himself. He never spoke of his own countrymen, without calling them "the most free and enlightened citizens on the face of the airth," or as "takin' the shine off of all creation." His country he boasted to be the "best atween the poles," "the greatest glory under heaven." The Yankees he considered (to use his expression) as "actilly the class-leaders in knowledge among all the Americans," and boasted that they have not only "gone ahead of all others," but had lately arrived at that most enviable *ne plus ultra* point, "goin' ahead of themselves." In short, he entertained no doubt that Slickville was the finest place in the greatest nation in the world, and the Slick family the wisest family in it.

I was about calling his attention to this national trait, when I saw him draw his reins under his foot (a mode of driving peculiar to himself, when he wished to economize the time that would otherwise be lost by an unnecessary delay), and taking off his hat (which, like a peddler's pack, contained a general assortment), select from a number of loose cigars one that appeared likely "to go," as he called it. Having lighted it by a lucifer, and ascertained that it was "true in draft," he resumed his reins, and remarked—

"This must be an everlastin' fine country beyond all doubt, for the folks have nothin' to do but to ride about and talk politics. In winter, when the ground is covered with snow, what grand times they have a-sleighin' over these here marshes with the gals, or playin' ball on the ice, or goin' to quiltin' frolics of nice long winter evenings, and then a-drivin' home like mad by moonlight. Natur' meant that season on purpose for courtin'. A little tidy scrumptious-looking sleigh, a real clipper of a horse, a string of bells as long as a string of inions round his neck, and a sprig on his back, lookin' for all the world like a bunch of apples broke off at gatherin' time, and a sweetheart alongside, all muffled up but her eyes and lips—the one lookin' right into you, and the other talkin' right at you—is e'enamost enough to drive one ravin', tarin', distracted mad with pleasure, ain't it? And then the dear critters say the bells make such a din, there's no hearin' one's self speak; so they put their pretty little mugs close up to your face, and talk, talk, talk, till one can't help lookin' right at them instead of the horse, and then whap you both go capsized into a snowdrift together, skins, cushions, and all. And then to see the little critter shake herself when she gets up, like a duck landin' from a pond, a-chatterin' away all the time like a canary bird, and you a-haw-hawin' with pleasure, is fun alive, you may depend. In this way Bluenose gets led on to offer himself as a lovier, afore he knows where he bees.

"But when he gets married, he recovers his eyesight in little less than half no time. He soon finds he's treed; his flint is fixed then, you may depend. She larns him how vinegar is made: *'Put plenty of sugar into the water aforehand, my dear,'* says she, *'if you want to make it real sharp.'* The larf is on the other side of his mouth then. If his sleigh gets upsot, it's no longer a funny matter, I tell you; he catches it right and left. Her eyes don't look right up to his'n any more, nor her little tongue ring, ring, ring, like a bell any longer; but a great big hood covers her head, and a whappin' great muff covers her face, and she looks like a bag of soiled clothes a-goin' to the brook to be washed. When they get out, she don't wait any more for him to walk lock and lock with her, but they march like a horse and a cow to water, one in each gutter. If there ain't a transmogrification it's a pity. The difference atween a wife and a sweetheart is near about as great as there is between new and hard cider: a man never tires of puttin' one to his lip, and makes plaguy wry faces at t'other. It makes me so kinder wamblecropt when I think on it, that I'm afeared to venture on matrimony at all. I have seen some Bluenoses most properly bit, you may depend. You've seen a boy a-slidin' on a most beautiful smooth bit of ice, hain't you, larfin', and hoopin', and hallowin' like one possessed, when presently souse he goes in over head and ears? How he outs, fins, and flops about, and blows like a porpoise properly frightened, don't he? and when he gets out, there he stands, all shiverin' and shakin', and the water a squish-squashin' in his shoes, and his trousers all stickin' slimsey-like to his legs. Well, he sneaks off home, lookin' like a fool, and thinkin' everybody he meets is a-larfin' at him: many folks here are like that 'ere boy, afore they have been six months married. They'd be proper glad to get out of the scrape too, and sneak off if they could, that's a fact. The marriage yoke is plaguy apt to gall the neck, as the ash bow does the ox in rainy weather, unless it be most particularly well fitted. You've seen a yoke of cattle that warn't properly mated? They spend more strength in pullin' agin each other, than in pullin' the load. Well, that's apt to be the case with them as choose their wives in sleighin' parties, quiltin' frolics, and so on, instead of the dairies, looms, and cheese-houses.

"Now the Bluenoses are all a-stirrin' in winter. The young folks drive out the gals, and talk love and all sorts of things as sweet as doughnuts. The old folks find it near about as well to leave the old woman to home, for fear they shouldn't keep tune together; so they drive out alone to chat about House of Assembly with their neighbours, while the boys and hired helps do the chores. When the spring comes, and the fields are dry enough to be sowed, they all have to be ploughed, *'cause fall rains wash the lands too much for fall ploughin'*. Well, the ploughs have to be mended and sharpened, *'cause what's the use of doin' that afore it's wanted?* Well, the wheat gets in too late, and then comes rust; but whose fault is that? *Why, the climate, to be sure, for Nova Scotia ain't a bread country.*

"When a man has to run ever so far as fast as he can clip, he has to stop and take breath; you must do that or choke. So it is with a horse; run him a mile, and his flanks will heave like a blacksmith's bellows; you must slack up the rein and give him a little wind, or he'll fall right down with you. It stands to reason, don't it? Atwixt spring and fall work is *'Blowin' time.'* Then courts come on, and grand jury business, and militia trainin', and race trainin', and what not; and a fine spell of ridin' about and doin' nothin', a real *'Blowin' time.'* Then comes harvest, and that is proper hard work: mowin' and pitchin' hay, and reapin' and bindin' grain, and potato diggin'. That's as hard as sole-leather, afore it's hammered on the lapstone; it's a'most next to anything. It takes a feller as tough as Old Hickory (General Jackson) to stand that.

"Ohio is 'most the only country I know of where folks are

saved that trouble; and where the freshets come jist in the nick of time for 'em, and sweep all the crops right up in a heap for 'em, and they have nothin' to do but take it home and house it; and sometimes a man gets more than his own crop, and finds a proper swad of it all ready piled up, only a little wet or so; but all countries ain't like Ohio. Well, arter harvest comes fall, and then there's a grand 'blowin' time' till spring. Now, how the Lord the Bluenoses can complain of their country, when it's only one-third work and two-thirds 'blowin' time,' no soul can tell.

"Father used to say, when I lived on the farm along with him, 'Sam,' says he, 'I vow I wish there was jist four hundred days in the year, for it's a plaguy sight too short for me. I can find as much work as all hands on us can do for three hundred and sixty-five days, and jist thirty-five days more, if we had 'em. We hain't got a minit to spare; you must shell the corn and winner the grain at night, clean all up slick, or I guess we'll fall astarn, as sure as the Lord made Moses.' If he didn't keep us all at it, a-drivin' away full chisel, the whole blessed time, it's a pity. There was no 'blowin' time' there, you may depend. We ploughed all the fall for dear life; in winter we thrashed, made and mended tools, went to market and mill, and got out our firewood and rails. As soon as frost was gone, came sowin' and plantin', weedin' and hoein'; then harvest and spreadin' compost; then gatherin' manure, fencin' and ditchin'; and then turn tu and fall ploughin' ag'in. It all went round like a wheel without stoppin', and so fast, I guess you couldn't see the spokes, just one long everlastin' stroke from July to etarnity, without time to look back on the tracks. Instead of racin' over the country like a young doctor, to show how busy a man is that has nothin' to do, as Bluenose does, and then take a 'blowin' time,' we kept a rale travellin 'gait, an eight-mile-an-hour pace, the whole year round. *They buy more nor they sell, and eat more than they raise*, in this country. What a pretty way that is, isn't it? If the critters knew how to cipher, they would soon find out that a sum stated that way always eends in a naught. I never knew it to fail, and I defy any soul to cipher it so as to make it come out any other way, either by Schoolmaster's Assistant or Algebra. When I was a boy, the Slickville Bank broke, and an awful disorderment it made, that's a fact; nothin' else was talked of. Well, I studied it over a long time, but I couldn't make it out : so says I, 'Father, how came that 'ere bank to break? Warn't it well built? I thought that 'ere Quincy granite was so amazin' strong all natur' wouldn't break it.' 'Why, you foolish critter,' says he, 'it ain't the buildin' that's broke, it's the consarn that's smashed.' 'Well,' says I, 'I know folks are plaguily consarned about it, but what do you call folks' "smashin' their consarns"?' Father, he larfed out like anything; I thought he never would stop; and sister Sall got right up and walked out of the room, as mad as a hatter. Says she, 'Sam, I do believe you are a born fool, I vow.' When father had done larfin', says he, 'I'll tell you, Sam, how it was. They ciphered it so that they brought out nothin' for a remainder.' 'Possible!' says I; 'I thought there was no eend to their puss. I thought it was like Uncle Peleg's musquash hole, and that no soul could ever find the bottom of. My!' says I. 'Yes,' says he, 'that 'ere bank spent and lost more money than it made, and when folks do that, they must smash at last, if their puss be as long as the national one of Uncle Sam.' This Province is like that 'ere bank of our'n; it's goin' the same road, and they'll find the little eend of the horn afore they think they are half way down to it.

"If folks would only give over talking about that everlastin' House of Assembly and Council, and see to their farms, it would be better for 'em, I guess; for arter all, what is it? Why it's only a sort of first chop Grand Jury, and nothin' else. It's no more like Congress or Parliament, than Marm Pugwash's keepin' room is like our State hall. It's jist nothin'. Congress makes war and peace, has a say in all treaties, confarms all great nominations of the President, regilates the army and navy, governs twenty-four independent States, and snaps its fingers in the face of all the nations of Europe, as much as to say, Who be you? I allot I am as big as you be. If you are six foot high, I am six foot six in my stockin' feet, by gum, and can lambaste any two on you in no time. The British can whip all the world, and we can whip the British. But this little House of Assembly that folks make such a touse about, what is it? Why jist a decent Grand Jury. They make their presentments of little money votes, to mend these everlastin' rottin' little wooden bridges, to throw a poultice of mud once a year on the roads, and then take a 'blowin' time' of three months and go home. The littler folks be, the bigger they talk. You never seed a small man that didn't wear high-heel boots, and a high-crowned hat, and that warn't ready to fight 'most any one, to show he was a man every inch of him.

"I met a member the other day, who swaggered near about as large as Uncle Peleg. He looked as if he thought you couldn't find his 'ditto' anywhere. He used some most particular educational words, genuine jaw-breakers. He put me in mind of a squirrel I once shot in our wood location. The little critter got a hickory nut in his mouth; well, he found it too hard to crack, and too big to swaller, and for the life and soul of him, he couldn't spit it out ag'in. If he didn't look like a proper fool, you may depend. We had a pond back of our barn, about the bigness of a good sizeable washtub, and it was chock full of frogs. Well, one of these little critters fancied himself a bull-frog, and he puffed out his cheeks, and took a rael 'blowin' time' of it; he roared away like thunder; at last he puffed and puffed out till he bust like a b'iler. If I see the Speaker this winter (and I shall see him to a sartainty if they don't send for him to London, to teach their new Speaker; and he's up to snuff, that 'ere man; he knows how to cipher), I'll jist say to him, 'Speaker,' says I, 'if any of your folks in the House go to swell out like dropsy, give 'em a hint in time. Says you, 'If you have 'ere a little safety valve about you, let off a little steam now and then, or you'll go for it; recollect the Clockmaker's story of the "Blowin' time" ' "

"TOMORROW will be Sabbath day," said the Clockmaker; "I guess we'll bide where we be till Monday. I like a Sabbath in the country; all natur' seems at rest. There's a cheerfulness in the day here, you don't find in towns. You have natur' before you here, and nothin' but art there. The deathly stillness of a town, and the barred windows, and shut shops, and empty streets, and great long lines of big brick buildin's look melancholy. It seems as if life had ceased tickin', but there hadn't been time for decay to take hold on there; as if day had broke, but man slept. I can't describe exactly what I mean, but I always feel kinder gloomy and wamblecropt there.

"Now in the country it's jist what it ought to be—a day of rest for man and beast from labour. When a man rises on the Sabbath, and looks out on the sunny fields and wavin' crops, his heart feels proper grateful, and he says, Come, this is a splendid day, ain't it? Let's get ready and put on our bettermost close, and go to meetin'. His first thought is prayerfully to render thanks; and then when he goes to worship he meets all his neighbours, and he knows them all, and they are glad to see each other, and if any two on 'em hain't exactly gee'd together durin' the week, why, they meet on kind of neutral ground, and the minister or neighbours make peace atween them. But it ain't so in towns. You don't know no one you meet there. It's the worship of neighbours, but it's the worship of strangers, too, for neighbours don't know nor care about each other. Yes, I love a Sabbath in the country."

While uttering this soliloquy, he took up a pamphlet from the table, and turning to the title page, said, "Have you ever seen this here book on the 'Elder Controversy'? (a controversy on the subject of Infant Baptism). This author's friends say it's a clincher; they say he has sealed up Elder's mouth as tight as a bottle."

"No," said I, "I have not; I have heard of it, but never read it. In my opinion the subject has been exhausted already, and admits of nothing new being said upon it. These religious controversies are a serious injury to the cause of true religion; they are deeply deplored by the good and moderate men of all parties. It has already embraced several denominations in the dispute in this Province, and I hear the agitation has extended to New Brunswick, where it will doubtless be renewed with equal zeal. I am told all the pamphlets are exceptionable in point of temper, and this one in particular, which not only ascribes the most unworthy motives to its antagonist, but contains some very unjustifiable and gratuitous attacks upon other sects unconnected with the dispute. The author has injured his own cause, for *an intemperate advocate is more dangerous than an open foe.*"

"There is no doubt on it," said the Clockmaker; "it is as clear as mud, and you are not the only one that thinks so, I tell you. About the hottest time of the dispute, I was to Halifax, and who should I meet but Father John O'Shaughnessy, a Catholic priest. I had met him afore in Cape Breton, and had sold him a clock. Well, he was a-leggin' it off hot foot. 'Possible!' says I, 'Father John, is that you? Why, what on airth is the matter of you? What makes you in such an everlastin' hurry, drivin' away like one ravin' distracted mad?' 'A sick visit,' says he; 'poor Pat Lanigan—him that you mind to Bradore Lake—well, he's near about at the p'int of death.' 'I guess not,' said I, 'for I jist heard tell he was dead.' Well, that brought him up all standin', and he 'bouts ship in a jiffy, and walks a little way with me, and we got a-talkin' about this very subject. Says he, 'What are you, Mr. Slick?' Well, I looks up to him, and winks—'A Clockmaker,' says I. Well, he smiled, and says he, 'I see'; as much as to say, I hadn't ought to have axed that 'ere question at all, I guess, for every man's religion is his own, and nobody else's business. 'Then,' says he, 'you know all about this country. Who does folks say had the best of the dispute?' Says I, 'Father John, it's like the battles up to Canada lines last war, each side claims victory; I guess there ain't much to brag on nary way—damage done on both sides, and nothin' gained, as far as I can learn.' He stopped short, and looked me in the face, and says he, 'Mr. Slick, you are a man that has seen a good deal of the world, and a considerable of an understandin' man, and I guess I can talk to you. Now,' says he, 'for gracious' sake do jist look here, and see how you heretics—Protestants I mean,' says he (for I guess that 'ere word slipped out without leave), 'are by the ears, a-drivin' away at each other the whole blessed time, tooth and nail, hip and thigh, hammer and tongs, disputin', revilin', wranglin', and beloutin' each other with all sorts of ugly names that they can lay their tongues to. Is that the way you love your neighbours as yourself? *We say this is a practical comment on schism,* and by the powers of Moll Kelly,' said he, 'but they all ought to be well lambasted together, the whole batch on 'em entirely.' Says I, 'Father John, give me your hand; there are some things I guess, you and I don't agree on, and most likely never will, seein' that you are a Popish priest; but in that idee I do opinionate with you, and I wish, with all my heart, all the world thought with us.'

"I guess he didn't half like that 'ere word Popish priest, it seemed to grig him like; his face looked kinder riled, like well water arter a heavy rain, and said he, 'Mr. Slick,' says he, 'your country is a free country, ain't it?' 'The freest,' says I, 'on the face of the airth; you can't "ditto" it nowhere. We are as free as the air, and when our dander's up, stronger than any hurricane you ever seed—tear up all creation 'most; there ain't the beat of it to be found anywhere.' 'Do you call this a free country?' said he. 'Pretty considerable middlin',' says I, 'seein' that they are under a king.' 'Well,' says he, 'if you were seen in Connecticut a-shakin' hands along with a Popish priest, as you are pleased to call me' (and he made me a bow, as much as to say, Mind your trumps the next deal), 'as you now are in the streets of Halifax along with me, with all your crackin' and boastin' of your freedom, I guess you wouldn't sell a clock ag'in in that State for one while, I tell you'; and he bid me good mornin' and turned away. 'Father John!' says I. 'I can't stop,' says he; 'I must see that poor critter's family; they must be in great trouble, and a sick visit is afore controvarsy in my creed.' 'Well,' says I, 'one word with you afore you go; if that 'ere name Popish priest was an ongenteel one, I ax your pardon; I didn't mean no offence, I do assure you, and I'll say this for your satisfaction, tu: you're the first man in this Province that ever gave me a real right down complete checkmate since I first sot foot in it, I'll be skinned if you ain't.'

"Yes," said Mr. Slick, "Father John was right; these antagonizing chaps ought to be well quilted, the whole raft of 'em. It fairly makes me sick to see the folks, each on 'em a-backin' up of their own man. 'At it ag'in!' says one; 'Fair play!' says another; 'Stick it into him!' says a third; and 'That's your sort!' says a fourth. Them are the folks who do mischief. They show such clear grit, it fairly frightens me. It makes my hair stand right up on eend to see ministers do that 'ere. *It appears to me that I could write*

*a book in favour of myself and my notions, without writin' agin
any one, and if I couldn't I wouldn't write at all, I snore.* Our
old minister, Mr. Hopewell (a real good man, and a larned man
too at that), they sent to him once to write agin the Unitarians,
for they are a-goin' ahead like statiee in New England, but he
refused. Said he, 'Sam,' says he, 'when I first went to Cambridge,
there was a boxer and wrastler came there, and he beat everyone wherever he went. Well, old Mr. Possit was the Church of
England parson at Charlestown, at the time, and a terrible
powerful man he was—a rael sneezer, and as *active* as a weasel.
Well, the boxer met him one day, a little way out of town,
a-takin' of his evenin' walk, and said he, "Parson," says he, "they
say you are a most plaguy strong man and uncommon stiff too."
"Now," says he, "I never seed a man yet that was a match for me;
would you have any objection jist to let me be availed of your
strength here in a friendly way, by ourselves, where no soul
would be the wiser? If you will I'll keep dark about it, I swan."
"Go your way," said the parson, "and tempt me not; you are a
carnal-minded, wicked man, and I take no pleasure in such vain,
idle sports." "Very well," said the boxer; "now here I stand,"
says he, "in the path, right slap afore you; if you pass round me,
then I take it as a sign that you are afeard on me, and if you
keep the path, why then you must first put me out—that's a
fact." The parson jist made a spring forrard and ketched him
up as quick as wink, and throwed him right over the fence whap
on the broad of his back, and then walked on as if nothin' had
happened—as demure as you please, and lookin' as meek as if
butter wouldn't melt in his mouth. "Stop," said the boxer, as
soon as he picked himself up, "stop Parson," said he, "that's a
good man, and jist chuck over my horse, too, will you, for I
swan I believe you could do one near about as easy as t'other.
My!" said he, "if that don't bang the bush; you are another
guess chap from what I took you to be, anyhow."

" 'Now,' said Mr. Hopewell, says he, 'I won't write, but if ary
a Unitarian crosses my path, I'll jist over the fence with him in
no time, as the parson did the boxer; *for writin' only aggravates
your opponents, and never convinces them. I never seed a con-
vart made by that way yet; but I'll tell you what I have seed: a
man set his own flock a-doubtin' by his own writin'. You may
happify your enemies, cantankerate your opponents, and injure
your own cause by it, but I defy you to sarve it.* These writers,'
said he, 'put me in mind of that 'ere boxer's pupils. He would
sometimes set two on 'em to spar; well, they'd put on their

gloves, and begin, larfin' and jokin', all in good humour. Presently one on 'em would put in a pretty hard blow; well, t'other would return it in airnest. "O," says the other, "if that's your play, off gloves and at it"; and sure enough, away would fly their gloves, and at it they'd go, tooth and nail.

" 'No, Sam, the misfortin' is, we are all apt to think Scriptur' intended for our neighbours, and not for ourselves. The poor all think it made for the rich. "Look at that 'ere Dives," they say, "what an all-fired scrape he got into by his avarice, with Lazarus; and ain't it writ as plain as anything, that them folks will find it as easy to go to heaven, as for a camel to go through the eye of a needle?" Well, then, the rich think it all made for the poor —that they shan't steal nor bear false witness, but shall be obedient to them that's in authority. And as for them 'ere Unitarians,' and he always got his dander up when he spoke of them, 'why, there's no doin' nothin' with them,' says he. 'When they get fairly stumped, and you produce a text that they can't get over, nor get round, why, they say, "It ain't in our version at all; that's an interpolation, it's an invention of them 'ere everlastin' monks"; there's nothin' left for you to do with them, but to sarve them as Parson Possit detailed the boxer—lay right hold of 'em and chuck 'em over the fence, even if they were as big as all out-doors. That's what our folks ought to have done with 'em at first, pitched 'em clean out of the State, and let 'em go down to Nova Scotia, or some such outlandish place, for they ain't fit to live in no Christian country at all.

" 'Fightin' is no way to make convarts; *the true way is to win 'em.* You may stop a man's mouth, Sam,' says he, 'by a-crammin' a book down his throat, but you won't convince him. It's a fine thing to write a book all covered over with Latin, and Greek, and Hebrew, like a bridle that's real jam, all spangled with brass nails, but who knows whether it's right or wrong? Why, not one in ten thousand. If I had my religion to choose, and warn't able to judge for myself, I'll tell you what I'd do: I'd jist ask myself *Who leads the best lives?* Now,' says he, 'Sam, I won't say who do, because it would look like vanity to say it was the folks who hold to our platform, but I'll tell you who don't. *It ain't them that makes the greatest professions always*; and mind what I tell you, Sam, when you go a-tradin' with your clocks away down East to Nova Scotia, and them wild provinces, keep a bright lookout on them as cant too much, for *a long face is plaguy apt to cover a long conscience*—that's a fact.' "

THE road from Amherst to Parrsboro' is tedious and uninteresting. In places it is made so straight that you can see several miles of it before you, which produces an appearance of interminable length, while the stunted growth of the spruce and birch trees bespeaks a cold, thin soil, and invests the scene with a melancholy and sterile aspect. Here and there occurs a little valley, with its meandering stream, and verdant and fertile interval, which though possessing nothing peculiar to distinguish it from many others of the same kind, strikes the traveller as superior to them all, from the contrast to the surrounding country. One of these secluded spots attracted my attention, from the number and neatness of the buildings which its proprietor, a tanner and currier, had erected for the purposes of his trade. Mr. Slick said he knew him, and he guessed it was a pity he couldn't keep his wife in as good order as he did his factory.

"They don't hitch their horses together well at all. He is properly henpecked," said he; "he is afeard to call his soul his own, and he leads the life of a dog; you never seed the beat of it, I vow. Did you ever see a rooster hatch a brood of chickens?"

"No," said I, "not that I can·recollect."

"Well, then, I have," said he, "and if he don't look like a fool all the time he is a-settin' on the eggs, it's a pity; no soul could help larfin' to see him. Our old nigger, January Snow, had a spite agin one of father's roosters, seein' that he was a coward, and wouldn't fight. He used to call him Dearborne, arter our General that behaved so ugly to Canada : and says he one day, 'I guess you are no better than a hen, you everlastin' old chicken-hearted villain, and I'll make you a larfin'-stock to all the poultry. I'll put a trick on you you'll bear in mind all your born days.' So he catches old Dearborne, and pulls all the feathers off his breast, and strips him as naked as when he was born, from his throat clean down to his tail, and then takes a bundle of nettles and gives him a proper switchin', that stung him and made him smart like mad; then he warms some eggs and puts them in a nest, and sets the old cock right atop of 'em. Well, the warmth of the eggs felt good to the poor critter's naked belly, and kinder kept the itchin' of the nettles down, and he was glad to bide where he was; and whenever he was tired and got off, his skin felt so cold, he'd run right back and squat down ag'in; and when his feathers began to grow, and he got obstropulous, he got another ticklin' with the nettles, that made him return double quick to his location. In a little time he larnt the trade real complete. Now, this John Porter (and there he is on the bridge, I vow; I never seed the beat o' that—speak of old Saytin and he's sure to appear), well, he's jist like old Dearborne, only fit to hatch eggs."

When we came to the bridge, Mr. Slick stopped his horse, to shake hands with Porter, whom he recognized as an old acquaintance and customer. He inquired after a bark-mill he had smuggled from the States for him, and enlarged on the value of such a machine, and the cleverness of his countrymen who invented such useful and profitable articles; and was recommending a new process of tanning, when a female voice from the house was heard, vociferating, "John Porter, come here this minute." "Coming, my dear," said the husband. "Come here, I say, directly; why do you stand talking to that Yankee villain there?" The poor husband hung his head, looked silly, and bidding us good-bye, returned slowly to the house.

As we drove on, Mr. Slick said, "That was me—I did that."

"Did what?" said I.

"That was me that sent him back; I called him, and not his wife. I had that 'ere bestowment ever since I was knee high or so; I'm a real complete hand at ventriloquism; I can take off any man's voice I ever heard to the very nines. If there was a law ag'in forgin' that, as there is for handwritin', I guess I should have been hanged long ago, I've had high goes with it many a time, but it's plaguy dangersome, and I don't practise it now but seldom. I had a real bout with that 'ere citizen's wife once, and completely broke her in for him : she went as gentle as a circus horse for a space, but he let her have her head ag'in, and she's as bad as ever now. I'll tell you how it was.

"I was down to the Island a-sellin' clocks, and who should I meet but John Porter; well, I traded with him for one, part cash, part truck and produce, and also put off on him that 'ere bark-mill you heerd me axin' about, and it was pretty considerable on in the evenin' afore we finished our trade. I came home along with him, and had the clock in the wagon to fix it up for him, and to show him how to regilate it. Well, as we neared his house, he began to fret and take on dreadful oneasy; says he, 'I hope Jane won't be abed, 'cause if she is she'll act ugly, I do suppose.' I had heard tell of her afore—how she used to carry a stiff upper lip, and make him and the broomstick well acquainted together; and says I, 'Why do you put up with her tantrums? I'd make a fair division of the house with her, if it was me; I'd take the inside and allocate her the outside of it pretty quick, that's a fact.' Well, when we came to the house, there was no light in it, and the poor critter looked so streaked and down in the mouth, I felt proper sorry for him. When he rapped at the door, she called out, 'Who's there?' 'It's me, dear,' says Porter. 'You, is it,' said she, 'then you may stay where you be; them as gave you your supper may give you your bed, instead of sendin' you sneakin' home at night like a thief.' Said I, in a whisper, says I, 'Leave her to me, John Porter; jist take the horses up to the barn, and see after them, and I'll manage her for you; I'll make her as sweet as sugary candy, never fear.' The barn, you see, is a good piece off to the eastward of the house; and as soon as he was cleverly out of hearin', says I, a-imitatin' of his voice to the life, 'Do let me in, Jane,' says I, 'that's a dear critter; I've brought you home some things you'll like, I know.' Well, she was an awful jealous critter; says she, 'Take 'em to her you spent the evenin' with; I don't want you nor your presents neither.' Arter a good deal of coaxin' I stood on t'other tack, and began to threaten to break the door down; says I, 'You old unhandsum-lookin' sinner, you vinergar cruet you, open the door this minit or I'll smash it right in.' That grigged her properly, it made her very wrathy (for nothin' sets up a woman's spunk like callin' her ugly; she gets her back right up like a cat when a strange dog comes near her; she's all eyes, claws, and bristles).

"I heerd her bounce right out of bed, and she came to the door as she was, ondressed, and onbolted it; and as I entered it, she fetched me a box right across my cheek with the flat of her hand, that made it tingle ag'in. 'I'll teach you to call names ag'in,' says she, 'you varmint.' It was jist what I wanted; I pushed the door tu with my foot, and seizin' her by the arm with one hand, I quilted her with the horsewhip real handsum with the other. At first she roared like mad; 'I'll give you the ten commandments,' says she (meaning her ten claws), 'I'll pay you for this, you cowardly villain, to strike a woman. How dare you lift your hand, John Porter, to your lawful wife!' and so on; all the time runnin' round and round, like a colt that's a-breakin', with the mouthin' bit, rarir', kickin', and plungin' like statiee. Then she began to give in. Says she, 'I beg pardon, on my knees I beg pardon; don't murder me, for Heaven's sake—don't, dear John, don't murder your poor wife, that's a dear; I'll do as you bid me; I promise to behave well, upon my honour I do; O! dear John, do forgive me, do dear.' When I had her properly brought to, for havin' nothin' on but a thin undergarment, every crack of the whip told like a notch on a baker's tally, says I, 'Take that as a taste of what you'll catch when you act that way, like Old Scratch. Now go and dress yourself, and get supper for me and a stranger I have brought home along with me, and be quick, for I vow I'll be master in my own house.' She moaned like a dog hit with a stone, half whine, half yelp. 'Dear, dear,' says she, 'if I ain't all covered over with welts as big as my finger; I do believe I'm flayed alive!' and she boo-hoo'd right out like any-thing. 'I guess,' said I, 'you've got 'em where folks won't see 'em, anyhow, and I calculate you won't be over forrard to show 'em where they be. But come,' says I, 'be a-stirrin', or I'll quilt you ag'in as sure as you're alive; I'll tan your hide for you, you may depend, you old ungainly tempered heifer you.'

"When I went to the barn, says I, 'John Porter, your wife made right at me, like one ravin' distracted mad, when I opened the door, thinkin' it was you; and I was obliged to give her a crack or two of the cowskin to get clear of her. It has effectuated a cure completely; now foller it up, and don't let on for your life it warn't you that did it, and you'll be master once more in your own house. She's all docity jist now—keep her so.' As we returned we saw a light in the keepin' room, the fire was blazin' up cheerfulsome, and Marm Porter moved about as brisk as a parched pea, though as silent as dumb, and our supper was ready in no time. As soon as she took her seat and sot down, she sprung right up on eend, as if she sot on a pan of hot coals, and coloured all over; and then tears started in her eyes. Thinks I to myself, I calculate I wrote that 'ere lesson in large letters anyhow; I can read that writin' without spellin', and no mistake; I guess you've got pretty well warmed thereabouts this hitch. Then she tried it ag'in; first she sot on one leg, then on t'other, quite oneasy, and then right atwixt both, a-fidgetin' about dreadfully; like a man that's rode all day on a bad saddle, and lost a little leather on the way. If you had seed how she stared at Porter, it would have made you snicker. She couldn't credit her eyes. He warn't drunk, and he warn't crazy, but there he sot as peeked and as meechin' as you please. She seemed all struck up of a heap at his rebellion. The next day when I was about startin', I advised him to act like a man, and keep the weather-gauge now he had it, and all would be well; but the poor critter only held on a day or two, she soon got the upper hand of him and made him confess all, and by all accounts he leads a worse life now than ever. I put that 'ere trick on him jist now to try him, and I see it's a gone goose with him; the jig is up with him; she'll soon call him with a whistle like a dog. I often think of the hornpipe she danced there in the dark along with me to the music of my whip; she touched it off in great style, that's a fact. I shall mind that go one while, I promise you. It was actilly equal to a play at old Bow'ry. You may depend, Squire, the only way to tame a shrew is by the cowskin. Grandfather Slick was raised all along the coast of Kent in Old England, and he used to say there was an old saying there, which, I expect, is not far off the mark :

> 'A woman, a dog, and a walnut tree,
> The more you lick them the better they be.' "

"This country," said Mr. Slick, "abounds in superior mill privileges, and one would naterally calculate that such a sight of water power would have led to a knowledge of machinery. I guess if a Bluenose was to go to one of our free and enlightened citizens, and tell him Nova Scotia was intersected with rivers and brooks in all directions, and nearly one quarter of it covered with water, he'd say, 'Well, I'll start right off and see it, I vow, for I guess I'll larn somethin'. I allot I'll get another wrinkle away down East there. With such splendid chances for experimentin', what first-chop mills they must have, to a sartainty. I'll see such new combinations, and such new applications of the force of water to motion, that I'll make my fortin', for we can improve on anything a'most.' Well, he'd find his mistake out, I guess, as I did once, when I took passage in the night at New York for Providence, and found myself the next mornin' clean out to sea, steerin' away for Cape Hatteras, in the Charleston steamer. He'd find he'd gone to the wrong place, I reckon; there ain't a mill of any kind in the Province fit to be seen. If we had 'em, we'd sarve 'em as we do the gamblin' houses down South —pull 'em right down; there wouldn't be one on 'em left in eight and forty hours.

"Some domestic factories they ought to have here: it's an essential part of the social system. Now we've run to the other extreme; it's got to be too big an interest with us, and ain't suited to the political institutions of our great country. Natur' designed us for an agricultural people, and our government was predicated on the supposition that we would be so. Mr. Hopewell was of the same opinion. He was a great hand at gardenin', orchardin', farmin', and what not. One evenin' I was up to his house, and says he, 'Sam, what do you say to a bottle of my old genuine cider? I guess I got some that will take the shine off of your father's by a long chalk, much as the old gentleman brags of his'n. I never bring it out afore him. He thinks he has the best in all Connecticut. It's an innocent ambition that; and, Sam, it would be but a poor thing for me to gratify my pride at the expense of humblin' his'n. So I never lets on that I have any better, but keep dark about this superfine particular article of mine, for I'd as lives he'd think so as not.' He was a real primi*tive* good man was minister. 'I got some,' said he, 'that was bottled that very year that glorious action was fought atween the *Constitution* and the *Guerriere*. Perhaps the whole world couldn't show such a brilliant whippin' as that was. It was a splendid deed, that's a fact. The British can whip the whole airth, and we can whip the British. It was a bright promise for our young eagle : a noble bird that, too—great strength, great courage, and surpassing sagacity.'

"Well, he went down to the cellar, and brought up a bottle, with a stick tied to its neck, and day and date to it, like the lye-bills on the trees in Squire Hendrick's garden. 'I like to see them 'ere cobwebs,' says he, as he brushed 'em off, 'they are like grey hairs in an old man's head; they indicate venerable old age.' As he uncorked it, says he, 'I guess, Sam, this will warm your gizzard, my boy; I guess our great nation may be stumped to produce more eleganter liquor than this here. It's the dandy, that's a fact. That,' said he, a-smackin' his lips, and lookin' at its sparklin' top, and layin' back his head, and tippin' off a horn mug brimful of it—'that,' said he, and his eyes twinkled ag'in, for it was plaguy strong—'that is the produce of my own orchard.' 'Well,' I said, 'minister,' says I, 'I never see you a-swiggin' it out of that 'ere horn mug, that I don't think of one of your texts.' 'What's that, Sam?' says he, 'for you always had a'most a special memory when you was a boy.' 'Why,' says I, 'that "the horn of the righteous man shall be exalted"; I guess that's what they mean by "exaltin' the horn," ain't it?' Lord, if ever you was to New Or*leens*, and seed a black thundercloud rise right up and cover the whole sky in a minit, you'd a thought of it if you had seed his face. It looked as dark as Egypt. 'For shame!' says he, 'Sam, that's ondecent; and let me tell you that a man that jokes on such subjects, shows both a lack of wit and sense too. I like mirth, you know I do, for it's only the Pharisees and hypocrites that wear long faces, but then mirth must be innocent to please me; and when I see a man make merry with serious things, I set him down as a lost sheep. That comes of your speculatin' to Lowell; and, I vow, them factorin' towns will corrupt our youth of both sexes, and become hotbeds of iniquity. Evil communications endamnify good manners, as sure as rates; one scabby sheep will infect a whole flock; vice is as catchin' as that nasty disease the Scotch have, it's got by shakin'

hands, and both eend in the same way—in brimstone. I appro-
bate domestic factories, but nothin' further for us. It don't suit
us or our institutions. A republic is only calculated for an enlightened and vartuous people, and folks chiefly in the farmin'
line. That is an innocent and a happy vocation. Agriculture was
ordained by Him as made us, for our chief occupation.'

"Thinks I, here's a pretty how do you do; I'm in for it now,
that's a fact; he'll jist fall to and read a regular sarmon, and he
knows so many by heart he'll never stop. It would take a Philadelphia lawyer to answer him. So, says I, 'Minister, I ax your
pardon; I feel very ugly at havin' given you offence, but I didn't
mean it, I do assure you. It jist popped out unexpectedly, like
a cork out of one of them 'ere cider bottles. I'll do my possibles
that the like don't happen ag'in, you may depend; so 'spose we
drink a glass to our reconciliation.' 'That I will,' said he, 'and
we will have another bottle too, but I must put a little water
into *my glass* (and he dwelt on that word, and looked at me, quite
feelin', as much as to say, Don't for goodness' sake make use of
that 'ere word *horn* ag'in, for it's a joke I don't like), 'for my
head han't quite the strength my cider has. Taste this, Sam,' said
he (openin' of another bottle); 'it's of the same age as the last,
but made of different apples, and I am fairly stumped sometimes
to say which is best.'

" 'These are the pleasures,' says he, 'of a country life. A man's
own labour provides him with food, and an appetite to enjoy it.
Let him look which way he will, and he sees the goodness and
bounty of his Creator, his wisdom, his power, and his majesty.
There never was anything so true, as that 'ere old sayin' "Man
made the town, but God made the country," and both bespeak
their different architects in terms too plain to be misunderstood.
The one is filled with virtue, and the other with vice. One is the
abode of plenty, and the other of want; one is a ware-duck of
nice pure water, and t'other one a cess-pool. Our towns are
gettin' so commercial and factoring, that they will soon generate
mobs, Sam' (how true that 'ere has turned out, hain't it? He
could see near about as far into a millstone as them that picks
the hole into it), 'and mobs will introduce disobedience and
defiance to laws, and that must eend in anarchy and bloodshed.
No,' said the old man, raising his voice, and giving the table a
wipe with his fist that made the glasses all jingle ag'in, 'give me
the country—that country to which He that made it said, "Bring
forth grass, the herb yieldin' seed, and the tree yieldin' fruit,"
and who saw it that it was good. Let me jine with the feathered

tribe in the mornin' (I hope you get up airly now, Sam; when you was a boy there was no gittin' you out of bed at no rate) and at sunset, in the hymns which they utter in full tide of song to their Creator. Let me pour out the thankfulness of my heart to the Giver of all good things, for the numerous blessings I enjoy, and intreat Him to bless my increase, that I may have wherewithal to relieve the wants of others, as He prevents and relieves mine. No! give me the country. It's——' Minister was jist like a horse that has the spavin; he sot off considerable stiff at first, but when he once got under way, he got on like a house afire. He went like the wind, full split. He was jist beginnin' to warm on the subject, and I knew if he did, what wonderful bottom he had; how he would hang on forever a'most; so says I, 'I think so too, Minister; I like the country; I always sleep better there than in towns; it ain't so plaguy hot nor so noisy neither; and then it's a pleasant thing to set out on the stoop and smoke in the cool, ain't it? I think,' says I, 'too, Minister, that 'ere uncommon handsum cider of your'n desarves a pipe; what do you think?' 'Well,' says he, 'I think myself a pipe wouldn't be amiss, and I got some rael good Varginny as you e'enamost ever seed, a present from Rowland Randolph, an old college chum; and none the worse to my palate, Sam, for bringin' bygone recollections with it. Phœbe, my dear,' said he to his darter, 'bring the pipes and tobacco.' As soon as the old gentleman fairly got a pipe in his mouth, I give Phœbe a wink, as much as to say, Warn't that well done? That's what I call a most particular handsum fix. He can talk now (and that I do like to hear him do); but he can't make a speech, or preach a sarmon, and that I don't like to hear him do, except on Sabbath day, or up to Town Hall, on oration times.

"Minister was an uncommon pleasant man—for there was nothin' a'most he didn't know—except when he got his dander up, and then he did spin out his yarns for everlastinly.

"But I'm of his opinion. If the folks here want their country to go ahead, they must honour the plough; and General Campbell ought to hammer that 'ere into their noddles, full chisel, as hard as he can drive. I could larn him somethin', I guess, about hammerin' he ain't up to. It ain't everyone that knows how to beat a thing into a man's head. How could I have sold so many thousand clocks, if I hadn't had that knack? Why, I wouldn't have sold half a dozen you may depend.

"Agriculture is not only neglected but degraded here. What a number of young folks there seem to be in these parts, a-ridin' about, titivated out real jam, in their go-to-meetin' clothes, a-doin' nothin'. It's melancholy to think on it. That's the effect of the last war. The idleness and extravagance of those times took root, and bore fruit abundantly, and now the young people are above their business. They are too high in the instep, that's a fact.

"Old Drivvle, down here to Maccan, said to me one day, 'For gracious' sake,' says he, 'Mr. Slick, do tell me what I shall do with Johnny. His mother sets great store by him, and thinks he's the makin's of a considerable smart man; he's growin' up fast now, and I am pretty well to do in the world, and reasonable forehanded, but I don't know what the dogs to put him to. The Lawyers are like spiders—they've eat up all the flies, and I guess they'll have to eat each other soon, for there's more on 'em than causes now every court. The Doctors' trade is a poor one, too; they don't get barely cash enough to pay for their medicines; I never seed a country practitioner yet that made anything worth speakin' of. Then, as for preachin', why church and dissenters are pretty much tarred with the same stick; they live in the same pastur' with their flocks, and, between 'em, it's fed down pretty close I tell you. What would you advise me to do with him?' 'Well,' says I, 'I'll tell you if you won't be miffy with me.' 'Miffy with you indeed,' said he, 'I guess I'll be very much obliged to you; it ain't every day one gets a chance to consult with a person of your experience; I count it quite a privilege to have the opinion of such an understandin' man as you be.' 'Well,' says I, 'take a stick and give him a rael good quiltin'; jist tantune him blazes, and set him to work. What does the critter want? You have a good farm for him, let him go and airn his bread; and when he can raise that, let him get a wife to make butter for it; and when he has more of both than he wants, let him sell 'em and lay up his money, and he will soon have his bread buttered on both sides. Put him to, eh! why, put him to the PLOUGH, *the most nateral, the most happy, the most innocent, and the most healthy employment in the world.*' 'But,' said the old man (and he did not look over half pleased), 'markets are so confounded dull, labour so high, and the banks and great folks a-swallerin' all up so, there don't seem much encouragement for farmers; it's hard rubbin', nowadays, to live by the plough—he'll be a hard workin' poor man all his days.' 'O!' says I, 'if he wants to get rich by farmin', he can do that too. Let him sell his wheat, and eat his oatmeal and rye; send his beef, mutton, and poultry to market, and eat his pork and toes; make his own cloth, weave his own linen, and keep out of shops, and he'll soon grow rich : there are more fortins got by savin' than by makin', I guess, a plaguy sight; he can't eat his cake and have it too, that's a fact. *No, make a farmer of him, and you will have the satisfaction of seeing him an honest, an independent, and a respectable member of society; more honest than traders, more independent than professional men, and more respectable than either.'*

" 'Ahem!' says Marm Drivvle, and she began to clear her throat for action; she slumped down her knittin' and clawed off her spectacles, and looked right straight at me, so as to take good aim. I seed a regular nor'wester a-brewin', I knew it would bust somewhere sartin, and make all smoke ag'in, so I cleared out and left old Drivvle to stand the squall. I conceit he must have had a tempestical time of it, for she had got her Ebenezer up, and looked like a proper sneezer. Make her Johnny a farmer, eh! I guess that was too much for the like o' her to stomach.

"Pride, Squire," continued the Clockmaker (with such an air of concern, that, I verily believe, the man feels an interest in the welfare of a Province in which he has spent so long a time), *"Pride, Squire, and a false pride, too, is the ruin of this country; I hope I may be skinned if it ain't."*

THE WHITE NIGGER

ONE of the most amiable, and at the same time most amusing traits, in the Clockmaker's character, was the attachment and kindness with which he regarded his horse. He considered "Old Clay" as far above a Provincial horse, as he did one of his "free and enlightened citizens" superior to a Bluenose. He treated him as a travelling companion, and when conversation flagged between us, would often soliloquize to him, a habit contracted from pursuing his journeys alone.

"Well, now," he would say, "Old Clay, I guess you took your time a-goin' up that 'ere hill—s'pose we progress now. Go along, you old sculpin, and turn out your toes. I reckon you are as deff as a shad, do you hear there? Go ahead! Old Clay. There now," he'd say, "Squire, ain't that dreadful pretty? There's action. That looks about right: legs all under him—gathers all up snug—no bobbin' of his head—no rollin' of his shoulders—no wabblin' of his hind parts, but steady as a pump bolt, and the motion all underneath. When he fairly lays himself to it, he trots like all vengeance. Then look at his ear—jist like rabbit's; none o' your flop-ears like them Amherst beasts, half horses, half pigs, but straight up and p'inted, and not too near at the tips; for that 'ere, I consait, always shows a horse ain't true to draw. *There are only two things, Squire, worth lookin' at in a horse, action and soundness; for I never saw a critter that had good action that was a bad beast.* Old Clay puts me in mind of one of our free and enlightened——"

"Excuse me," said I, "Mr. Slick, but really you appropriate that word 'free' to your countrymen, as if you thought no other people in the world were entitled to it but yourselves."

"Neither be they," said he. "We first sot the example. Look at our Declaration of Independence. It was writ by Jefferson, and he was the first man of the age; perhaps the world never seed his ditto. It's a beautiful piece of penmanship that; he gave the British the but-eend of his mind there. I calculate you couldn't fault it in no particular; it's generally allowed to be his capsheaf. In the first page of it, second section, and first varse, are these words: 'We hold this truth to be self-evident, that all men are created equal.' I guess King George turned his quid when he read that. It was somethin' to chaw on he hadn't been used to the flavour of, I reckon."

"Jefferson forgot to insert one little word," said I; "he should have said, 'all white men'; for as it now stands, it is a practical untruth in a country which tolerates domestic slavery in its worst and most forbidding form. It is a declaration of *shame*, and not of *independence*. It is as perfect a misnomer as ever I knew."

"Well," said he, "I must admit there is a screw loose somewhere thereabouts, and I wish it would convene to Congress to do somethin' or another about our niggers, but I am not quite certified how that is to be sot to rights; I consait that you don't understand us. But," said he, evading the subject with his usual dexterity, "we deal only in niggers—and those thick-skulled, crooked-shanked, flat-footed, long-heeled, woolly-headed gentlemen don't seem fit for much else but slavery, I do suppose; they ain't fit to contrive for themselves. They are just like grasshoppers; they dance and sing all summer, and when winter comes they have nothin' provided for it, and lay down and die. They require someone to see arter them. Now, we deal in black niggers only, but the Bluenoses sell their own species—they trade in white slaves."

"Thank God!" said I, "slavery does not exist in any part of his Majesty's dominions now; we have at last wiped off that national stain."

"Not quite, I guess," said he, with an air of triumph, "it ain't done with in Nova Scotia, for I have seed these human cattle sales with my own eyes; I was availed of the truth of it up here to old Furlong's last November. I'll tell you the story," said he; and as this story of the Clockmaker's contained some extraordinary statements which I had never heard of before, I noted it in my journal, for the purpose of ascertaining their truth; and, if founded on fact, of laying them before the proper authorities.

"Last fall," said he, "I was on my way to Partridge Island, to ship off some truck and *produce* I had taken in, in the way of trade; and as I neared old Furlong's house, I seed an amazin' crowd of folks about the door; I said to myself, says I, Who's dead, and what's to pay now? What on airth is the meanin' of all this? Is it a vandew, or a weddin', or a rollin' frolic, or a religious stir, or what is it? Thinks I, I'll see; so I hitches Old

Clay to the fence, and walks in. It was some time afore I was able to wiggle my way through the crowd, and get into the house. And when I did, who should I see but Deacon Westfall, a smooth-faced, slick-haired, meechin'-lookin' chap as you'd see in a hundred, a-standin' on a stool, with an auctioneer's hammer in his hand; and afore him was one Jerry Oaks and his wife, and two little orphan children, the prettiest little toads I ever beheld in all my born days. 'Gentlemen,' said he, 'I will begin the sale by putting up Jerry Oaks, of Apple River; he's a considerable of a smart man yet, and can do many little chores besides feedin' the children and pigs; I guess he's near about worth his keep.' 'Will you warrant him sound, wind and limb?' says a tall, ragged-lookin' countryman, 'for he looks to me as if he was foundered in both feet, and had a string halt into the bargain.' 'When you are as old as I be,' says Jerry, 'mayhap you may be foundered too, young man; I have seen the day when you wouldn't dare to pass that joke on me, big as you be.' 'Will any gentleman bid for him,' says the Deacon, 'he's cheap at 7s. 6d.' 'Why, Deacon,' said Jerry, 'why surely your honour isn't a-goin' for to sell me separate from my poor old wife, are you? Fifty years have we lived together as man and wife, and a good wife has she been to me, through all my troubles and trials, and God knows I have had enough of 'em. No one knows my ways and my ailments but her; and who can tend me so kind, or who will bear with the complaints of a poor old man but his wife? Do, Deacon, and Heaven bless you for it, and yours, do sell us together; we have but a few days to live now, death will divide us soon enough. Leave her to close my old eyes, when the struggle comes, and when it comes to you, Deacon, as come it must to us all, may this good deed rise up for you, as a memorial before God. I wish it had pleased Him to have taken us afore it came to this, but His will be done'; and he hung his head, as if he felt he had drained the cup of degradation to its dregs. 'Can't afford it, Jerry—can't afford it, old man,' said the Deacon, with such a smile as a November sun gives, a-passin' atween clouds. 'Last year they took oats for rates, now nothin' but wheat will go down, and that's as good as cash; and you'll hang on, as most of you do, yet these many years. There's old Joe Crowe, I believe in my conscience he will live forever.' The biddin' then went on, and he was sold for six shillings a week. Well, the poor critter gave one long, loud, deep groan, and then folded his arms over his breast, so tight that he seemed tryin' to keep in his heart from bustin'. I pitied the misfortunate wretch from my soul; I don't know as I ever felt so streaked afore. Not so his wife—she was all tongue. She begged, and prayed, and cried, and scolded, and talked at the very tip eend of her voice, till she became, poor critter, exhausted, and went off in a faintin' fit, and they ketched her up and carried her out to the air, and she was sold in that condition.

"Well, I couldn't make head or tail of all this, I could hardly believe my eyes and ears; so says I to John Porter—him that has that catamount of a wife, that I had such a touse with—'John Porter,' says I, 'who ever seed or heerd tell of the like of this? What under the sun does it all mean? What has that 'ere critter done that he should be sold arter that fashion?' 'Done?' said he, 'why nothin', and that's the reason they sell him. This is town-meetin' day, and we always sell the poor for the year, to the lowest bidder. Them that will keep them for the lowest sum, gets them.' 'Why,' says I, 'that feller that bought him is a pauper himself, to my sartin knowledge. If you were to take him up by the heels and shake him for a week, you couldn't shake six-pence out of him. How can he keep him? It appears to me the poor buy the poor here, and that they all starve together.' Says I, 'There was a very good man once lived to Liverpool, so good, he said he hadn't sinned for seven years : well, he put a mill-dam across the river, and stopped all the fish from goin' up, and the court fined him fifty pounds for it; and this good man was so wrathy, he thought he should feel better to swear a little, but conscience told him it was wicked. So he compounded with conscience, and cheated the devil, by calling it a "dam fine busi-ness." Now, friend Porter, if this is your poor-law, it is a damn poor law, I tell you, and no good can come of such hard-hearted doins. It's no wonder your country don't prosper, for who ever heerd of a blessin' on such carryins on as this?' Says I, 'Did you ever hear tell of a sartain rich man, that had a beggar called Lazarus laid at his gate, and how the dogs had more compassion than he had, and came and licked his sores? Cause if you have, look at that forehanded and 'sponsible man there, Deacon West-fall, and you see the rich man. And then look at that 'ere pauper, dragged away in that ox-cart from his wife forever, like a feller to States' Prison, and you see Lazarus. Recollect what follered, John Porter, and have neither art nor part in it, as you are a Christian man.'

"It fairly made me sick all day. John Porter follered me out of the house, and as I was a-turnin' Old Clay, said he, 'Mr. Slick,' says he, 'I never seed it in that 'ere light afore, for it's our custom, and custom, you know, will reconcile one to 'most anything. I must say, it does appear, as you lay it out, an unfeelin' way of providin' for the poor; but, as touchin' the matter of dividin' man and wife, why' (and he peered all round to see that no one was within hearin'), 'why, I don't know, but if it was my allotment to be sold, I'd as lieves they'd sell me separate from Jane as not, for it appears to me it's about the best part of it.'

"Now, what I have told you, Squire," said the Clockmaker, "is the truth; and if members, instead of their everlastin' politics, would only look into these matters a little, I guess it would be far better for the country. So, as for our Declaration of Independence, I guess you needn't twit me with our slave sales, for we deal only in blacks; but Bluenose approbates no distinction in colours, and when reduced to poverty, is reduced to slavery, and is sold—*a white nigger*."

As we approached within fifteen or twenty miles of Parrsboro', a sudden turn of the road brought us directly in front of a large wooden house, consisting of two storeys and an immense roof, the height of which edifice was much increased by a stone foundation, rising several feet above ground.

"Now, did you ever see," said Mr. Slick, "such a catamaran as that? There's a proper goney for you, for to go and raise such a buildin' as that 'ere, and he as much use for it, I do suppose, as my old wagon here has for a fifth wheel. Bluenose always takes keer to have a big house, 'cause it shows a big man, and one that's considerable forehanded, and pretty well to do in the world. These Nova Scotians turn up their blue noses as a bottle-nose porpoise turns up his snout, and puff and snort exactly like him at a small house. If neighbour Carrit has a two-storey house, all filled with winders, like Sandy Hook lighthouse, neighbour Parsnip must add jist two feet more on to the post of his'n, and about as much more to the rafter, to go ahead of him, so all these long sarce gentlemen strive who can get the furdest in the sky, away from their farms. In New England our maxim is a small house, and a'most an everlastin' almighty big barn; but these critters revarse it; they have little hovels for their cattle, about the bigness of a good sizeable bear trap, and a house for the humans as grand as Noah's Ark. Well, jist look at it and see what a figur' it does cut. An old hat stuffed into one pane of glass, and an old flannel petticoat, as yaller as jaundice, in another, finish off the front; an old pair of breeches, and the pad of a bran' new cart-saddle worn out, titivate the eend, while the backside is all closed up on account of the wind. When it rains, if there ain't a pretty how-do-you-do, it's a pity—beds toted out of this room and tubs set in t'other to catch soft water to wash; while the clapboards, loose at the eends, go clap, clap, clap, like gals a-hacklin' flax, and the winders and doors keep a-dancin' to the music. The only dry place in the house is in the chimbley corner, where the folks all huddle up, as an old hen and her chickens do under a cart of a wet day. 'I wish I had the matter of half a dozen pound of nails,' you'll hear the old gentleman in the grand house say, 'I'll be darned if I don't, for if I had I'd fix them 'ere clapboards; I guess they'll go for it some o' these days.' 'I wish you had,' his wife would say, 'for they do make a most particular unhandsum clatter, that's a fact'; and so they let it be till the next tempestical time comes, and then they wish ag'in. Now, this grand house has only two rooms downstairs that are altogether slicked up and finished off complete; the other is jist petitioned off rough like, one half great dark entries, and t'other half places that look a plaguy sight more like packin' boxes than rooms. Well, all upstairs is a great onfarnished place, filled with every sort of good-for-nothin' trumpery in natur'—barrels without eends; corn-cobs half husked; cast-off clothes and bits of old harness; sheep-skins, hides, and wool; apples, one half rotten, and t'other half squashed; a thousand or two of shingles that have bust their withes, and broke loose all over the floor; hay rakes, forks, and sickles, without handles or teeth; rusty scythes, and odds and eends without number. When anything is wanted, then there is a general overhaul of the whole cargo, and away they get shifted forrard, one by one, all handled over and chucked into a heap together till the lost one is found; and the next time, away they get pitched to the starn ag'in, higglety pigglety, heels over head, like sheep takin' a split for it over a wall; only they increase in number each move, cause some on 'em are sure to get broke into more pieces than there was afore. Whenever I see one of these grand houses, and a hat lookin' out o' the winder with nary head in it, think I, I'll be darned if that's a place for a wooden clock—nothin' short of a London touch would go down with them folks, so I calculate I won't alight.

"Whenever you come to such a grand place as this, Squire, depend on't the farm is all of a piece—great crops of thistles, and an everlastin' yield of weeds, and cattle the best fed of any in the country, for they are always in the grain fields or mowin' lands, and the pigs a-rootin' in the potato patches. A spic and span new gig at the door, shinin' like the mud banks of Windsor, when the sun's on 'em, and an old wrack of a hay wagon, with its tongue onhitched, and stickin' out behind, like a pig's tail, all indicate a big man. He's above thinkin' of farmin' tools : he sees to the bran' new gig; and the hired helps look arter the carts. Catch him with his go-to-meetin' clothes on, a-rubbin' ag'in their nasty greasy axles, like a tarry nigger; not he, indeed, he'd stick you up with it.

"The last time I came by here, it was a little bit arter daylight down, rainin' cats and dogs, and as dark as Egypt; so, thinks I, I'll jist turn in here for shelter to Squire Bill Blake's. Well, I knocks away at the front door, till I thought I'd a-split it in; but arter a-rappin' awhile to no purpose, and findin' no one come, I gropes my way round to the back door, and opens it, and feelin' all along the partition for the latch of the keepin' room, without finding it, I knocks ag'in, when someone from inside calls out 'Walk!' Thinks I, I don't cleverly know whether that indicates 'walk in,' or 'walk out'; it's plaguy short metre, that's a fact; but I'll see anyhow. Well, arter gropin' about awhile, at last I got hold of the string and lifted the latch and walked in, and there sot old Marm Blake, close into one corner of the chimbley fireplace, a-see-sawin' in a rockin' chair, and a half-grown black house-help, half asleep in t'other corner, a-scroudgin' up over the embers. 'Who be you?' said Marm Blake, 'for I can't see you.' 'A stranger,' said I. 'Beck!' says she, speakin' to the black heifer in the corner, 'Beck!' says she ag'in, raisin' her voice, 'I believe you are as def as a post; get up this minit and stir the coals, till I see the man.' Arter the coals were stirred into a blaze, the old lady surveyed me from head to foot; then she axed me my name, and where I came from, where I was a-goin', and what my business was. 'I guess,' said she, 'you must be reasonable wet; sit to the fire and dry yourself, or mayhap your health may be endamnified p'r'aps.'

"So I sot down, and we soon got pretty considerably well acquainted, and quite sociable like, and her tongue, when it fairly waked up, began to run like a mill-race when the gate's up. I hadn't been talkin' long, 'fore I well nigh lost sight of her altogether ag'in, for little Beck began to flourish about her broom, right and left in great style, a-clearin' up, and she did raise such an awful thick cloud o' dust, I didn't know if I should ever see or breathe either ag'in. Well, when all was sot to rights and the fire made up, the old lady began to apologize for havin' no candles; she said she'd had a grand tea-party the night afore, and used them all up, and a whole sight of vittles too; the old man hadn't been well since, and had gone to bed airly. 'But,' says she, 'I do wish with all my heart you had a-come last night, for we had a most a special supper—punkin pies and doughnuts, and apple sarce, and a roast goose stuffed with Indian puddin', and a pig's harslet stewed in molasses and onions, and I don't know what all; and the fore part of today folks called to finish. I actilly have nothin' left to set afore you; for it was none o' your skim-milk parties, but superfine upper crust, real jam, and we made clean work of it. But I'll make some tea, anyhow, for you, and perhaps, after that,' said she, alterin' of her tone, 'perhaps you'll expound the Scriptures, for it's one while since I've heerd them laid open powerfully. I hain't been fairly lifted up since that good man Judas Oglethrop travelled this road,' and then she gave a groan and hung down her head, and looked corner-ways, to see how the land lay thereabouts. The tea-kettle was accordingly put on, and some lard fried into oil, and poured into a tumbler; which, with the aid of an inch of cotton wick, served as a makeshift for a candle.

"Well, arter tea we sot and chatted awhile about fashions, and markets, and sarmons, and scandal, and all sorts o' things; and, in the midst of it, in runs the nigger wench, screamin' out at the tip eend of her voice, 'O Missus! Missus! there's Fire in the dairy, Fire in the dairy!' 'I'll give it to you for that,' said the old lady, 'I'll give it you for that, you good-for-nothin' hussy; that's all your carelessness; go and put it out this minit; how on airth did it get there? My night's milk gone, I dare say; run this minit and put it out, and save the milk.' I am dreadful afeard of fire, I always was from a boy, and seein' the poor foolish critter seize a broom in her fright, I ups with the tea-kettle and follows her; and away we clipped through the entry, she callin' out 'Mind the cellar door on the right!' 'Take kear of the close-horse on the left!' and so on, but as I couldn't see nothin', I kept right straight ahead. At last my foot kotched in somethin' or another, that pitched me somewhat less than a rod or so, right agin the poor black critter, and away we went heels over head. I heerd a splash and a groan, and I smelt somethin' plaguy sour, but I couldn't see nothin'; at last I got hold of her and lifted her up, for she didn't scream, but made a strange kind of chokin' noise, and by this time up came Marm Blake with a light. If poor Beck didn't let go then in airnest, and sing out for dear life, it's a pity, for she had gone head first into the swill-tub, and the tea-kettle had scalded her feet. She kept a-dancin' right up and down, like one ravin' distracted mad, and boo-hoo'd like anything, clawin' away at her head the whole time, to clear away the stuff that stuck to her wool.

"I held in as long as I could, till I thought I should have busted, for no soul could help a-larfin', and at last I haw-hawed right out. 'You good-for-nothin' stupid slut, you,' said the old lady to poor Beck, 'it sarves you right, you had no business to leave it there—I'll pay you.' 'But,' said I, interferin' for the unfortunate critter, 'good gracious, marm! you forget the fire.' 'No I don't,' said she, 'I see him,' and seizin' the broom that had fallen from the nigger's hand, she exclaimed, 'I see him, the nasty varmint,' and began to belabour most onmarcifully a poor half-starved cur that the noise had attracted to the entry. 'I'll teach you,' said she, 'to drink milk; I'll larn you to steal into the dairy,' and the besot critter joined chorus with Beck, and they both yelled together, till they fairly made the house ring ag'in. Presently old Squire Blake popped his head out of a door, and rubbin' his eyes, half asleep and half awake, said, 'What the devil's to pay now, wife?' 'Why nothin',' says she, 'only, *Fire's in the dairy*, and Beck's in the swill-tub, that's all.' 'Well, don't make such a touse, then,' said he, 'if that's all,' and he shot tu the door and went to bed ag'in. When we returned to the keepin' room, the old lady told me that they always had had a dog called '*Fire*' ever since her grandfather, Major Donald Fraser's time, 'and what was very odd,' says she, 'every one on 'em would drink milk if he had a chance.'

"By this time the shower was over, and the moon shinin' so bright and clear that I thought I'd better be up and stirrin', and arter slippin' a few cents into the poor nigger wench's hand, I took leave of the grand folks in the big house. Now, Squire, among these middlin'-sized farmers you may lay this down as a rule: *The bigger the house the bigger the fools be that's in it.*

"But howsomever, I never call to mind that 'ere go in the big house up to the right, that I don't snicker when I think of '*Fire in the dairy.*' "

"I ALLOT you had ought to visit our great country, Squire," said the Clockmaker, "afore you quit for good and all. I calculate you don't understand us. The most splendid location atween the poles is the United States, and the first man alive is Gineral Jackson, the hero of the age, him that's skeered the British out of their seven senses. Then there's the great Daniel Webster; it's generally allowed he's the greatest orator on the face of the airth, by a long chalk; and Mr. Van Buren, and Mr. Clay, and Amos Kindle, and Judge White, and a whole raft of statesmen, up to everything and all manner of politics; there ain't the beat of 'em to be found anywhere. If you was to hear 'em I consait you'd hear genuine pure English for once, anyhow; for it's generally allowed we speak English better than the British. They all know me to be an American citizen here, by my talk, for we speak it complete in New England.

"Yes, if you want to see a free people—them that makes their own laws, accordin' to their own notions—go to the States. Indeed, if you can fault them at all, they are a little grain too free. Our folks have their head a trifle too much, sometimes, particular in elections, both in freedom of speech and freedom of press. One hadn't ought to blart right out always all that comes uppermost. A horse that's too free frets himself and his rider too, and both on 'em lose flesh in the long run. I'd e'enamost as lives use the whip sometimes, as to be for everlastinly a-pullin' at the rein. One's arm gets plaguy tired, that's a fact. I often think of a lesson I larnt Jehiel Quirk once, for lettin' his tongue outrun his good manners.

"I was down to Rhode Island one summer, to larn gildin' and bronzin', so as to give the finishin' touch to my clocks. Well, the folks elected me a hog-reeve, jist to poke fun at me, and Mr. Jehiel, a beanpole of a lawyer, was at the bottom of it. So one day, up to Town Hall, where there was an oration to be delivered on our Independence, jist afore the orator commenced, in runs Jehiel in a most all-fired hurry; and says he, 'I wonder,' says he, 'if there's ary a hog-reeve here? because if there be I require a turn of his office.' And then, said he, a-lookin' up to me, and callin' out at the tip eend of his voice, 'Mr. Hog-reeve Slick,' says he, 'here's a job out here for you.' Folks snickered a good deal, and I felt my spunk a-risin' like half flood, that's a fact; but I bit in my breath, and spoke quite cool. 'Possible?' says I; 'well, duty, I do suppose, must be done, though it ain't the most agreeable in the world. I've been a-thinkin',' says I, 'that I would be liable to a fine of fifty cents for sufferin' a hog to run at large, and as you are the biggest one, I presume, in all Rhode Island, I'll jist begin by ringin' your nose, to prevent you for the futur' from pokin' your snout where you hadn't ought to'; and I seized him by the nose and nearly wrung it off. Well, you never heerd such a shoutin' and clappin' of hands, and cheerin', in your life; they haw-hawed like thunder. Says I, 'Jehiel Quirk, that was a superb joke of your'n; how you made the folks larf, didn't you? You are e'enamost the wittiest critter I ever seed. I guess you'll mind your parts o' speech, and study the *accidence* ag'in afore you let your clapper run arter that fashion, won't you?' "

"I thought," said I, "that among you republicans, there were no gradations of rank or office, and that all were equal, the Hog-reeve and the Governor, the Judge and the Crier, the master and his servant; and although from the nature of things, more power might be entrusted to one than the other, yet that the rank of all was precisely the same."

"Well," said he, "it is so in theory, but not always in practice; and when we do prac*tise* it, it seems to go a little ag'in the grain, as if it warn't quite right neither. When I was last to Baltimore there was a court there, and Chief Justice Marshall was detailed there for duty. Well, with us in New England, the Sheriff attends the Judge to court, and says I to the Sheriff, 'Why don't you escort that 'ere venerable old Judge to the State House? He's a credit to our nation, that man; he's actilly the first pothook on the crane; the whole weight is on him; if it warn't for him the fat would be in the fire in no time. I wonder you don't show him that respect—it wouldn't hurt you one morsel, I guess.' Says he, quite miffy like, 'Don't he know the way to court as well as I do? If I thought he didn't, I'd send one of my niggers to show him the road. I wonder who was his lackey last year, that he wants me to be his'n this time. It don't convene to one of our free and enlightened citizens to tag arter any man, that's a fact; it's too English, and too foreign for our glorious institutions. He's bound by law to be there at ten o'clock, and so be I, and we both know the way there I reckon.'

"I told the story to our minister, Mr. Hopewell (and he has some odd notions about him, that man, though he don't always let out what he thinks). Says he, 'Sam, that was in bad taste' (a great phrase of the old gentleman's, that), 'in bad taste, Sam. That 'ere sheriff was a goney; don't cut your cloth arter his pattern, or your garment won't become you, I tell you. We are too enlightened to worship our fellow citizens as the ancients did, but we ought to pay great respect to vartue and exalted talents in this life, and, arter their death, there should be statues of eminent men placed in our national temples, for the veneration of arter ages, and public ceremonies performed annually to their honour. Arter all, Sam,' said he (and he made a considerable of a long pause, as if he was dubersome whether he ought to speak out or not), 'arter all, Sam,' said he, 'atween ourselves (but you must not let on I said so, for the fullness of time hain't yet come), half a yard of blue ribbon is a plaguy cheap way of rewardin' merit, as the English do; and, although we larf at 'em (for folks always will larf at what they hain't got, and never can get), yet titles ain't bad things as objects of ambition, are they?' Then tappin' me on the shoulder, and lookin' up and smilin', as he always did when he was pleased with an idee, 'Sir Samuel Slick would not sound bad, I guess, would it, Sam?'

"'When I look at the English House of Lords,' said he, 'and see so much larning, piety, talent, honour, vartue, and refinement collected together, I ax myself this here question : Can a system which produces and sustains such a body of men as the world never saw before and never will see ag'in, be defective? Well, I answer myself, perhaps it is, for all human institutions are so, but I guess it's e'enabout the best arter all. It wouldn't do here now, Sam, nor perhaps for a century to come; but it will come sooner or later with some variations. Now the Newtown pippin, when transplanted to England, don't produce such fruit as it does in Long Island, and English fruits don't presarve their flavour here neither; allowance must be made for difference of soil and climate (O Lord! thinks I, if he turns into his orchard I'm done for; I'll have to give him the dodge somehow or another, through some hole in the fence, that's a fact; but he passed on that time). 'So it is,' said he, 'with constitutions; our'n will gradually approximate to their'n, and their'n to our'n. As they lose their strength of executive, they will varge to republicanism, and as we invigorate the form of government (as we must do, or go to the old boy), we shall tend towards a monarchy.

If this comes on gradually, like the changes in the human body, by the slow approach of old age, so much the better; but I fear we shall have fevers and convulsion-fits, and colics, and an everlastin' gripin' of the intestines first; you and I won't live to see it, Sam, but our posteriors will, you may depend.'

"I don't go the whole figur' with minister," said 'he Clock-maker, "but I do opinionate with him in part. In ou. business relations we belie our political principles; we say every man is equal in the Union, and should have an equal vote and voice in the government; but in our Banks, Railroad Companies, Factory Corporations, and so on, every man's vote is regilated by his share and proportion of stock; and if it warn't so, no man would take hold on these things at all

"Natur' ordained it so : a father of a family is head, and rules supreme in his household; his eldest son and darter are like first leftenants under him, and then there is an overseer over the niggers; it would not do for all to be equal there. So it is in the univarse, it is ruled by one Superior Power; if all the angels had a voice in the government I guess——" Here I fell fast asleep; I had been nodding for some time, not in approbation of what he said, but in heaviness of slumber, for I had never before heard him so prosy since I first overtook him on the Colchester road. I hate politics as a subject of conversation; it is too wide a field for chit-chat, and too often ends in angry discussion. How long he continued this train of speculation I do not know, but, judging by the different aspect of the country, I must have slept an hour.

I was at length aroused by the report of his rifle, which he had discharged from the wagon. The last I recollected of his conversation was, I think, about American angels having no voice in the government, an assertion that struck my drowsy faculties as not strictly true; as I had often heard that the American ladies talked frequently and warmly on the subject of politics, and knew that one of them had very recently the credit of breaking up General Jackson's cabinet. When I awoke, the first I heard was, "Well! I declare, if that ain't an amazin' fine shot, too, considerin' how the critter was a-runnin' the whole blessed time; if I hain't cut her head off with a ball, jist below the throat, that's a fact. There's no mistake in a good Kentucky rifle, I tell you."

"Whose head?" said I, in great alarm, "whose head, Mr. Slick? for Heaven's sake what have you done?" (for I had been dream-ing of those angelic politicians, the American ladies).

MR. SLICK, like all his countrymen whom I have seen, felt that his own existence was involved in that of the Constitution of the United States, and that it was his duty to uphold it upon all occasions. He affected to consider its government and its institutions as perfect, and if any doubt was suggested as to the stability or character of either, would make the common reply of all Americans, "I guess you don't understand us," or else enter into a laboured defence. When left, however, to the free expression of his own thoughts, he would often give utterance to those apprehensions which most men feel in the event of an experiment not yet fairly tried, and which has in many parts evidently disappointed the sanguine hopes of its friends. But, even on these occasions, when his vigilance seemed to slumber, he would generally cover them, by giving them as the remarks of others, or concealing them in a tale. It was this habit that gave his discourse rather the appearance of thinking aloud than a connected conversation.

"We are a great nation, Squire," he said, "that's sartain; but I'm afeard we didn't altogether start right. It's in politics as in racin', everything depends upon a fair start. If you are off too quick, you have to pull up and turn back ag'in, and your beast gets out of wind and is baffled; and if you lose in the start you hain't got a fair chance arterwards, and are plaguy apt to be jockeyed in the course. When we set up housekeepin', as it were, for ourselves, we hated our stepmother, Old England, so dreadful bad, we wouldn't foller any of her ways of managin' at all, but made new receipts for ourselves. Well, we missed it in many things most consumedly, somehow or another. Did you ever see," said he, "a congregation split right in two by a quarrel, and one part go off and set up for themselves?"

"I am sorry to say," said I, "that I have seen some melancholy instances of the kind."

"Well, they shoot ahead, or drop astern, as the case may be, but they soon get on another tack, and leave the old ship clean out of sight. When folks once take to emigratin' in religion in this way, they never know where to bide. First they try one location, and then they try another; some settle here, and some improve there, but they don't hitch their horses together long. Sometimes they complain they *have too little water*, at other times that they *have too much*; they are never satisfied, and, wherever these separatists go, they onsettle others as bad as themselves. *I never look on a desarter as any great shakes.*

"My poor father used to say, 'Sam, mind what I tell you : if a man don't agree in all particulars with his church, and can't go the whole hog with 'em, he ain't justified on that account, nohow, to separate from them, for, Sam, "*Schism is a sin in the eye of God.*" The whole Christian world,' he would say, 'is divided into two great families, the Catholic and Protestant. Well, the Catholic is a united family, a happy family, and a strong family, all governed by one head; and Sam, as sure as eggs is eggs, that 'ere family will grub out t'other one, stalk, branch, and root; it won't so much as leave the seed of it in the ground, to grow by chance as a natural curiosity. Now the Protestant family is like a bundle of refuse shingles, when withed up together (which it never was and never will be to all etarnity), no great of a bundle arter all; you might take it up under one arm, and walk off with it without winkin'. But, when all lyin' loose as it always is, jist look at it, and see what a sight it is : all blowin' about by every wind of doctrine, some away up e'enamost out of sight, others rollin' over and over in the dirt, some split to pieces, and others so warped by the weather and cracked by the sun—no two of 'em will lie so as to make a close j'int. They are all divided into sects, railin', quarrelin', separatin', and agreein' in nothin' but hatin' each other. It is awful to think on. T'other family will some day or other gather them all up, put them into a bundle and bind them up tight, and condemn 'em as fit for nothin' under the sun, but the fire. Now he who splits one of these here sects by schism, or he who preaches schism, commits a grievous sin, and Sam, if you vally your own peace of mind, have nothin' to do with such folks.

" 'It's pretty much the same in politics. I ain't quite clear in my conscience, Sam, about our glorious Revolution. If that 'ere blood was shed justly in the rebellion, then it was the Lord's doin', but if unlawfully, how am I to answer for my share in it? I was at Bunker's Hill (the most splendid battle it's generally allowed that ever was fought); what effect my shots had, I can't tell, and I am glad I can't, all except one, Sam, and that shot——'
Here the old gentleman became dreadful agitated, he shook like

an ague fit, and he walked up and down the room, and wrung his hands, and groaned bitterly. 'I have wrastled with the Lord, Sam, and have prayed to Him to enlighten me on that p'int, and to wash out the stain of that 'ere blood from my hands. I never told you that 'ere story, nor your mother, neither, for she could not stand it, poor critter, she's kinder narvous.

" 'Well, Doctor Warren (the first soldier of his age, though he never fought afore) commanded us all to resarve our fire till the British came within p'int-blank shot, and we could cleverly see the whites of their eyes, and we did so; and we mowed them down like grass, and we repeated our fire with awful effect. I was among the last that remained behind the breastwork, for most on 'em, arter the second shot, cut and run full split. The British were close to us; and an officer, with his sword drawn, was leading on his men, and encouragin' them to the charge. I could see his features; he was a rael handsum man : I can see him now with his white breeches and black gaiters, and red coat, and three-cornered cocked hat, as plain as if it was yesterday instead of the year '75. Well, I took a steady aim at him, and fired. He didn't move for a space, and I thought I had missed him, when all of a sudden he sprung right straight up on eend, his sword slipped through his hands up to the p'int, and then he fell flat on his face atop of the blade, and it came straight out through his back. He was fairly skivered. I never seed anything so awful since I was raised; I actilly screamed out with horror; and I threw away my gun and joined them that were retreatin' over the neck to Charlestown. Sam, that 'ere British officer, if our rebellion was onjust or onlawful, was murdered, that's a fact; and the idee, now I am growin' old, haunts me day and night. Sometimes I begin with the Stamp Act, and I go over all our grievances, one by one, and say, Ain't they a sufficient justification? Well, it makes a long list, and I get kinder satisfied, and it appears as clear as anything. But sometimes there come doubts in my mind, jist like a guest that's not invited or not expected, and takes you at a short like, and I say, Warn't the Stamp Act repealed, and concessions made, and warn't offers sent to settle all fairly? and I get troubled an oneasy ag'in. And then I say to myself, says I, O yes, but them offers came too late. I do nothin' now, when I am alone, but argue it over and over ag'in. I actilly dream on that man in my sleep sometimes, and then I see him as plain as if he was afore me; and I go over it all ag'in till I come to that 'ere shot, and then I leap right up in bed and scream like all vengeance, and your mother, poor old critter, says, "Sam," says she, "what on airth ails you, to make you act so like Old Scratch in your sleep? I do believe there's somethin' or another on your conscience." And I say, "Polly, dear, I guess we're a-goin' to have rain, for that plaguy cute rheumatiz has seized my foot, and it does antagonize me so I have no peace. It always does so when it's like for a change." "Dear heart," she says (the poor simple critter), "then I guess I had better rub it, hadn't I, Sam?" and she crawls out of bed and gets her red flannel petticoat, and rubs away at my foot ever so long. O, Sam, if she could rub it out of my heart as easy as she thinks she rubs it out of my foot, I should be at peace, that's a fact.

" 'What's done, Sam, can't be helped, there is no use in cryin' over spilt milk, but still one can't help a-thinkin' on it. But I don't love schisms, and I don't love rebellion.

" 'Our Revolution has made us grow faster and grow richer; but, Sam, when we were younger and poorer, we were more pious and more happy. We have nothin' fixed, either in religion or politics. What connection there ought to be atween Church and State, I am not availed, but some there ought to be, as sure as the Lord made Moses. Religion, when left to itself, as with us, grows too rank and luxuriant. Suckers and sprouts, and intersecting shoots, and superfluous wood, make a nice shady tree to look at, but where's the fruit, Sam? That's the question—where's the fruit? No; the pride of human wisdom, and the presumption it breeds will ruinate us. Jefferson was an infidel, and avowed it, and gloried in it, and called it the enlightenment of the age. Cambridge College is Unitarian, 'cause it looks wise to doubt, and every drumstick of a boy ridicules the belief of his forefathers. If our country is to be darkened by infidelity, our government defiled by every State, and every State ruled by mobs —then, Sam, the blood we shed in our Revolution will be atoned for in the blood and suffering of our fellow citizens. The murders of that civil war will be expiated by a political suicide of the State.'

"I am somewhat of father's opinion," said the Clockmaker, "though I don't go the whole figur' with him; but he needn't have made such an everlastin' touse about fixin' that 'ere British officer's flint for him, for he'd a died of himself by this time, I do suppose, if he had a missed his shot at him. P'r'aps we might have done a little better, and p'r'aps we mightn't, by stickin' a little closer to the old Constitution. But one thing I will say: I think, arter all, your colony government is about as happy and as good a one as I know on. A man's life and property are well protected here at little cost, and he can go where he likes, and do what he likes, provided he don't trespass on his neighbour.

"I guess that's enough for any on us, now ain't it?"

"I ALLOT," said Mr. Slick, "that the Bluenoses are the most gullible folks on the face of the airth—regular soft horns, that's a fact. Politics and such stuff set 'em a-gapin', like children in a chimbley corner listenin' to tales of ghosts, Salem witches, and Nova Scotia snowstorms; and while they stand starin' and yawpin', all eyes and mouth, they get their pockets picked of every cent that's in 'em. One candidate chap says, 'Feller citizens, this country is goin' to the dogs hand over hand; look at your rivers, you have no bridges; at your wild lands, you have no roads; at your treasury, you hain't got a cent in it; at your markets, things don't fetch nothin'; at your fish, the Yankees ketch 'em all. There's nothin' behind you but sufferin', around you but poverty, afore you but slavery and death. What's the cause of this unheerd-of awful state of things, aye, what's the cause? Why, Judges, and Banks, and Lawyers, and great folks, have swallered all the money. They've got you down, and they'll keep you down to all etarnity, you and your posteriors arter you. Rise up, like men! Arouse yourselves like freemen, and elect me to the legislatur', and I'll lead on the small but patriotic band; I'll put the big wigs through their facins, I'll make 'em shake in their shoes, I'll knock off your chains and make you free.' Well, the goneys fall tu and elect him, and he desarts right away, with balls, rifle, powder, horn, and all. *He promised too much.*

"Then comes a rael good man, and an everlastin' fine preacher, a'most a special spiritual man; renounces the world, the flesh, and the devil, preaches and prays day and night, so kind to the poor, and so humble, he has no more pride than a babe, and so short-handed, he's no butter to his bread—all self-denial, mortifyin' the flesh. Well, as soon as he can work it, he marries the richest gal in all his flock, and then his bread is buttered on both sides. *He promised too much.*

"Then comes a doctor, and a prime article he is, too. 'I've got,' says he, 'a screw auger emetic and hot crop, and if I can't cure all sorts o' things in natur' my name ain't Quack.' Well, he turns stomach and pocket both inside out, and leaves poor Bluenose—a dead man. *He promised too much.*

"Then comes a lawyer, an honest lawyer too, a rael wonder under the sun, as straight as a shingle in all his dealin's. He's so honest he can't bear to hear tell of other lawyers; he writes agin 'em, raves agin 'em, votes agin 'em; they are all rogues but him. He's jist the man to take a case in hand, 'cause *he* will see justice done. Well, he wins his case, and fobs all for costs, 'cause he's sworn to see justice done to—himself. *He promised too much.*

"Then comes a Yankee clockmaker" (and here Mr. Slick looked up and smiled) "with his 'soft sawder,' and 'human natur',' and he sells clocks warranted to run from July to Etarnity, stoppages included, and I must say they do run as long as—as long as wooden clocks commonly do, that's a fact. But I'll show you presently how I put the leake into 'em, for here's a feller a little bit ahead on us, whose flint I've made up my mind to fix this while past." Here we were nearly thrown out of the wagon by the breaking down of one of those small wooden bridges, which prove so annoying and so dangerous to travellers. "Did you hear that 'ere snap?" said he; "well, as sure as fate, I'll break my clocks over them 'ere etarnal log bridges, if Old Clay clips over them arter that fashion. Them 'ere poles are plaguy treacherous; they are jist like old Marm Patience Doesgood's teeth, that keeps the great United Independent Democratic Hotel at Squaw Neck Creek, in Massachusetts—one half gone, and t'other half rotten eends."

"I thought you had disposed of your last clock," said I, "at Colchester, to Deacon Flint."

"So I did," he replied, "the last one I had to sell to him, but I've got a few left for other folks yet. Now there is a man on this road, one Zeb Allen, a rael gen*u*ine skinflint, a proper close-fisted customer as you'll a'most see anywhere, and one that's not altogether the straight thing in his dealin' neither. He don't want no one to live but himself; and he's mighty handsum to me—sayin' my clocks are all a cheat, and that we ruinate the country, a-drainin' every drop of money out of it, a-callin' me a Yankee broom, and what not. But it ain't all jist gospel that he says. Now I'll put a clock on him afore he knows it; I'll go right into him as slick as a whistle, and play him to the eend of my line like a trout. I'll have a hook in his gills, while he's a-thinkin' he's only smellin' at the bait. There he is now, I'll be darned if he ain't, standin' afore his shop door, lookin' as strong as high proof Jamaiky; I guess I'll whip out of the bung while he's a-lookin' arter the spicket, and p'r'aps he'll be none o' the wiser till he finds it out, neither."

"Well, Squire, how do you do?" said he; "how's all at home?"

"Reasonable well, I give you thanks, won't you alight?"

"Can't today," said Mr. Slick, "I'm in a considerable of a hurry to ketch the packet; have you any commands for Sou'west? I'm goin' to the Island, and across the Bay to Windsor. Any word that way?"

"No," says Mr. Allen, "none that I can think on, unless it be to inquire how butter's goin'; they tell me cheese is down, and produce of all kind particular dull this fall."

"Well, I'm glad I can tell you that question," said Slick, "for I don't calculate to return to these parts; butter is risin' a cent or two; I put mine off mind at tenpence."

"Don't return! possible? why, how you talk. Have you done with the clock trade?"

"I guess I have; it ain't worth follerin' now."

" 'Most time," said the other, laughing, "for by all accounts the clocks warn't worth havin', and most infarnal dear too; folks begin to get their eyes open."

"It warn't needed in your case," said Mr. Slick, with that peculiarly composed manner that indicates suppressed feeling, "for you were always wide awake; if all the folks had cut their eye-teeth as airly as you did, there'd be plaguy few clocks sold in these parts, I reckon; but you are right, Squire, you may say that, they actually were *not* worth havin', and that's the truth. The fact is," said he, throwing down his reins, and affecting a most confidential tone, "I felt almost ashamed of them myself, I tell you. The long and short of the matter is jist this : they don't make no good ones nowadays, no more, for they calculate 'em for shippin' and not for home use. I was all struck up of a heap, when I seed the last lot I got from the States; I was properly bit by them, you may depend—they didn't pay cost; for I couldn't recommend them with a clear conscience, and I must say I do like a fair deal, for I'm straight up and down, and love to go right ahead, that's a fact. Did you ever see them I fetched when I first came, them I sold over the Bay?"

"No," said Mr. Allen, "I can't say I did."

"Well," continued he, "they *were* a prime article, I tell you —no mistake there—fit for any market; it's generally allowed there ain't the beat of them to be found anywhere. If you want a clock, and can lay your hands on one of them, I advise you not to let go the chance; you'll know 'em by the 'Lowell' mark, for they were all made at Judge Beler's factory. Squire Shepody, down to Five Islands, axed me to get him one, and a special job I had of it, near about more sarch arter it than it was worth; but I did get him one, and a particular handsum one it is, copal'd and gilt superior. I guess it's worth ary half-dozen in these parts, let t'others be where they may. If I could a got supplied with the like o' them, I could a made a grand spec out of them, for they took at once, and went off quick."

"Have you got it with you?" said Mr. Allen, "I should like to see it."

"Yes, I have it here, all done up in tow, as snug as a bird's egg, to keep it from jarrin', for it hurts 'em consumedly to jolt 'em over them 'ere etarnal wooden bridges. But it's no use to take it out, it ain't for sale; it's bespoke, and I wouldn't take the same trouble to get another for twenty dollars. The only one that I know of that there's any chance of gettin', is one that Increase Crane has up to Wilmot, they say he's a-sellin' off."

After a good deal of persuasion, Mr. Slick unpacked the clock, but protested against his asking for it, for it was not for sale. It was then exhibited, every part explained and praised, as new in invention and perfect in workmanship. Now Mr. Allen had a very exalted opinion of Squire Shepody's taste, judgment, and saving knowledge; and, as it was the last and only chance of getting a clock of such superior quality, he offered to take it at the price the Squire was to have it, at seven pounds ten shillings. But Mr. Slick vowed he couldn't part with it at no rate, he didn't know where he could get the like again (for he warn't quite sure about Increase Crane's), and the Squire would be confounded disappointed; he couldn't think of it. In proportion to the difficulties, rose the ardour of Mr. Allen; his offers advanced to £8, to £8 10s., to £9.

"I vow," said Mr. Slick, "I wish I hadn't let on that I had it at all. I don't like to refuse you, but where am I to get the like?" After much discussion of a similar nature, he consented to part with the clock, though with great apparent reluctance, and pocketed the money with a protest that, cost what it would, he should have to procure another, for he couldn't think of putting the Squire's pipe out arter that fashion, for he was a very clever man, and as fair as a bootjack.

"Now," said Mr. Slick, as we proceeded on our way, "that 'ere feller is properly sarved; he got the most inferior article I had, and I jist doubled the price on him. It's a pity he should be a-tellin' of lies of the Yankees all the time; this will help him now to a little grain of truth." Then mimicking his voice and manner, he repeated Allen's words with a strong nasal twang, " 'Most time for you to give over the clock trade, I guess, for by all accounts they ain't worth havin', and most infarnal dear too; folks begin to get their eyes open.' Better for you, if you'd a had your'n open, I reckon; a joke is a joke, but I consait you'll find that no joke. The next time you tell stories about Yankee peddlers, put the wooden clock in with the wooden punkin seeds, and hickory hams, will you? The Bluenoses, Squire, are all like Zeb Allen; they think they know everything, but they get gulled from year's eend to year's eend. They expect too much from others, and do too little for themselves. They actilly expect the sun to shine, and the rain to fall, through their little House of Assembly. 'What have you done for us?' they keep axin' their members. 'Who did you spunk up to last session?' jist as if all legislation consisted in attackin' some half-dozen puss-proud folks at Halifax, who are jist as big noodles as they be themselves. You hear nothin' but politics, politics, politics, one ever-lastin' sound of give, give, give. If I was Governor I'd give 'em the butt-end of my mind on the subject; I'd crack their pates till I let some light in 'em, if it was me, I know. I'd say to the members, Don't come down here to Halifax with lockrums about politics, making a great touse about nothin'; but open the country, foster agricultur', encourage trade, incorporate companies, make bridges, facilitate conveyance, and above all things make a railroad from Windsor to Halifax; and mind what I tell you now—write it down for fear you should forget it, for it's a fact; and if you don't believe me, I'll lick you till you do, for there ain't a word of a lie in it, by gum—*One such work as the Windsor Bridge is worth all your laws, votes, speeches, and resolutions, for the last ten years, if tied up and put into a meal-bag together. If it ain't, I hope I may be shot!*"

WE had a pleasant sail of three hours from Parrsboro' to Windsor. The arrivals and departures by water are regulated at this place by the tide, and it was sunset before we reached Mrs. Wilcox's comfortable inn. Here, as at other places, Mr. Slick seemed to be perfectly at home; and he pointed to a wooden clock, as a proof of his successful and extended trade, and of the universal influence of "soft sawder," and a knowledge of "human natur'." Taking out a penknife, he cut off a splinter from a stick of firewood, and balancing himself on one leg of his chair, by the aid of his right foot, commenced his favourite amusement of whittling, which he generally pursued in silence. Indeed, it appeared to have become with him an indispensable accompaniment of reflection.

He sat in this abstracted manner until he had manufactured into delicate shavings the whole of his raw material, when he very deliberately resumed a position of more ease and security, by resting his chair on two legs instead of one, and putting both his feet on the mantelpiece. Then, lighting his cigar, he said in his usual quiet manner—

"There's a plaguy sight of truth in them 'ere old proverbs. They are distilled facts steamed down to an essence. They are like portable soup, an amazin' deal of matter in a small compass. They are what I vally most—experience. Father used to say, 'I'd as lieves have an old homespun, self-taught doctor as ary a professor in the college at Philadelphia or New York to attend me; for what they do know, they know by experience, and not by books; and experience is everything; it's hearin', and seein', and tryin'; and arter that, a feller must be a born fool if he don't know.' That's the beauty of old proverbs; they are as true as a plumb line, and as short and sweet as sugar candy. Now when you come to see all about this country you'll find the truth of that 'ere one—'A man that has too many irons in the fire is plaguy apt to get some on 'em burnt.'

"Do you recollect that 'ere tree I showed you to Parrsboro'? It was all covered with black knobs, like a wart rubbed with caustic. Well, the plum-trees had the same disease a few years ago, and they all died, and the cherry-trees I consait will go for it too. The farms here are all covered with the same 'black knobs,' and they do look like Old Scratch. If you see a place all gone to wrack and ruin, it's mortgaged you may depend. The 'black knob' is on it. My plan, you know, is to ax leave to put a clock in a house, and let it be till I return. I never say a word about sellin' it, for I know when I come back, they won't let it go arter they are once used to it. Well, when I first came, I knowed no one, and I was forced to inquire whether a man was good for it, afore I left it with him; so I made a p'int of axin' all about every man's place that lived on the road. 'Who lives up there in the big house?' says I; 'it's a nice location that, pretty considerable improvements, them.' 'Why, sir, that's A. B.'s; he was well to do in the world once, carried a stiff upper lip, and keered for no one; he was one of our grand aristocrats—wore a long-tailed coat, and a ruffled shirt; but he must take to ship buildin', and has gone to the dogs.' 'O,' said I, 'too many irons in the fire. Well, the next farm, where the pigs are in the potato field, whose is that?' 'O, sir, that's C. D.'s; he was a considerable fore-handed farmer, as any in our place, but he sot up for an Assembly-man, and opened a store, and things went agin him somehow; he had no luck arterwards. I hear his place is mortgaged, and they've got him cited in chancery.' ' "The black knob" is on him,' said I. 'The black what, sir?' says Bluenose. 'Nothin',' says I. 'But the next, who improves that house?' 'Why, that's E. F.'s; he was the greatest farmer in these parts, another of the aristocracy; had a most noble stock o' cattle, and the matter of some hundreds out in j'int notes. Well, he took the contract for beef with the troops; and he fell astarn, so I guess it's a gone goose with him. He's heavy mortgaged.' 'Too many irons ag'in,' said I. 'Who lives to the left there? That man has a most special fine interval, and a grand orchard too; he must be a good mark, that.' 'Well he was once, sir, a few years ago; but he built a fullin' mill, and a cardin' mill, and put up a lumber establishment, and speculated in the West Indy line; but the dam was carried away by the freshets, the lumber fell, and faith he fell too; he's shot up, he hain't been seed these two years; his farm is a common, and fairly run out.' 'O,' said I, 'I understand now, my man; these folks had too many irons in the fire, you see, and some on 'em have got burnt.' 'I never heerd tell of it,' says Bluenose; 'they might, but not to my knowledge'; and he scratched his head, and looked as if he would ask the meanin' of it, but didn't like to. Arter that I axed no more questions; I knew a mortgaged farm as far as I could see it. There was a strong family likeness in 'em all—the same ugly features, the same cast o' countenance. The black knob was discernible, there was no mistake: barn doors broken off, fences burnt up, glass out of windows; more white crops than green, and both lookin' weedy; no wood pile, no sarce garden, no compost, no stock; moss in the mowin' lands, thistles in the ploughed lands, and neglect everywhere; skinnin' had commenced—takin' all out and puttin' nothin' in—gittin' ready for a move, *so as to leave nothin' behind.* Flittin' time had come. Foregatherin', for fore-closin'. Preparin' to curse and quit. That beautiful river we came up today, what superfine farms it has on both sides of it, hain't it? it's a sight to behold. Our folks have no notion of such a country so far down East, beyond creation most, as Nova Scotia is. If I was to draw up an account of it for the 'Slickville Gazette,' I guess few would accept it as a bona fide draft, without some 'sponsible man to indorse it, that warn't given to flammin'. They'd say there was a land speculation to the bottom of it, or a water privilege to put into the market, or a plaister rock to get off, or some such scheme. They would, I snore. But I hope I may never see daylight ag'in, if there's sich a country in all our great nation, as the *vi*-cinity of Windsor.

"Now it's jist as like as not, some goney of a Bluenose, that seed us from his fields, sailin' up full split, with a fair wind on the packet, went right off home and said to his wife, 'Now do for gracious' sake, mother, jist look here, and see how slick them folks go along; and that captain has nothin' to do all day, but sit straddle legs across his tiller, and order about his sailors, or talk like a gentleman to his passengers: he's got 'most as easy a time of it as Ami Cuttle has, since he took up the fur trade, a-snarin' rabbits. I guess I'll buy a vessel, and leave the lads to do the ploughin' and little chores; they've growed up now to be considerable lumps of boys.' Well, away he'll go, hot foot (for I know the critters better nor they know themselves), and he'll go and buy some old wrack of a vessel, to carry plaister, and mortgage his farm to pay for her. The vessel will jam him up tight for repairs and new riggin', and the sheriff will soon pay him a visit (and he's a most particular troublesome visitor that; if he once only gets a slight how-d'ye-do acquaintance, he becomes so amazin' intimate arterwards, a-comin' in without knockin', and a-runnin' in and out at all hours, and makin' so plaguy free and easy, it's about as much as a bargain if you can get clear of him arterwards). Benipt by the tide, and benipt by the sheriff, the vessel makes short work with him. Well, the upshot is, the farm gets neglected while Captain Cuddy is to sea a-drogin' of plaister. The thistles run over his grain fields, his cattle run over his hay land, the interest runs over its time, the mortgage runs over all, and at last he jist runs over to the lines to Eastport, himself. And when he finds himself there, a-standin' in the street, near Major Pine's tavern, with his hands in his trouser pockets, a-chasin' of a stray shillin' from one eend of 'em to another, afore he can catch it, to swap for a dinner, won't he look like a ravin' distracted fool, that's all? He'll feel about as streaked as I did once, a-ridin' down the St. John River. It was the fore part of March; I'd been up to Frederickton a-speculatin' in a small matter of lumber, and was returnin' to the city, a-gallopin' along on one of old Buntin's horses, on the ice, and all at once I missed my horse : he went right slap in and slid under the ice out of sight as quick as wink, and there I was a-standin' all alone. Well, says I, what the dogs has become of my horse and portmantle? they have given me a proper dodge, that's a fact. That is a narrer squeak, it fairly bangs all. Well, I guess he'll feel near about as ugly, when he finds himself brought up all standin' that way; and it will come so sudden on him, he'll say, Why, it ain't possible I've lost farm and vessel both, in tu tu's, that way, but I don't see neither on 'em. Eastport is near about all made up of folks who have had to cut and run for it.

"I was down there last fall, and who should I see but Thomas Rigby, of Windsor. He knew me the minit he laid eyes upon me, for I had sold him a clock the summer afore. (I got paid for it though, for I seed he had too many irons in the fire not to get some on 'em burnt; and besides, I knew every fall and spring the wind set in for the lines from Windsor very strong—a regular trade-wind—a sort of monshune, that blows all one way for a long time without shiftin'.) Well, I felt proper sorry for him, for he was a very clever man, and looked cut up dreadfully, and amazin' down in the mouth. 'Why,' says I, 'possible? is that you, Mr. Rigby? why, as I am alive! if that ain't my old friend—why how do you?' 'Hearty, I thank you,' said he, 'how be you?' 'Reasonable well, I give you thanks,' says I; 'but what on airth brought you here?' 'Why,' says he, 'Mr. Slick, I couldn't well avoid it; times are uncommon dull over the Bay; there's nothin' stirrin' there this year, and never will, I'm thinkin'. No mortal soul *can* live in Nova Scotia. I do believe that our country was made of a Sunday night, arter all the rest of the univarse was finished. One half of it has got all the ballast of Noah's Ark thrown out there; and the other half is eat up by bankers, lawyers, and other great folks. All our money goes to pay salaries, and a poor man has no chance at all.' 'Well,' says I, 'are you done up stock and fluke—a total wrack?' 'No,' says he, 'I have two hundred pounds left yet to the good, but my farm, stock, and utensils, them young blood horses, and the bran' new vessel I was a-buildin', are all gone to pot—swept as clean as a thrashin' floor, that's a fact; Shark and Co. took all.' 'Well,' says I, 'do you know the reason of all that misfortin'?' 'O,' says he, 'any fool can tell that—bad times to be sure; everything has turned ag'in the country; the banks have it all their own way, and much good may it do 'em.' 'Well,' says I, 'what's the reason the banks don't eat us up too, for I guess they are as hungry as your'n be, and no way particular about their food neither; considerable sharp set—cut like razors, you may depend. I'll tell you,' says I, 'how you got that 'ere slide, that sent you heels over head—*You had too many irons in the fire*. You hadn't ought to have taken hold of ship buildin' at all; you knowed nothin' about it. You should have stuck to your farm, and your farm would have stuck to you. Now go back, afore you spend your money; go up to Douglas, and you'll buy as good a farm for two hundred pounds as what you lost, and see to that, and to that only, and you'll grow rich. As for banks, they can't hurt a country no great, I guess, except by breakin', and I consait there's no fear of your'n breakin'; and as for lawyers, and them kind o' heavy coaches, give 'em half the road, and if they run ag'in you, take the law of 'em. *Undivided, unremitting attention paid to one thing, in ninety-nine cases out of a hundred, will insure success; but you know the old sayin' about "too many irons."*

" 'Now,' says I, 'Mr. Rigby, what o'clock is it?' 'Why,' says he, 'the moon is up a piece, I guess it's seven o'clock or thereabouts. I suppose it's time to be a-movin'.' 'Stop,' says I, 'jist come with me; I got a rael nateral curiosity to show you—such a thing as you never laid your eyes on in Nova Scotia, I know.' So we walked along towards the beach. 'Now,' says I, ' look at that 'ere man, old Lunar, and his son, a-sawin' plank by moonlight, for that 'ere vessel on the stocks there; come ag'in tomorrow mornin' afore you can cleverly discern objects the matter of a yard or so afore you, and you'll find 'em at it ag'in. I guess that vessel won't ruinate those folks. *They know their business and stick to it.*' Well, away went Rigby, considerable sulky (for he had no notion that it was his own fault; he laid all the blame on the folks to Halifax); but I guess he was a little grain posed, for back he went, and bought to Sowack, where I hear he has a better farm than he had afore.

"I mind once we had an Irish gal as a dairy help; well, we had a wicked devil of a cow, and she kicked over the milk pail, and in ran Dora, and swore the Bogle did it. Jist so poor Rigby, he wouldn't allow it was nateral causes, but laid it all to politics. Talkin' of Dora, puts me in mind of the gals, for she warn't a bad-lookin' heifer, that. My! what an eye she had, and I con-saited she had a particular small foot and ankle too, when I helped her up once into the haymow, to sarch for eggs; but I can't exactly say, for when she brought 'em in, mother shook her head and said it was dangerous; she said she might fall through and hurt herself, and always sent old Snow arterwards. She was a considerable of a long-headed woman, was mother; she could see as far ahead as most folks. She warn't born yesterday, I guess. But that 'ere proverb is true as respects the gals too. Whenever you see one on 'em with a whole lot of sweethearts, it's an even chance if she gets married to any on 'em. One cools off, and another cools off, and before she brings any one on 'em to the right weldin' heat, the coal is gone, and the fire is out. Then she may blow and blow till she's tired; she may blow up a dust, but the deuce of a flame can she blow up ag'in to save her soul alive. I never see a clever lookin' gal in danger of that, I don't long to whisper in her ear, You dear little critter, you, take care! *You have too many irons in the fire; some on 'em will get stone cold, and t'other ones will get burnt so, they'll never be no good in natur'.*"

THE next morning the Clockmaker proposed to take a drive round the neighbourhood. "You hadn't ought," says he, "to be in a hurry; you should see the vicinity of this location; there ain't the beat of it to be found anywhere."

While the servants were harnessing Old Clay, we went to see a new bridge which had recently been erected over the Avon River. "That," said he, "is a splendid thing. A New Yorker built it, and the folks in St. John paid for it."

"You mean of Halifax," said I; "St. John is in the other Province."

"I mean what I say," he replied, "and it is a credit to New Brunswick. No, sir, the Halifax folks neither know nor keer much about the country; they wouldn't take hold on it, and if they had a waited for them, it would have been one while afore they got a bridge, I tell you. They've no spirit, and plaguy little sympathy with the country, and I'll tell you the reason on it. There are a good many people there from other parts, and always have been, who come to make money and nothin' else, who don't call it home, and don't feel to home, and who intend to up killoch and off, as soon as they have made their ned out of the Bluenoses. They have got about as much regard for the country as a peddler has, who trudges along with a pack on his back. He *walks*, 'cause he intends to *ride* at last; *trusts*, 'cause he intends to *sue* at last; *smiles*, 'cause he intends to *cheat* at last; *saves all*, 'cause he intends to *move all* at last. It's actilly overrun with transient paupers, and transient speculators; and these last grumble and growl like a bear with a sore head, the whole blessed time, at everything; and can hardly keep a civil tongue in their head, while they're fobbin' your money hand over hand. These critters feel no interest in anything but cent per cent; they deaden public spirit; they hain't got none themselves, and they larf at it in others; and when you add their numbers to the timid ones, the stingy ones, the ignorant ones, and the poor ones, that are to be found in every place, why, the few smart-spirited ones that's left are too few to do anything, and so nothin' is done. It appears to me if I was a Bluenose I'd—but thank fortin' I ain't, so I says nothin'; but there is somethin' that ain't altogether jist right in this country, that's a fact.

"But what a country this Bay country is, isn't it? Look at that medder; bean't it lovely? The prayer-eyes of Illanoy are the top of the ladder with us, but these dykes take the shine off them by a long chalk, that's sartin. The land in our Far West, it is generally allowed, can't be no better; what you plant is sure to grow and yield well, and food is so cheap, you can live there for half nothin'. But it don't agree with us New England folks; we don't enjoy good health there; and what in the world is the use of food, if you have such an etarnal dyspepsy you can't digest it? A man can hardly live there till next grass, afore he is in the yaller leaf. Just like one of our bran' new vessels built down in Maine, of best hackmatack, or what's better still, of our rael American live oak (and that's allowed to be about the best in the world); send her off to the West Indies, and let her lie there awhile, and the worms will riddle her bottom all full of holes like a tin cullender, or a board with a grist of duck-shot through it; you wouldn't believe what *a bore* they be. Well, that's jist the case with the Western climate. The heat takes the solder out of the knees and elbows, weakens the joints, and makes the frame rickety.

"Besides, we like the smell of the salt water; it seems kinder nateral to us New Englanders. We can make more a-ploughin' of the seas, than ploughin' of a prayer-eye. It would take a bottom near about as long as Connecticut River, to raise wheat enough to buy the cargo of a Nantucket whaler, or a Salem tea ship. And then to leave one's folks, and na*tive* place, where one was raised, halter broke, and trained to go in gear, and exchange all the comforts of the Old States for them 'ere new ones, don't seem to go down well at all. Why, the very sight of the Yankee gals is good for sore eyes, the dear little critters! They do look so scrumptious, I tell you, with their cheeks bloomin' like a red rose budded on a white one, and their eyes like Mrs. Adams's diamonds (that folks say shine as well in the dark as in the light), neck like a swan, lips chock full of kisses—lick! It fairly makes one's mouth water to think on 'em. But it's no use talkin', they are just made critters, that's a fact, full of health and life, and beauty. Now, to change them 'ere splendid white water-lilies of Connecticut and Rhode Island for the yaller crocuses of Illanoy, is what we don't like. It goes most confoundedly agin the grain, I tell you. Poor critters, when they get away back there, they grow as thin as a sawed lath; their little peepers are as dull as a boiled codfish; their skin looks like yaller fever, and they seem all mouth like a crocodile. And that's not the worst of it, neither; for when a woman begins to grow saller it's all over with her; she's up a tree then, you may depend, there's no mistake. You can no more bring back her bloom, than you can the colour to a leaf the frost has touched in the fall. It's a gone goose with her, that's a fact. And that's not all, for the temper is plaguy apt to change with the cheek too. When the freshness of youth is on the move, the sweetness of temper is amazin' apt to start along with it. A bilious cheek and a sour temper are like the Siamese twins, there's a nateral cord of union atween them. The one is a signboard, with the name of the firm written on it in big letters. He that don't know this, can't read, I guess. It's no use to cry over spilt milk, we all know, but it's easier said than done, that. Womenkind, and especially single folks, will take on dreadful at the fadin' of their roses, and their frettin' only seems to make the thorns look sharper. Our minister used to say to sister Sall (and when she was young she was a rael witch, a'most an everlastin' sweet girl), 'Sally,' he used to say, 'now's the time to larn, when you are young; store your mind well, dear, and the fragrance will remain long arter the rose has shed its leaves. *The otter of roses is stronger than the rose, and a plaguy sight more valuable.*' Sall wrote it down; she said it warn't a bad idee, that: but father larfed; he said he guessed minister's courtin' days warn't over, when he made such pretty speeches as that 'ere to the gals. Now, who would go to expose his wife, or his darters, or himself, to the dangers of such a climate, for the sake of thirty bushels of wheat to the acre instead of fifteen? There seems a kinder somethin' in us that rises in our throat when we think on it, and won't let us. We don't like it. Give me the shore, and let them that like the Far West go there, I say.

"This place is as fertile as Illanoy or Ohio, as healthy as any part of the globe, and right alongside of the salt water; but the folks want three things—*Industry, Enterprise, Economy.* These Bluenoses don't know how to vally this location; only look at it, and see what a place for bisness it is: the centre of the Province; the nateral capital of the Basin of Minas, and part of the Bay of Fundy; the great thoroughfare to St. John, Canada, and the United States; the exports of lime, gypsum, freestone, and grindstone; the dykes—but it's no use talkin'; I wish we had it, that's all. Our folks are like a rock-maple tree: stick 'em in anywhere but eend up and top down, and they will take root and grow; but put 'em in a rael good soil like this, and give 'em a fair chance, and they will go ahead and thrive right off, most amazin' fast, that's a fact. Yes, if we had it, we would make another guess place of it from what it is. *In one year we would have a railroad to Halifax, which, unlike the stone that killed two birds, would be the makin' of both places.* I often tell the folks this, but all they can say is, 'O we are too poor and too young.' Says I, 'You put me in mind of a great long legged, long tail colt father had. He never changed his name of colt as long as he lived, and he was as old as the hills; and though he had the best of feed, was as thin as a whippin' post. He was colt all his days—always young—always poor; and young and poor you'll be I guess to the eend of the chapter.' "

On our return to the inn, the weather, which had been threatening for some time past, became very tempestuous. It rained for three successive days, and the roads were almost impassable. To continue my journey was wholly out of the question. I determined, therefore, to take a seat in the coach for Halifax, and defer until next year the remaining part of my tour. Mr. Slick agreed to meet me here in June, and to provide for me the same conveyance I had used from Amherst. I look forward with much pleasure to our meeting again. His manner and idiom were to me perfectly new, and very amusing; while his good sound sense, searching observation, and queer humour, rendered his conversation at once valuable and interesting. There are many subjects on which I should like to draw him out; and I promised myself a fund of amusement in his remarks on the state of society and manners at Halifax, and the machinery of the local government, on both of which he appears to entertain many original and some very just opinions.

As he took leave of me in the coach he whispered, "Inside of your great big cloak you will find wrapped up a box, containin' a thousand rael genuine first chop Havanas—no mistake—the clear thing. When you smoke 'em, think sometimes of your old companion, SAM SLICK THE CLOCKMAKER."

THE END

THOMAS CHANDLER HALIBURTON was born in Windsor, Nova Scotia, in 1796. He practised law for a time in Annapolis Royal, and in 1826 was elected to the provincial House of Assembly. After his withdrawal from active politics in 1829, he became in turn a Justice of the Court of Common Pleas and, in 1841, a Judge of the Supreme Court. In 1856 he removed to England, where he represented Launceston in the House of Commons for six years prior to his death in 1865.

Haliburton's career as a writer began with the publication of his *Historical and Statistical Account of Novia Scotia* in 1829. But in the thirties, stimulated by his connection with "The Club," an institution organized by Joseph Howe, he turned increasingly to satirical and humorous writing as an outlet for his strong opinions on political and social questions. In 1835 he contributed to Howe's *Novascotian* the first sketches of *The Clockmaker: or, the Sayings and Doings of Samuel Slick, of Slickville*, and the series was published in book form in 1836. This was followed by a second series in 1838, and a third in 1840. Further adventures of Mr. Slick are recorded in *The Attaché: or, Sam Slick in England* (1843, 1844), and *Sam Slick's Wise Saws and Modern Instances* (1853). Of the remaining books by Haliburton, the most important are *The Old Judge* (1849) and *The Season Ticket* (1860).

THE NEW CANADIAN LIBRARY LIST

Asterisks (*) denote titles of New Canadian Library Classics

McCLELLAND AND STEWART LIMITED
publishers of The New Canadian Library
would like to keep you informed about
new additions to this unique series.

For a complete listing of titles and
current prices – or if you wish to be added
to our mailing list to receive future catalogues
and other new book information – write:

BOOKNEWS
McClelland and Stewart Limited
25 Hollinger Road
Toronto, Canada M4B 3G2

McClelland and Stewart books are
available at all good bookstores.

Booksellers should be happy to order from our catalogues
any titles which they do not regularly stock.